ASTRAY

by

Scarlet Clover Publishers, L.L.C.

Littleton, Colorado

Covers Design Director – Karen D. Badger
Interior Design and Formatting – Karen D. Badger
Cover Artwork – Kelly Jo Stevens

Edited by – Denise Nash, Kathie Solie, and Barbara Oatley

Published by Scarlet Clover Publishers L.L.C.
P.O. Box 621002
Littleton, Colorado 80162

Printed and bound in the United States of America, UK, and Europe

ISBN-13: 978-0692609729
ISBN-10: 0692609725

ASTRAY

by

Kieran York

Books Also Written by Kieran York

Primrose
Trevar's Team: 1 (A Beryl Trevar Mystery)
Within Our Celebration (Short Stories)
Touring Kelly's Poem
Loitering on the Frontier
Night Without Time
Earthen Trinkets
Careful Flowers
Appointment with a Smile
Shinney Forest Cloaks: Book 3 (A Royce Madison Mystery)
Crystal Mountain Veils: Book 2 (A Royce Madison Mystery)
Timber City Masks: Book 1 (A Royce Madison Mystery)
Sugar With Spice (Short Stories)
Blushing Aspen (Poetry)
Realm of Belonging (Poetry)

Contributor to Sappho's Poetry Series, edited by Beth Mitchum

Wet Violets, Volume 2
Roses Read, Volume 3
Delectable Daisies, Volume 4
Fallen Petals, Volume 5

Kieran York

DEDICATION

I dedicate this book to my friend, Karen D. Badger.

The irony of the dedication is that this book is about an antagonist with an evil soul.

In contrast, this book is dedicated to one of kindest, finest women I know, or have ever known. She is a true Warrior Protagonist. I knew of her kindness before becoming her friend. Word gets around. When Scarlet Clover Publishers began, Karen helped to get releases on my other books, and get them into print. For that I am eternally grateful.

We have worked together since then. Her brilliance, knowledge of all things computer, creativity, and deft hand at the artistic, always astounds me. Working with her is a pleasure and a privilege.

Thank you, my friend!

ACKNOWLEDGEMENTS

I acknowledge the many fine folks who made this Scarlet Clover book. Karen D. Badger, Denise Nash, Kathie Solie, Barbara Oatley, Kelly Jo Stevens, and Brenda Starr. AND CEO, Clover York.

Another acknowledgement is important with this book. I wish to recognize the victims of violence. It was out of violence when my decision to write this story began.

For over three and a half decades I have lived a dozen blocks from Columbine High School in Littleton, Colorado. It is an area nestled against the glorious Rocky Mountain foothills. Those of us living in this community of Columbine had always felt fairly secure.

We were not prepared to experience the violation of innocence that shattered our hearts April 20, 1999. I recall TV camerapersons and reporters commenting that it was difficult to understand how this horrific crime could have happened in such a beautiful, unsullied area. Thirteen victims lost their lives.

Perhaps the soul of crime was what I searched for in this book, *Astray.* There might have been answers that will forever go unexplained.

For me there is a stark reality about the perpetrators. No matter how one may attempt to peer into the face of evil, to most of us it remains an enigmatic stranger. So it is with fiction - so it was with the reality that forged itself into our community one morning in the confines of a high school.

I am no nearer understanding violence than I've ever been. The difference, after completing *Astray,* is that it is no longer important that I comprehend savagery. Perhaps it is most vital that we never accept terror as a condition for sharing this planet with those gone astray. No matter the format. No matter the degree. From prevention to justice – it must improve.

After the Columbine tragedy, our community had banners and bumper stickers reading: **We are all Columbine**. Survivors still wear pain in their eyes. There are two wheelchair ramps in my immediate neighborhood. This book acknowledges Columbine.

My heartfelt admiration goes to the valor and courage of victims, enforcers, first responders, medics, media, and caregivers. My sorrow goes to those we lost. Compassion begins with that loss. We are Colorado – and we are *all* – *all* Columbine.

I am proudly a victim's rights advocate.

ASTRAY

Midwinter - Denver, Colorado

PROLOGUE

Improbable as murder might be, when it happens there are always consequences that impact those living through it. This was the maxim I'd come to accept over years of attempting to understand the homicidal event. Certainly it was not set forth in my brain by a group of professors. No, this thought was superimposed over my heart by days and nights of viewing corpses, and of witnessing loved-ones after such crime's intrusion. This concept became in my day-to-day consideration, and it also inveigled its way into my dreams.

"Florez," I muttered as sharply as possible. I was not fully awake. I impatiently fumbled with the phone receiver. "And this better be good."

"Better than good," City Editor Kenny Erickson snapped. "Randa Florez, *if* you haul it out of bed and race across town, you've got the scoop of a lifetime. We have a bloody mess of a murder. Got it all. Kinky sex."

"Kenny, what is this? You've got no rookies to bother, so it's my turn in the sleep deprivation barrel? I've got a full agenda tomorrow." I was now fully awake. I temporarily despised Kenny Erickson. He was full of himself with his important title of *Mile High Mirror's* city desk editor.

"This isn't a joke. Come on, Randa. I know I'm disconnecting your dreams, but you'll thank me."

"Mine was the only name on the roster?"

"I'm doing you a favor. We're talking damned ugly. A woman carved up her drug dealer. Got your attention?"

"Crime of the century at..." I paused, squinting back at the red digital reading on my clock. "At one fifty-seven A.M. And yes, the dream has dissolved."

"I'm sure the killer didn't intend to intrude on your dreams, but she couldn't help herself. Jona Beck. That's what she told the arresting officer. Couldn't help herself. And she's one of you."

I swallowed the raw phlegm of sleep. "A woman?"

"A lesbian."

"She stabbed a drug dealer?"

"Not stabbed. She butchered the guy. Let's talk grizzly."

I reached for my jacket on the floor. I rummaged through my pockets, wrestling a small reporter's notebook from its hiding place. Paper fluttered back until an empty page appeared. With my free hand I uncapped a fountain pen. Once it was poised, I murmured, "Lesbian fillets man. What a headline! That ought to excite my Sapphic sorority sisters. Like the alliteration?"

"You'll like the byline: Randa Florez, writer of yet another award-winning newspaper crime feature series."

I made a notation in the margin. "Make it gory," I emphasized as I wrote the words. "And I've got the exclusive?"

"The exclusive is yours. The dyke asked for you. Crush maybe?"

"Let's cut the dainty crap about my sexual orientation. It's old news. And speaking of news, I trust you mean it about my getting the exclusive? No sending in the feature desk after I've wallowed through the sewage?"

Blank moments told me he was swaying back away ever so slightly. "I'd never do that to you again. It's yours. And I won't comment on the Sapphic angle."

"Right," I muttered with heavy sarcasm - without a quaver of regret.

There was a pinched pause. He then asked, "What do lesbians dream about?"

"It is about eight extraordinary hours. In my case, six or less." I wasn't going to divulge my carnality by telling him that I dreamed about warm, soft skin wrapping my entirety. Nor about kisses that reached my soul. Certainly not about the feel of another woman's breasts pressing against my own. Nor dreams about burying my face in fistfuls of fragrant, cascading silky hair as I kiss a woman's neck. Nor about passion as it begins to unleash. The levitating-on-the-ceiling climaxes were never to be mentioned.

"No comment?"

"Absolutely none. You couldn't understand, Kenny. You think foreplay is remembering a woman's first name."

His laugh was brief, but there. "Randa, you'll never understand the male animal."

"I was raised by a father and I have two male siblings. I do have a clue. Now, I'm on my way. I'll call you from the station."

There was a click on the other end of the telephone. There was a judgmental moment of telling myself that it's okay to assassinate a drug dealer. Then my liberalism snatched me back. Law is law.

My crawl from the bed began with a labored attempt to retract my sprawling limbs. I don't have time for a shower. Time, my mind mulled. I don't have time to scour a compact, dusty loft. Nor to run through my spartanly furnished rooms with a feather duster. Time. Even romance was often edged from my hectic schedule.

Slipping first into my denims, I shook my head to fully awaken myself. A soft, beige cable-knit sweater ruffled my tapered, shoulder-length sable hair as it cleared my head. Socks and penny loafers were an afterthought.

My cell phone was tucked into my leather aviatrix jacket's abundant pocket. Often I believed my jacket was a satellite desk. It served me as well as any branch office might.

It would only take a tick to dash down the street to the parking garage where I kept my car. I would then drive my silver 1983 Datsun 280ZX to the station. My automobile was the love of my life. For it reflected what I wished to be all about. The body, of classic lineage, was designed to look as if it were a racer. Before being given the numerical-alphabetical title, it was almost named *Fairlady*. I called my vehicle 'Garbo.' I'd always hated vanity license plates. But my Z deserved a name - not to mention a visual calling card. Garbo's engine purred. Her only sign of age was a few rusty pockmarks on the lower rear fenders.

Pausing, I glanced back at my semi-decorated loft. Maybe I should take along a towel to wipe my hand after this killer's blood-stained handshake. I envisioned Jona Beck to be blood-soaked. My own hands were certain to be tainted by the handshake of a bona fide slash and gash killer. I nixed the towel idea. With a grimace, I confessed I probably couldn't find a pristine towel to take with me. The laundry piled in the corner was becoming a monument to my unmanageable schedule. I gave a final sigh before locking the door. Just another magic moment in show biz.

I was to meet the murderer, Jona Beck. An 'out' outlaw.

* * *

Established: My LoDo loft was a mess. But my true home was *The Mile High Mirror*, Denver, Colorado, where I worked. I honestly believed the newspaper had become my actual lover. Others, those wondrous women, became surrogates. At least that's the theory of my most recent ex. I call her my *ex* because we constantly broke up and then reunited. Only to again break it all off. Alison Pagette claimed my heart was between the pages of a newspaper. And my playground was located at police headquarters and the city administration buildings. They're located directly across the street from *The Mirror*. And my beat was analogous, Alison believed, to my heartbeat.

Not exactly Sapphic recommendation of the year. I worked the crime beat. Homicide, to be precise. It became all powerful. That represented a sad admission. However, I would never admit to another woman, a lover, that my bed becomes larger, and much emptier, when spending a night alone.

* * *

At the police station, I waited while paperwork was being processed. My nemesis and competitor, a fellow crime beat reporter named Lanny Ventura, called the wait 'loitering with intent'. It was part of our profession that Lanny and I both despised. She claimed she could actually feel her body decompose while awaiting verification on some stories. For all the purported excitement my profession was supposed to ignite, it could be tedious. Verifying facts meant waiting for centuries at a chunk - a mega chunk.

I'd long ago accepted the stalls and runarounds of City Hall. But waiting was becoming more difficult. This story might be the kick-start needed to rejuvenate my journalistic fervor. Or it might be another exercise through a maze of police procedures. Finally, we were off to battle with a vigilant public defender's office for *as is* interviews.

There were also endless source checks.

When checks are completed and the story fully developed – it would be edited. If it were an important scoop, it immediately became an e-extra. *The Mirror's* digital edition would break the news. That was *The Mirror's E-Edition*. The 'live time' news story would be available to subscribers. Printed papers appeared daily at their prescribed time – and on occasions, there would also be newsstand extras.

One thing seemed certain. My heart needed this story. Muggings, drug busts, and corporate fraud scams were getting me down. A good old fashioned, highfalutin crime of the decade was due in.

* * *

"I'm Randa Florez," I stated, extending my hand. I'm expecting reflexive lies, excuses, and certainly a display of all the pain moldering away within her soul.

Jona Beck's cuffed handshake was weak. Her eye contact was a series of skittering, blinking pauses. "I didn't think they'd let you talk with me."

"I've had numerous interviews in the interrogation rooms before. Guess they know I'm not about to sneak a metal file in for you." I studied her as we sat opposite one another at the dented and worn table. I glanced up at the guard, who was stationed inconspicuously at the door. I thought I'd seen her smile slightly in my direction. "And I've got protection." To her I asked, "There isn't a problem with my taking a few photos with my phone?"

She muttered no, and then shrugged. As I snapped a few preliminary shots of Jona, the guard resumed her stiff-backed stance.

Placing a palm-sized audio recorder on the table, I switched the ON button. Then I folded back the cover of my reporter's notebook.

"I saw pictures of you in the paper," she spoke with a childlike awe. "I knew you're *family*."

"And so you decided you'd give me your exclusive story? A lesbian loyalty?"

"Yeah. Maybe so. They're gonna put me away forever. Or maybe kill me."

I was struck with her youthful appearance. There was an overwhelming frailness about her. Although we were about the same height of five-eight, she seemed taller because of her rail-like thinness. She was a good ten pounds lighter than my hundred-and-twenty. The paleness of her skin made her piercing blue eyes appear to bulge. She was lime-white - even her hands and arms. In my story I'd use the description 'hauntingly pallid' to explain her coloring. Although her frame was delicate, Jona Beck's demeanor was rough. She'd been around. Short, straggly blonde hair pressed back behind her ears. Her expressions flickered like a spent candle.

"I knew you were family because I saw you before," she announced. "In person."

"Where?" I cautiously asked.

"You were in a bar. Big drag show. I told my girl, Lucia, that I know you're a reporter. She says I'm makin' it up. It was you. Randa Florez. It was a drag show."

"Could have been." I searched my memory. "Drag show. Must have been the AIDS benefit last year." Trawling her face for a recollection was totally ineffective. Her emotions were sturdy granite blocks that excluded recognition.

"I was wearing a denim jacket with *vesica piscis* embroidered on the back."

Memories flooded like tidal waves. "Yes. I remember now. You told me I was the only one who had ever recognized the symbol." The almond shaped, pointed oval sign had intrigued me when taking a mythology class at the university. I'd commented that it looked rather vagina like. The professor smiled and told me that it did indeed signify the divine female genitalia. I had quickly memorized the name. "Your hair was longer and you wore shades."

"Yeah. I figured you'd remember me." Her tone was boasting. "Not many women know what we know."

"What do you know, Jona?"

"They're callin' me a cold-blooded killer. *Cold-blooded*!"

Her eyes glowed. They were chilling. I questioned, "You like being called that?"

"Shit, yes."

Leaning back, I crossed my arms. My hands restlessly clasped the band of muscles in my upper arm. I needed a moment to catch my breath. Jona Beck wasn't jamming the offertory boxes with acts of contrition. I realized that this was the first time I'd really seen a gleam within the eyes of a murderer. Other members of the Forth Estate had told me about seeing a killer's eyes light up as they bragged while discussing their crime. The conceit of an outlaw wasn't uncommon. However, I'd never seen eyes relishing the verbal reenactment of murder.

But when Jona Beck began recounting her crime, I witnessed that look. I broke out in a cold sweat. I'd talked with killers who were conning for their lives, and/or freedom. Often their eyes reflected the look of a trapped, frightened animal. Some of those eyes feigned a pathetic, soulful innocence. But I'd never seen such swaggering contempt. Jona wasn't begging for a pardon, nor was she faking contrition. There was no pretend search for redemption - only haughtiness.

She sat back. She saw my eyes register amazement. She licked her thin upper lip. With a belligerent wink, she continued recounting the gruesome crime.

"The cops busted in. Busted the fuckin' door down. I was standing over Bull's body."

"Bull? You mean the murder victim, Maynard Jones?"

"Yeah. We always called him Bulldog. 'Cause he's ugly as a bulldog's backside. Mean as a bulldog, too. Feisty as hell. Even dying. I carved both his names in his skin 'cause he was so stinkin' feisty. He didn't like his lacerations."

I glanced away. "The officer's report said that you were looking down at the mutilated body with a taunting gaze." I gave her the exact quotation.

"I wanted him to get back up. So I could kill him again. I wanted to do it all over again."

"And you confessed?" I figured her answer would be quick off the mark, and I was correct. This was a grandstand occasion if ever there was one. I recognized it, as well as the remote gaze of neutrality in Jona Beck's eyes.

"Sure. I tell 'em I don't know what got into me. Then I laugh. Tough like." Jona's face twisted into a cruel smile. "The dumb fuck cop asks what I meant. I say, I meant that I didn't know what the fuck got into me. The dumb asshole can't understand English." Her chained feet are nonchalantly planted under the table. There was a moment's intermission as she casually crossed her ankles. She smiled at the sound of clanking chains. "These jerks here at headquarters interrogate me. They tell me I can call someone. Well, I tell 'em how I wanna talk with you. Give you my story."

"Why not an attorney first?"

"They'll appoint one for me."

She knew the system, the script, and verse. "Why did you *really* kill him?"

Jona's shrill laugh allowed her eyes to glow. "You want me to come up with a reason? No need. The fuckin' public defender will give me a reason. Make me out to be a victim. Old Bull always shorted me. Maybe it tossed me over the edge. Maybe they'll make me out to be a victim of drugs. Maybe some kind of wacko."

"You've got to admit, it isn't rational."

Jona leaned forward. Her legs swung back under the marred wooden chair. "You think I'm criminally insane. But maybe I got my reason."

"Reason?"

"I only kill if somebody gets in my way. So that makes me crazy?" Her grin was that of a sun-baked skull.

"You might be giving me that impression for a reason."

"Yeah, you got all the answers. You been to some jackoff college and learned to be a smart ass."

"I went to Denver University."

"D.U." She whistled through her teeth. "You must have bucks."

"No. The university is actually too pricey for me. But I got a few grants and loans. I learned how to live on the cheap. With a Hispanic surname, I often recognized dubious looks being traded when I divulge my alma mater. Stereotypically, we're a low-income race," I said with a trace of bitterness.

"Yeah. You got the Mexican name, but you look kinda different."

Women have called me exotic. My medium-tall trim frame was a gift from my tall, gentlemanly Anglo grandfather on my mother's side. My square face came from my mother's mother. She, my maternal grandmother, wasn't a progenitor I claimed. I wanted my own DNA imprint. My grandmother, Lenora Randolph, perhaps more than any other human being, had harmed my life.

From my father's Hispanic lineage evolved my olive skin tone, dark soulful eyes, and my brooding temperament that converted to a fiesta at the drop of a sombrero. My heredity was truly one given me by my father's family. These people were the family of my soul and spirit. Although my blood was mixed, the *familia* Florez rightfully claimed me as theirs. But it was too complicated to explain to Jona Beck. "I'm a mongrel," I offered.

"As long as you ain't a bitch," Jona said with a snap to her voice. She resumed her anger. "And you pronounce my name John-a. Not like that fella with the fuckin' whale."

"John-a," I stressed.

She reached across the table and snapped off the recorder. "I'm done talkin' with you."

"Might we talk again?"

"Yeah. Maybe. When you write your story, you tell the world that I'm a badass. Tell those fuckers out there to beware. I'm all the evil they ever want to know." When I didn't respond immediately, her eyes sparked. "What you thinking?"

"I was thinking about a Gertrude Stein line. From a book called, *The Geographical History of America*."

"Yeah?"

"Yes. She wrote a phrase that seems somehow appropriate." I cited the passage: "Has anything to do with the human mind. It might. It can have nothing to do with human nature that can easily be seen."

Jona Beck rolled her eyes. "You aren't using that crap in my story, are you?"

"No." I doubted that my readers would appreciate it any more than this twenty-three year old killer did. "I'm not even certain why it sprung into my mind."

"I'll tell you why. Because that ritzy university ruined you. That's why."

"What ruined you, Jona?"

"Fuck off." She would be abstemious from additional interview questions.

She stood. I heard the rattle of her leg chains as she walked to the door. The guard escorted her out. She was probably on her way to another interrogation. Or perhaps they'd sweat her until a public defender was appointed. It didn't make much difference. They had her name on a guilty verdict. Pronounced John-a Beck.

I glanced at the area where she walked. As if some of the residue of Jona Beck remained, I felt her presence. Although in chains, hers seemed to be a soul traveling with no curbs - no barriers. Why the crime? Why the brutality? I wondered what broke Jona's heart. There was a longing to know more about this woman. I realized there must be some reason why she'd gone terribly astray.

Her *evil* excuse was good copy, but what about the invisible nature of the human mind? I wanted to find out. I planned to make an inquiry into this killer's elaborately complex mind. Her past was a start. I'd gone in search of more elusive stories. At least this one had a name and a face. Both name and face were like no others I'd ever known.

My heart was heated. For if I explored another human being, I must know myself. I wanted to view the demons wriggling from Jona Beck's soul. The science of carnage is sad and ugly. I knew there would be a costly intrusion. For anguish was breeding deeply within my own heart. Pretense could emerge from its fugue state. Fear hovered as a divining-rod over my willingness to explore myself.

To locate Jona Beck, I must take an odyssey to locate my pain. That would soap the dirty contents of my own heart. Bathing one's heart is usually a pubertal struggle. My own purgation had often been put on hold. I thought of Ovid's story of Daedalus and his son, Icarus. When one soars too near the sun with wax wings, the result was obvious. If I found Jona's hell, I also faced my own. Perhaps hell was too deep, wide, and furious to describe. As Icarus fell helplessly to earth, so might I.

If I was truly able to locate the message of others, I must decode myself. It was the human face filling itself with language that most intrigued me. Just as there are parts of the vast heavens above that I can't see from here, there are also parts of my reflection lost from my vision. So often life was a cavernous, maze-like chamber.

ASTRAY

CHAPTER 1

Midsummer - Denver, Colorado
Wednesday

"It's been a long time since we've dined together," I admitted with a sigh.

"By your own decision," she replied. My mother sat across from me. She was upset because I hadn't dressed formally for our dinner at the Palace Arms. She withheld conversation. Although my maternal grandparent's estate was located in the prestigious old Cherry Creek gated area, my mother elected to stay downtown at the renowned Brown Palace Hotel. She told me she didn't wish to disrupt her parents. I asked how she can disrupt them in a home as big as a soccer field. She replied there will be a reporter at the hotel to interview her later, and that might upset her parent's agenda.

I'd worn my usual casual tan trousers, a paisley maroon blouse, loafers, and a hastily-retrieved-from-the-closet, mismatched brown jacket. Mother was impeccably dressed in a fashionable light blue suit. Its designer label needn't be seen to be recognized. Mother's shoes and shoulder bag matched. She'd selected a pricey perfume with a scent to capture the thin summer air of Denver.

There was a pause while we ordered. The waiter recognized her. His smile told us both he'd seen her perform. She nodded, returning his good will and fond remembrances of her at the Met. Having been affectionately referred to as America's opera sweetheart by critics, she was always gracious to fans. Admired by those with whom she worked, my mother was a much-beloved mezzo-soprano. Her smile flashed like an explosion. At fifty-three, Erika Randolph had entered a new stage of loveliness.

That unique beauty seemed never to change. Her eyes were always clear, sparkling, and intelligent. Their blueness was near the color of a mountain lake in full sunshine. Her skin, fair and perfect, matched magnificently with light honey-colored hair. Streaks had started to gray slightly. She'd pulled her hair back, gathering it at the base of her neck. Her makeup was skillfully, artfully, done. She had always reminded me of a flawless cameo. Perhaps that was something I'd once read.

When the waiter left, I asked, "Mother, why are you in Denver?"

"I was planning to wait until later to inform you of your grandmother's illness."

"I'm sorry to hear she's unwell." My tone was passably impartial. I swallowed away the bitterness with a small gulp of Scotch on the rocks. My mother sipped mineral water. She silently chastised me with a swirl of her glass.

"She's gravely ill."

I looked away. "Has she been hospitalized?"

"No. Your grandfather has hired a twenty-four hour nursing service."

Timothy Randolph was nothing if not attentive to his wife. He had married Lenora Randolph over fifty-five years ago. They had one child - my mother. Then he became attentive to both his wife and child. Part of his fortune came to him by way of his wealthy East Coast family. The other part was obtained through oil and mineral purchases. He lavished his family with advantage.

"I'm certain she's getting the best care possible." I attempted to make my voice one of confidence. Indifference existed a moment. "I truly hope she recovers."

"Yes." Her word was one of lost confidence. She continued watching me. As if I'm a stranger she's evaluating, she glanced from my lips to my eyes, to my hair. "Randa, you look well."

"I'm doing fine."

"And your career is certainly impressive. Last winter I happened, *quite by accident*, to see the first installment in a series about the young woman psychotic murderer. Naturally, I made it a point to continue reading the series. It was excellent work. But I needn't tell you that. You received the highest possible recognition." She smiled briefly before continuing. "I was extremely proud of your achievement. The series interested the nation as well as your mother."

"It made the wire services. Denver doesn't have many murders of that magnitude." I caught my breath quickly before diving into the next sentence. "It was a major story here. Because of the brutality. I had the exclusive throughout the trial. I was the only reporter Jona Beck allowed to interview her."

"I understand she was found not guilty. And then institutionalized."

"Yes, not guilty by reason of insanity. She was immediately transferred to the institution for the criminally insane division of Corrections."

"Do you believe she is insane?"

"She carved profanities upon a living body. She then continued with his name and her initials on his corpse. The police said she'd tortured Maynard Jones unmercifully. His street name was Bull or Bulldog. She included that name in her carving."

"Did she ever relate to you her reason?"

"Reason," I repeated. "The psychiatrist testified that she's without reason. The leading authority is a woman named Dr. Simone Milton. She believes Jona Beck is unable to control her impulses. The jury agreed that there was mental instability. But that she was capable of distinguishing right from wrong at the time of the crime. That meant she could have been given the death penalty. However in the final sentencing phase, one juror hung the jury. The death sentence was eliminated and it became life without chance of release."

"And you concur?"

"I'm not qualified to evaluate her. But it seems as if she killed as an act of retribution against every transgression of her life. In getting to know her, as much as I might understand the circumstances, I did find that she's very disturbed. Her past set her up with a life of pain. And when she struck back, it was with a vengeance."

"Your father - is he still also a devoted liberal?"

Her eye contact communicated her true question. Had I become a philosophic duplicate that replicated Paulo Florez's political leanings? What wasn't registering in her eyes was concern for my father. She rarely asked about him unless there was a connection with me. It was as if they'd never met, fallen in love, married, and had a child. It was as if he were a dream she'd had thirty-plus years ago. He'd disappointed her, as I had.

"Randa," she intruded on my musings, "will you see your grandmother?"

Wrapped tightly in a moment of heartache, I disconnected our stare. "There's no reason for my seeing her."

"Perhaps not." My mother took a drink of her mineral water. "I thought you might want to see her one final time."

Her words remained a darkness harbored within me. They were gently said, but scathing in intent. I knew they'd cut against my sleep as a paring knife whittling into soft butter. For me, the true wounds of conversation come with verbal artillery.

Dinner was served with elegance. Sparse dialogue was as though my mother and I were two strangers residing behind the glacial barrier of a past gone astray. Words, like stepping stones, moved us toward a dessert tray, and flavored coffees. My mind hiked the rocky silences between pleasantries. Our past had enclosed us in too many skins. To begin disrobing now seemed pointless.

It was as if our grief showed only within closed-circuitry.

* * *

I refused to return home to my nearly vacant loft. I entered my favorite piano bar. Called Marlene's, it had been in business nearly ten years.

Giselle Lamond was singing "Chances Are" with her bedroom blues voice. She nodded as I walked past to take a corner table. Pianist and friend, Del Croft, played piano in his inimitable style. Without asking, my favorite waiter, James, delivered a glass of white wine. Inhaling its aroma, I thought it could be described as being so delicate the goblet might very well be holding Vanda orchids. I sipped slowly before holding it up for a midair toast with the bartender and owner, Alicia Ortiz. Alicia and I knew one another from our youth in our neighborhood. I lifted my thumb with total approval for Alicia's choice of wine.

Giselle finished the set in time to join me before I began a second glass of wine. "Wine is my downfall," Giselle commented. She gave her long, auburn hair a shake. Curls bounced against her bare shoulders. A pale yellow, strapless evening gown highlighted her trimness. She searched Denver's Broadway thrift shops for vintage gowns. Her dark brown eyes glowed with the flicker of candlelight. Her smile widened. Nearing forty, she'd been singing in Denver nightclubs for years. Her songs were from the past about love, parting, and often reuniting. She took another sip of wine. "Mellow," she stated her approval.

"Yes. Hope it makes the wine list. It has my vote." I wanted to tell her it had a tender quality. *Tender* was a word not descriptive of wine, but of women. It was a quality I appreciated in both.

The room began clearing out at midnight on most week nights. Tonight the stools at the bar and around the piano were still occupied. Tables were filled with chattering, laughing men and women. With an upscale art deco atmosphere, the bar was dedicated to Marlene Dietrich. Grays, lavenders, teals, and polished chrome were combined with mirrors and life-sized photo images of Marlene. I'd sat nearest the sultry femme fatales' Blue Angel visage.

"How did things go with your mother?"

I turned my wine glass. "Ours is a relationship of great formality."

"Did you ask if she might drop by for a quick aria or two at the piano bar?"

I released a brief smile. "If you're willing to bring in a string and brass section. Actually she told me that my grandmother is ill. Perhaps dying."

"And?"

"And for the first time she seemed interested in my job. It was the story series I'd filed last winter about Jona Beck. My mother was in New York. She happened to see my byline. The story had gained national attention."

"Did you mention that the kid is seducing her shrink?"

I smiled. "I'm not sure she is."

"One of the guys tells me it isn't a rumor. There is something going on. He dates a fellow who works at the state institution. Claims it's all true. Jona and Dr. Simone Milton are very sweet on one another."

"Somewhat of an age difference," I commented. "Jona is twenty-three and Dr. Milton must be in her forties."

"Forty-two. From what I hear Jona's ex-lover made a big scene last time she visited."

"Lucia Gomez. I interviewed her several times when I was covering the Beck story."

"You probably didn't mention the seamier side of Jona Beck's life to your mother."

"No. She has enough to contend with by admitting I'm not only a primary Hispanic, but also a lesbian."

"Primary Hispanic," Giselle repeated with a laugh. "Because you were raised by your father's family, you consider yourself *primary Hispanic*?"

"I lived my first few years, for the most part, with my maternal grandparents. The Courts relegated my keeping to the pedigreed, moneyed, influential branch of my family tree. My mother was traveling too extensively to be burdened with me. She originally studied opera in Europe. My father went to court claiming he could offer a much more stable life. Custody was granted him, so I lived with my father and paternal grandparents from then on – with the exception of part of my summer vacations."

"You'd think the courts would've given you to your rich grandparents and famous mother."

"Perhaps the courts wisely decided there's more to life than money and fame." My words struck with precision. I choose not to explain that I could still recall being a child of five. Some introspective moments were where knots of grief resided. The difference between sorrow and farce blended. I'd barely become a preschooler. Then, sitting in the judge's chambers, I was diminished into a very small child grasping at the armrests. My breathing was shallow and difficult when answering questions. I wanted to stay with my father and his parents. There I was loved. I have since lived with the recrimination of hurting my mother. My decision, however, I've never felt to be wrong.

I was glad when Alicia brought the bottle of wine to our table. She poured us each another drink and then herself one. She was an amateur eavesdropper, but with a professional ranking of not letting on she'd been listening. "What's the verdict?" she asked.

"Excellent wine," I answered. "What do you think?"

"I'll put it on the list." Alicia Ortiz had entered her mid-forties. With a rubicund face, a bright smile, eyes that appeared to have the darkness of a brooding joke, and short salt and pepper hair, she was attractive. "I want to replace that weak Italian wine I had last month. The only lousy Italian wine I can remember serving."

"It was pixy piss," Giselle agreed. "But this," she said holding it up to the light, "makes me want to fall in love."

I nodded in agreement. "Yes. The wine is definitely romantic."

"Any romantic candidates now that Alison is a person of the past?" Giselle inquired. "Or *is* she finally out of your life?"

"We see one another as friends," I answered. Ali's relationships are always in the chronic state of impending demise. "I care. Of course I do."

They shared a knowing glance at one another. They needn't bother telling me that when Alison was finally done with me, I'll be emotionally pummeled until every filament of life ached. They knew she was a Sapphic scalp collector. Alison wouldn't be neglected. Her ultimatum was implied from day one. My profession often got in the way of her profession. She'd hoped some of her suggestions that were babbled in my ear between breathless love scenes might turn me around. Unresolved love always left a struggle showing within my eyes.

My cell phone rang its annoying whirlybird bell sound. I removed it from my pocket. When finished listening to the message, I quickly stood. I tipped a final gulp from my glass. "I'm on my way."

"Assignment?" Alicia asked.

"No. One of the police officers just called to let me know they've arrested my youngest brother Benjy."

"Serious?" Giselle questioned.

"It will be when my father finds out." I slipped into my jacket. "Joy riding again." I passed by Del Croft's piano and tossed a couple bills into his tip stein. "Keep on playing," I said with as much joy as I could manage.

He giggled. His hand went up, and then he playfully gave a partial wave in my direction. "I'm known for playing," he chirped. "You too, dear."

"Not going to be playing tonight," I forecasted. I began my trek to the parking lot. I'd bail out seventeen-year old Benjamin Augustine Florez. Then I'd want to scream my disapproval at him. But I'd probably only look into his pathetic face through the swimming view of my tears.

On the way to my car, I gazed up at the tincture of iodine-colored Denver skyline. I'm most saddened that my father will suffer because of Benjy. Father deserved sorrow less than anyone else I know.

* * *

"I'm Officer O'Bryan," she spoke as she outstretched her hand. "Nevada O'Bryan."

Nevada O'Bryan was an attractive woman, I guessed to be in her mid-twenties. Thick light brown hair had streaks the color of caramel. It was tied back and wrapped. Her eyes were a golden green. They shone brightly, with intelligence, from behind long-lashed lids. Her face was angular and her jaw softly cleft. Her smile was rapid fire with front teeth slightly crooked behind well-formed pouty lips. She stood about an inch taller than me. Her uniformed frame was toned.

"Thanks for calling," I said as I quickly released her hand. "Benjy loves cars. My father and other brother are mechanics. They have a small shop down on Federal Boulevard. Benjy probably borrowed one of the cars they'd been working on."

"That's your story and you're sticking to it," she commented with amusement. Her right eyebrow lifted. Her smile dimpled. "Your brother was picked up for speeding. He was not only without a driver's license, but there was no auto registration or proof of insurance."

I stood wand straight. "Look, Officer O'Bryan, he's not a bad kid."

"If he were a bad kid, we'd have already hauled him to a detention center." She paused, looking at her watch. "I'm ready to get off duty. Let's go grab a cup of coffee. Maybe a little breakfast."

"My brother is in a cell."

"Safe and sound."

"He should be home, Officer O'Bryan."

"Call me Nevada. And he'll be home before the night is over. But for now, my advice is to sweat him a little."

"Sweat him or stew him. He's just a kid," I argued.

"Your confrontational glare is bringing a knife to a gunfight," she teased.

My frown deepened. "You're new on the force?"

"But not new to enforcement. I've been a cop for five years. I've learned that it doesn't hurt to give a kid some time to think about how small those cells are. Come on, I'll spring for the breakfast special at Ruby's Coffee Shop. Just down the street."

It was my turn to grin. "I know where it is. It's one of Denver's lesbian-owned businesses."

"Uh huh, that's the one." As we walked to the door, she told the desk sergeant she'd be back in an hour. Then, to me, she whispered, "One of the officers mentioned that you're a reporter over at *The Mirror*. Crime reporter, right?"

"That would be me."

"She also mentioned you're family."

"That would also be me."

"You're lovely enough to be a TV news anchor," she stated with a flirtatious grin.

"My voice is too raspy. That delegates me to newspapers," I replied. "And I like ink."

When we reached Ruby's, we entered and were seated. Ruby Ryder was a huge, black woman in her late fifties. She had owned the hole-in-the-wall coffee shop and café for nearly thirty years. She greeted us by throwing the menus down with a slap on the booth's table.

"You don't want sausage," she informed us. "They musta taken it from a mean mule's ass."

"Make mine the special with *bacon*," I stressed.

"Same, please," Nevada ordered.

"Randa," Ruby began, "you tryin' to pump this little gal for information or get a date and be lucky?" Her laugh slammed the airway. She left to prepare our order, still chuckling.

Nevada blushed, but only momentarily. She looked away, down the aisle toward the front window. We had automatically sat in the back booth. I knew uniformed cops always try to sit against the wall, never to become a willing target.

"Your brother doesn't look like you," Nevada said.

"No. We share the same father, but different mothers. My mother and father were divorced when I was an infant. My father remarried over twenty years ago. I was just entering my preteen years then."

"So you have a stepmother?"

"Yes. Angie is my brother's mother. She was in her early twenties when she married my father. He was older than she. Angie was actually like my older sister. But I lived with my grandparents most of the time."

"You have two half-brothers?"

"Yes. Rogerio is twenty-one. And you've met Benjy. He just turned seventeen. How about you?"

"I'm from Nevada. I picked up the nickname while working in Wyoming. I've always had a handle. Mostly Lefty – because I'm left-handed."

"I'm usually observant, but I didn't notice your gun is on

the left side."

"I hope you didn't notice because you're looking into my eyes." She snickered slightly. "Anyway, let's not call me Lefty. Or Margaret. Do I look like a Margaret?" She smiled.

"Not especially. Why did you leave Nevada?"

"I wanted to travel and I liked cool weather. And there was a job opening in Wyoming. When a slot opened in Denver, well…that had been my first choice so I quickly accepted."

"Why did you become a police officer?" I delved.

"Simple. The hours are wonderful. The money great. Add to that the benefit of being in a nice, safe occupation. Can't be beat."

I laughed. "The hours stink, the money is lousy, and it's dangerous. So much for honesty."

"I think I can make a difference. Keep the streets sweet. If punks would stop *borrowing* cars it would be sweeter."

"When my father is finished with Benjy, I'd be willing to bet the streets sweeten up."

"Your dad likes corporal punishment?"

"Worse than flogging," I replied. I didn't tell her, but maybe she deciphered it in my somber expression. It was going to make my father weep. And that broke our hearts far worse than a thrashing.

"Let's hope Benjy gets the cure before he turns eighteen."

"It will take him that long to saw through his leg irons."

* * *

"Why Benj?" I asked as I drove toward my loft.

"I needed some space. Did you call our folks?"

"Yes. I told them you'd be staying the night with me. I'll drop you back home in the morning after they've had a chance to cool. Father said he'll pick up the car in the morning. And he's very disappointed in you."

Benjy shifted his slight frame, and then slid down into the bucket seat. "Sorry I got you up."

"I was up. So you needed an outing. You steal a car from your own father's shop. He's responsible for the cars he's working on. Benj, you need some sense dinned into your head. You've already lost your license for a year because you pulled this last winter. Are you going for broke? Do you want to serve detention time?"

"I've borrowed cars before and only got caught once."

"Twice counting tonight," I reminded him. Benjy operated under the presumption that when all else fails, the truth must be manipulated. "Just don't lie to me. I hate that worse than anything."

"You've always been Father's favorite," he indicted. "You've got it made. Lighter than me, tall, and your mother's famous. You've been to the university. Your talk is fancy. What the hell do I have?"

"Benj, I worked my way through school. And I earned scholarships along the way. No one handed me anything."

"That's bullshit. I'm the runt of the family."

"Why do you always compare yourself to Rogerio and me? You may be darker and shorter, but that adds to your charm. You're a good looking kid. As is, you are a handsome guy. You're not done growing. You're a sweet kid. If you'll just apply yourself and study you can do anything. You've got to work hard."

"It's too late when I'm a D-student."

"I told you I'll help you. For years I've also told you that I'll help pay for your education. And if college doesn't appeal, you know you have another option. You love cars. Father will let you join him and Rog at the shop. He'll train you to be a master mechanic. It's time you stop with the excuses, grow up, and take responsibility."

His silence told me volumes. Perhaps he knew that although I loved him, my favorite had always been Rogerio. Benjy was difficult to love. Once when I was watching after him, and he was about seven, he called me patron saint of shit-heads everywhere. I wasn't certain if he'd heard that from his mother or not. Angie was known to use that language, adding her own unique twists.

Angie often used her volatile vocabulary when referring to

my mother. I assumed Father loved Angie for her ability to make him laugh. Her humor and her sexuality might have helped snare him. I had never been convinced he was over my mother. My father believed it was his fault that Angie was resentful. Although he attempted to deny feelings for my mother, I've heard him listening to the compact discs of Erika Randolph.

Paulo Florez and Erika Randolph had met while studying music. He played classical guitar, taught by his grandfather. He also composed songs. Many were written for my mother. She sang like an angel. Although he played his guitar after my mother left, it was rare. And when she married a famous conductor, my father put his guitar in the attic. I hadn't heard his wondrous renditions since.

His first wife had stabbed a knife in his heart. Now his youngest son was doing the same. I reached over, took Benjy's hand and squeezed it. "Please don't hurt Father. He loves the three of us. Maybe he loves you most of all."

One thing I knew about my father. His love went where it was most needed.

* * *

After clearing papers from the sofa in my office, or as it was intended - a second bedroom, I took a quilt to my brother. He was already sleeping, so I carefully covered his thin limbs. I turned out the light and went up to my loft bedroom. There I considered the day's events. On the nightstand was my journal. There I tracked my thoughts, hopes, inspirations, and daily happenings.

Yesterday I had written that I remained in a romantic wilderness. Tonight I wrote: DITTO in big, block letters. Then: Dinner with Mother - similar to all other dinners with Mother; Wine at Marlene's; Benjy steals auto; Breakfast at Ruby's with a woman called Nevada O'Bryan. Benjy's arresting officer.

There was little more to report. I might have gone back to write in the margin that my grandmother Randolph was seriously ill, perhaps dying. But there was no previous mention of Lenora Randolph within my journal, so why make the entry at this late date.

I closed my journal, turned off the light, and considered that the day had taken me from the warm side of hell, to a slightly more comfortable cool area. If true happiness was an inside job, I vowed to work on some heavenly dreams.

CHAPTER 2

Thursday

LoDo became the abbreviation for Lower Downtown Denver's chic area years ago. The restored historic district between the newer downtown and the Central Platte Valley, was a trendy, hip area with a European air. Built for early generations, it was rebuilt with Coors Field, clusters of fashionable restaurants, street and rooftop cafes, microbreweries, art galleries, exclusive shops, very costly lofts, and equally expensive condos.

I had purchased my loft while the costs were not prohibitive to my newspaper reporter's budget. Admittedly, it was under the beautiful Alison Pagette's influence. Much of what I'd done in the past few years had been to please her; to acquiesce to her desires; to prove my love of her and for her and to her. And perhaps prove my love of her to myself.

Alison's luxury penthouse condo was only two blocks away from mine. Her elaborately decorated three bedroom condo displayed views of our extraordinary city and majestic mountains. She believed in being part of Denver's 'new energy' crowd. If I were to be at her side, in her bed, or even remotely near her, I was also to become a card-carrying member of her clique.

When she turned thirty, four years ago, her public relations firm was already taking the city by storm. Today her charm and talent had catapulted her to being owner of one of the top ten agencies in Denver. She was a force to be reckoned with in the business community - also in bed, as well as life in general.

Morning began with Alison's two messages on my phone service. The second was always her 'urgent' call. She urgently needed a response. I returned her call only after delivering

Benjy home. Alison was perturbed that I hadn't immediately contacted her. I offered to take her to lunch. She thought about declining. She said she'd meet me at an expensive little Moroccan restaurant. She then commented that if I were left to select, I'll take her to a taco stand on Pecos Street. Hot sauce would drip from her chin, she jabbed. I agreed to a sumptuous, lavish meal. It would cost me, but I realized that fact when I failed to call her on her first request.

The morning was used up in my home office, seated in front of my computer. I finished the story on a drug bust that yielded weaponry, and meth-amphetamines. After e-mailing the completed story to *The Mirror*, I showered and dressed in casual, neutral clothing. With minimal makeup, I glanced into the mirror's image. Ali would certainly challenge my scruffy look. I relented and changed from a cotton shirt to a satiny rose-colored dress blouse. I deepened the hue of my lipstick from frosty coral to rosy magenta.

When I arrived at the restaurant, Alison was waiting. I kissed her cheek. It was warm. Her elegant perfume lifted to excite my senses. Blonde curls stylishly surrounded her thin model's face. Her eyes were amethyst. Their sparkle blazed when she loves. Her smile was the enchanting secret between her lips. Just as with the Rubens portrait *Chapeau de paille*, one knows those lips will kiss back, but never entirely. They kept you anticipating.

Alison's clothing was always elegant and chic. Although she attracted both men and women, her love was purely Sapphic. Her magnetic draw was with the dynamics of a tornado's eye. She was perhaps the most charismatic, sensual woman I'd ever known, or ever seen for that matter.

"Finally," she snapped. "You know if you quit babysitting your family you might have time for your own life."

"Benjy needed bailing. He is my brother."

"Half-brother."

"That was the half I rescued," I retorted. "Look, let's not quarrel. You look magnificently beautiful." And she truly did. Her summer orchid-colored dress was purely business, but very feminine. "Great outfit, Ali."

"You could afford to smarten up if you stopped spending your income on the *familia*. What did bail put you back?"

"One of the officers pulled some strings. She's a *sister*. No one pressed charges, so she got the joyriding and other charges dropped. It was reduced to driving with a suspended license. Hardly a capital offense."

"She? Probably some corn-goddess woman turned bulldyke cop."

My silence refuted her comment. "She's a new officer on the force."

"Pretty?"

"Very."

"Interested?"

"Alison, I just met her. I'll probably never see her again."

"Of course you will. You hang around with Gypsies, tramps and thieves."

"Rather appropriate for a crime reporter." I ordered a bottle of wine that she probably would not approve. "How has your day gone?"

"Very damned grim. I've got to go to New York for a day or two."

"A mini-vacation?"

"Not hardly. Kissing client butts."

I grinned. "At least I'm not required to kiss any body parts of those Gypsies, tramps and thieves with whom I work."

"And I was going to pick up the luncheon tab before that remark," she chided.

"Don't let me stop you," I said with an accompanying smile.

"Randa, you're impossible at times." She paused. "How is your grandmother?"

"I'm assuming you're inquiring about my maternal grandmother Randolph. I have no idea how she is." I neglected to add that she never asked about my grandparents Florez.

"If she kicks off, you could be wealthy."

"Me wealthy?" I offered the question with a smile. I shook my head, and then sipped the wine. "Actually, no. Not really.

My grandfather is very fit. And my mother is next in line. The only time Mother ever spoke with me concerning her will, I requested that I not be included. I imagine her plans are to leave her money to a foundation of beleaguered opera singers."

"That will certainly give those old folks something to hit a high note about." We laughed. She took my hand. "Want to come by later? I'll be home after nine."

"Won't you need to pack?"

"Not as desperately as I'll need to achieve a dramatic, passionate orgasm." She rubbed her foot against the calf of my leg. "Any volunteers to give me a hand?" She bit her lower lip. "Well?"

As an apprentice lesbian might nod in agreement, my head tucked down first, and then lifted. If my heart was party to chaos for the homage I paid the exquisite Alison, I had only one answer. Her kiss was a great luxury in my life. The song claims that breaking up is so very hard to do. And indeed it was. Perhaps it would be inevitable, but I clung to desire for all I was worth.

From the adventures of Aeneas I recalled reading about the Fields of Mourning where unhappy lovers dwelt in the underworld. Lost souls resided there. I can only imagine Alison with her multitudes of castaway lovers. There were days when I'd be damned if I'd be one of them. And there are nights when the Field of Mourning looked like a box office smash.

* * *

My afternoon was shared between Denver County Court and *The Mile High Mirror*. After I'd filed my story, I decided to go by my grandparent's home. I had lived most of my life there with them. Before my father remarried, we lived with my grandmother, Mama Carmina, and grandfather, Papa Gus. Augustine and Carmina Florez were in their mid-seventies. They'd produced a daughter and three sons. My aunt Irene, or Renie to friends and family, had always lived at home with my grandparents. Uncles Diego and Dante, and their families, like my father and Angie, lived in the neighborhood.

Growing up was with Mama and Papa, Aunt Renie, and before my father married Angie, with my father. After he married, I wanted to stay behind with my grandparents. And why not? The cozy small brick bungalow home was the family's core. The home always had food cooking on an oversized range, laughter, and many cousins and friends. It was located in the Highland area, one of Denver's first residential neighborhoods.

There was a rich ethnic mix, and had become a diversified district of the city. Before the Highland's recent real estate popularity, property prices were low, affording women the opportunity of home ownership. Many Sapphic *sisters* had moved into the area in the last decade. We jokingly called the area Lesbian Heights.

When I came out to my family, my Uncle Dante joked that the neighborhood had so many lesbians I might lose my identity. Mama hushed him, but I simply laughed. Mama Carmina maintained there were to be no harsh words in her home. Although her own commanding voice often reached a volume my mother and her league of opera pals would envy.

My grandmother was tall and thin. She attributed her height to her mother's linage. My great-grandmother was full-blooded Native American. Mama was now gray-haired, with taut face. Her dark eyes peered through spectacles. Slightly stooped, she still moved quickly. She had become my confidante, my friend, my benefactor, and certainly my hero.

If the home was Mama Carmina's castle, Papa Gus's domain was the garden. Winters the converted garage became his greenhouse. His three sons built skylights and installed heating. There Papa Gus grew strange and wondrous plants. He specialized in scented geraniums. Our name, Florez, was derived from the word *flower*. All the pots of geraniums he'd provided to me eventually succumbed. He was baffled that a Florez could kill off a plant.

Stockily built, Papa Gus had a circular face beneath a shock of gray hair. Stern, that face also teased unmercifully, but always playfully. His motto had always been *Vivimus, vivamus.*

Let us live while we live. When I told him I'm lesbian his eyes overflowed with tears. He took my hand in his rough hands. He wanted me to sing lullabies to my children. Children are life's joy, he believed. We never spoke of it after that. He had accepted me.

My Aunt Renie was a different story. She began by telling me that the Catholic Church doesn't accept such behavior. I would argue. Finally, she would throw her hands in the air and scream, "What's the use of mending a chair on a sinking ship?" She had come to simply ignore my plight. Perhaps she thought I had a longing for the fires of hell.

Renie had never missed a Sunday Mass, and firmly believed they should give her an award for devout attendance. My Uncle Diego asked if she thought she should be given the Pope's Most Valuable Player cup. She chased him for several blocks. When she returned, she said if not the MVP, she should at least get a game ball. She resembled Mama Carmina, but with larger Bo-Peep eyes.

Renie refused to talk about my lesbianism with me. In spite of her ostracism where my sexual orientation was concerned, Aunt Renie had been wonderful to me. Her true nemesis was her sister-in-law - Angie. When my father brought Angie to the house, Renie had fits. Her smile became stone. She had tormented Angie with biblical reference for any sins Angie may have committed, or planned to commit.

Renie had her own ideas when it came to love and lust. She believed she must live a highly antiseptic life. She also expected the same from those around her. Some she was more forgiving of - and luckily, I was one who had her absolution. Angie had no such luck. She was fated to be on Renie's bad side. And as with most of life's destiny - it was fate that remained the ultimate boss.

Most families perpetuated the axiom that love was not easily recognized - and almost never understood. It did, however, exist within my *familia*. That much I recognized *and* understood.

* * *

"I made the *polla almendrado* especially for you," Mama Carmina told me. "Now you eat another helping." She scooped a brimming serving spoon filled with almond-sprinkled chicken that had been baked with tomatoes, peppers, assorted herbs, and lime juice. She dumped it into the center of my plate. "Randa, you haven't been here all week. Papa tells me you have forgotten us."

"No, Mama. Never that," I responded. I took a fork heaped with falling-apart tender chicken. "It's delicious. I don't want to be too full to exercise." I kept my bicycle at the house so that I could stop by after work to ride. It seemed a more peaceful ride than trying to cycle through the center of LoDo.

"Go," Mama commanded. "Ride your bike. When you come back, I'll reheat it for you. And your Aunt Renie has made *flan de naranja*."

"I'll need to ride to Pikes Peak if I'm to be treated with Renie's orange flan." We shared a laugh. I hugged my grandmother on the way to the door. "I'll be back within an hour or so."

I moved quickly to the shed where I retrieved my royal purple bike. I pedaled rapidly several blocks before slowing down. That, I considered, was my warm-up cycling. The rest of the ride was to be used only to observe and delight in the late afternoon's summer warmth. My destination was a small, nearby park. I'd been on the park's path for about ten minutes when I heard my name being called. I turned as I slowed the bike.

"Remember me?" Nevada O'Bryan asked.

"Yes." I smiled, gliding to a stop as she rode her bronze bike next to mine. "Officer O'Bryan."

"Call me Nevada. Most people don't recognize me when I'm out of uniform. People often find dealing with enforcers unpleasant. The quicker they forget the face, the better. I live nearby. Do you live here in West Denver, too?"

"No. My grandparent's home is a few blocks away. I was raised with them, so it's like a second home. I have a loft in

LoDo."

"That's impressive."

"A very small loft. And I purchased it when it was more affordable. It's nearer my office."

"The desk sergeant told me that you live to work."

"Guilty as charged."

Her laugh was sweet. "Yes. I can relate to that. Even now, I'm not just biking, I'm exercising for my next major chase. And I'm pooped. Would you like to go over to the Java Brew for a cup of iced coffee?"

"Sure. A drink called 'Mocha Madness' is my favorite drink in the world."

"Mine also. I've been going to the Brew for a couple of weeks now and just discovered the owners are *family*," she said as we escorted our bikes along the path.

"Lots of it going around in this neighborhood," I joked. "I'd gone there for years before I found out the proprietors are lesbian. It's nice to be able to support business in the community."

"I subscribe to your newspaper."

"Every subscription counts. I'll race you."

I jumped on my bike and began peddling toward Java Brew. It was little more than a small storefront shop, but it had atmosphere. Walls were painted with murals of famous world scenes. Many of them I recognize from summer vacations spent with my mother in Europe. My mother took me sightseeing, but the lion's share of the time was spent in dressing rooms of opera houses. I saw more of *Covent Garden* than of Big Ben. I didn't miss not seeing Spain's bullfights, but at the time, I resented spending hours waiting in the wings at *Teatro alla Scala*. While in Salzburg, my days were at the *Grosses Festspielhous.* In Vienna it was the *Staatsoper*; and in Rome the *Teatro dell' Opera.* I tired very quickly of the fussy garments, the backstage frenzy, and in general, of the large production atmosphere. I was a child in the background, and in the way.

Nevada breathlessly sat opposite of me at the table by the wall. When our iced coffees were delivered, we sipped slowly. I allowed the mocha flavor to seep into my taste buds. "Terrific," I commented.

"I like the Java Brew's ambiance. Books, magazines, games, and art."

"I'm glad you didn't suggest the corner tavern. My grandfather is having his post-supper glass of *cervaza* at Lena's Bar. Over two blocks and on the corner."

"I've hauled a few patrons from there," she said with a laugh. "Probably not your grandfather."

"No. Papa Gus only has one beer. It is his custom to have a brew before sleep. Also it helps him escape from his *casa de mujeres* to an atmosphere where he can converse with his cronies."

"And your father?"

"Most of the time he stays at home with Angie, Benjy's mom. After they were first married my father tried on the tradition of a drink with his pals after dinner. Angie followed him, shouted obscenities at him in the bar, and drug him home by the shirt sleeve."

"Is she a shrew?"

"No, not at all. It's just that her father was an alcoholic, so she wanted no part of that behavior in her husband. She has since relented. My father is free to stop in the tavern from time to time. I've only seen him loaded twice. Once was at my Uncle Diego's wedding. I was young. My father was just being *very* silly. I'm not sure I even realized he was drunk. I just thought he was hilarious. My father is a sweet, kind man. Very calm and quiet, actually. The only other time I saw him drunk was when I was eleven or so. My mother had remarried. My father took his guitar to the attic. He wept, saying that the song was gone from his life."

I remembered the agony in Father's voice. Not only was his heart broken, he was worried about my mother. And he was terrified of turning his daughter over to a man like my mother's new husband. I was to spend summers with them. Mother had married the world-famous conductor, Sanford Winton. Sanford was a self-absorbed man who relentlessly chased women and his own celebrity status.

My father sensed Sanford was also a cunning, cruel man. My father was correct in his insightful evaluation. My mother divorced Sanford after five years. By that time the damage had been done to us all.

After a moment's silence, I added, "My father enjoys the tavern mostly to meet his brothers, friends, and clients. He says it's an opportunity to pass out cards for their auto repair shop. Rogerio, my law-abiding brother, agrees."

"Tell your non-law-abiding brother that if I catch him borrowing any more cars, I'll cloud up and rain all over him. He has you and Rogerio as role models."

"Rog married several months ago. I'm going to be an aunt anytime now. My father is thrilled about it, and so is Angie. Although she says she's too young to be a grandmother."

Rogerio's wife, Teresa, was very well-suited for Rogerio. They were high school sweethearts, and so it had lasted the prelude-test of time. She possessed an even temper, quick wit, and was much more outgoing that my quiet brother. She was small in stature, but she had an energetic enthusiasm that made her capture a room. Most importantly to the family, and to me, she's made Rogerio happy.

We passed nearly an hour talking about our respective families. Nevada related her history, love affairs, and her love of job. We joked, and we shared thoughts. I was enjoying myself, I thought, as we ordered another round of Mocha Madness.

"A penny for your thoughts," she said.

"My thoughts aren't worth a penny this afternoon."

"And I was told you're an intellectual. Award-winning, ace reporter - Denver's own Randa Pilar Florez."

My face was flush with embarrassment. I leaned back against my chair as my hand automatically reached to rub my chin. "You've even remembered my middle name. It's my grandmother's middle name also." I smiled. "I use it as part of my byline to honor Mama Carmina."

"She must be pleased. You've done some terrific work."

"I've been lucky on an assignment or two."

"I recall reading the Jona Beck series when I was in Wyoming. I'm amazed you got her to open up and talk with you."

"It amazed me as well. Because I was the only one with a pipeline to her, I was even becoming tabloid fodder. I found that a great annoyance."

"Think they'll ever spring Jona Beck?"

"You're the law. You'd know much more about that possibility than I would. My guess is that she'll never see the light of day again. And your best guess?"

"I'm becoming a cynic. I think she'll pull down a couple years. Then a shrink's arrogance will claim to have tightened her bolts. They'll say she's sane. She may serve another year or two in prison to make certain she repents. Finally, she's out to make room for a new pretender."

"You might be right. She's very cagey."

"Cagey, not screwy?"

"After all the time I spent with her, all the days I chased her history - friends and family, anyone who knew her, I should know the answer." I paused, recounting in my mind the terror of the murder scene photos. "It has become a great riddle in my life. There were times when I was in her presence that I felt to be a shadow within a galloping heartbeat. Sometimes I barely felt able to breathe. She radiated an evil that was difficult to explain. If her love ever existed, it had been bitten away by darkness. She once asked me if I knew the secret color of dark. She bolted up from her chair, screaming. Then her eyes rolled. She muttered that passion is the true killer."

"Sounds weird to me."

"I honestly don't know if she is insane and impersonates reason. Or perhaps she's sane, imitating insanity. When the case began, I vowed to do the most in-depth, extensive study of the criminal mind possible. I still failed to understand Jona Beck. As thorough as my attempts might have seemed at the time, I did little more than write a story about her. Her motives, her mindset - they remain her own. She remains a mystery in the annals of crime."

"Speaking of crime," Nevada said, glancing at her

wristwatch, "I'd better make a move to get home. I'm working the graveyard shift tonight."

"I'd better get back, too."

"Hot date?"

My blush answered her question. "I'm going to visit a friend."

"My source tells me you date a ravishing, luscious woman. Might she be the friend?"

"Yes. Her name is Alison Pagette. We're in what's known as the 'make it or break it' stage of our relationship. It's been dicey for nearly a year. For all practical purposes, it's ended. The final farewell is difficult."

"Are you in love with her?"

Ending love seemed difficult to describe. There remained impressions against the memory's lining. They included first sight, first kiss, first touch, first contact, and first fight. They were the graphics of a smile that made tender my soul; a wink that lifted my spirits through the galaxies; and the come-hither glance that still melted my heart. Now the streamers had fallen. The confetti had drifted elsewhere. "I'm not certain," I answered.

Nevada stood. "Well, get certain, in case I decided I want you." Her laugh wasn't over-confident, nor was it teasing. It was a cop's tone of assured, recommended procedure.

I allowed a brief smile. Her words may have originated in her heart, but she said them with her *badge*. "I'll remember that," I replied with a heavy dose of my own editorializing.

* * *

When I returned to my grandparent's home, I saw my father's teal-colored Jeep in the driveway. Father met me as I entered the house, and we hugged briefly. "Thanks again," he said, "for taking care of Benjy last night."

"Is he grounded?"

"For the rest of his natural life," Angie answered. She was seated at the kitchen table. Her spoon nervously pushed Renie's *flan de naranja* around in the dessert bowl. She acted suspicious of its contents. In Angie's heart of hearts, she believed Renie capable of offing her with poison orange flan.

There was tension when Aunt Renie and Angie entered the same vicinity. Aunt Renie usually quoted scripture, never neglecting her biblical appreciation. Rankled, Angie retaliated by reminding Renie that she was married to Renie's favorite brother. That was her niche in the family diagram. To say nothing of the fact that from Angie's womb two Florez males had sprung. Angie enjoyed the indisputable fact that she was tight-wound *familia*. Renie did not enjoy that fact.

Renie sat opposite Angie with a scowl in her direction that was dwarfed only by intermittent pious smiles toward my father. "Eat your flan, Paulo," she encouraged. "And Randa, try some."

I knew better than to resist Renie. I sat in the most neutral seat at the table. After a large scoop of luscious flan, I announced, "Renie, this is the best orange flan you've ever created."

Renie gave Angie an additional glare. "Angie, you aren't eating yours. You don't like it maybe?"

"I had a big dinner," Angie replied with her own attitude. "And who the hell appointed you the damned flan cop?"

Renie checked my father for his reprimand. "Paulo doesn't approve of that kind of language," she denounced her sister-in-law.

"My *husband* doesn't like your picking at me," Angie retorted.

"I pick only at sin and sinners," Renie said. Her jaw clamped.

"I'd rather live with the sinners than die with the saints!" Angie retaliated.

My father's discomfort was obvious. I asked, "Father, do you have time to look at my car? I'm still having problems with the accelerator."

He stood to follow me away from the chaos. "I'll check it now. You might need to bring it in to the shop."

"I can swing by first thing tomorrow morning."

We walked together to the street where my silver Z was parked. His arm slid around my shoulder. "Thanks for getting me out of that mess," he said with a sigh of appreciation. "It is truly being detached from the horns of a dilemma. I wish Renie wouldn't be so hard on Angie. Angie now calls my parent's home *Renie's dungeon*."

"I love Aunt Renie, but she seems to search her targets," I replied. I got into the driver's seat to pull the hood release. "Before Angie, did Renie pick on my mother?"

"No." Father's answer was swift. "No." I studied him as he frowned. He had inherited his mother's rapier trimness. Standing six-feet tall, he had a distinguished, polished stance and walk. It seemed one of great nobility. Handsome in a stately way, opposed to *cute* handsome. With a medium complexion, his eyes were very dark. His short hair, mustache and beard were salt and pepper. The beard was precisely clipped with the dignity of the *Man of La Mancha*. Father was a proud man. Yet great humility was within his soul.

Father was college educated, having earned a music scholarship with his mastery of guitar. He had continued to learn throughout his life. His brothers and buddies referred to him as 'Professor' Paulo because of his sense of inquiry, along with his soft-spoken nature. Father's voice usually implied something of great importance was about to be communicated. When now he spoke, I realized his frown meant that he wanted to ask something vital to him.

"Have you talked with Erika today?" he questioned.

"She hasn't called."

"Randa, you might call your mother. Her own mother is in grave condition." His expression reflected compassion. Even when talking about the ex-wife that broke his heart. "I'm certain she wants to hear from you."

"She called you?"

"Only to ask if you were doing all right."

"I had dinner with her. She saw that I'm doing fine." My tone was one of exasperation. "You've got your own troubles with Benjy. I don't see why she's trying to complicate your life."

"Your mother wants a relationship with you. If nothing else I've tried to teach you to respect your parents." His voice scolded, yet with a gentle reprimand.

"She wants a formal relationship. She gets formality. Let's face it - we've been estranged for years." I started my auto's engine. I revved it for several moments, and then turned off the ignition. My father leaned over the fender. I joined him. Together we peered into the cavernous under-hood area to view an immaculately well-kept engine. "Mother doesn't really want to be bothered unless it's on her terms."

"That's not true, Randa."

"Of course it is," I disputed. "Other than her love of opera and her parents, her heart is a corpse."

"No. She's more loving than you know. She's an artist. She is a very sensitive artist. She's sacrificed greatly to have achieved acclaim. She must feel very alone at times." His low, well-modulated voice dipped, "Times like now."

"It's her decision. Opera was always more important to her than we were."

"You aren't being fair. Randa, you don't know how it was for her. For us."

"I know how it was to be her abandoned child," my brittle accusation was spoken with difficulty.

"You were never that. Her mother is dying."

"Sorrow is easier than guilt."

He turned to look into my face. His own face was drawn. "Your mother is one of life's special people. Gifted. Her voice brings audiences joy. She's like a very rare jewel."

"I don't care if she's sleeping with the Muse, she's hurt us both."

"The difference is that my hurt has healed." He reached for my hand. His touch was gentle. "Randa, I don't believe she intended to harm either of us. Her art took her from us."

"She whistles, and like a well-behaved mourning dove, I'm supposed to fly to her side to assist with deathwatch duty. Some morbidity assignment. Why should I watch a stranger die? They both betrayed me." I felt my jaw clamping tightly.

"Your mother hasn't always been there for you. But she does love you."

"Do you believe her quest for fame excuses the fact that she has been a bogus mother to me?" I asked with rancor.

"You should never call her bogus." There was anger in his voice.

"I was the mistake of her passion. She never wanted me. She handed me over without a fight."

His eyes batted rapidly. "She didn't fight for custody of you because you wanted to be with me."

"I was five-years old."

He emphasized, "But you *were* old enough to tell a judge you wanted to live with your father and grandparents Florez. She believed those words."

"It's too damned bad she didn't believe all of my words." I glanced away quickly, as if being slapped. I fought back the dampness burning my eyes.

"She loved you enough to grant your wish. She gave you exactly what you wanted. I was to be the custodial parent." His arms gathered me to his side. "Randa, you and your mother grew apart through the years. You expected more of her than she was able to give."

I moved away, turning from my father. I looked into the windshield's reflection. My eyes were reddened, my mouth contorted. "You know what happened with Sanford Winton. She stood by him. She believed him. And she believed him, in part, because of *her* mother's lies. My own grandmother knew what she was doing by lying."

"Your dying grandmother's untruth did serve to back him up when Sanford denied trying to assault you."

"Mother said that everyone thought I made it up because I wanted her to divorce him."

"Your mother did divorce Sanford."

"Eventually. But even before that, she elected to believe him, and her mother."

"Her mother has always been domineering. Lenora Randolph's influence over your mother put an end to our marriage. But I've forgiven. Now, it's your turn. For your own sake, forgive her."

"No." With emptiness, I slammed the car's hood down. My unspoken words were an army of outraged warriors.

"Bring Garbo in for a tune-up anytime tomorrow. Rogerio loves working on your Z."

With silent nobility, my father turned to walk toward the house. I drove away. The return trip to my loft made me consider that even at summer's mid-marker, I felt to have a wintry heart.

* * *

Although in her embrace, I wasn't in Alison's heart. She'd rebuked me for being late. My assignment now was to make it up to her. I was to take her to the land of erotica as she'd never experienced it before. This was part of Ali's Code of Expectations. She called me her Sapphic balladeer. My song of passion would be composed upon her skin. My poetry was to sketch out orgasmic enchantment. Romance was required, but love needed not be intersected.

Within the confines of her huge bed, I felt the emotional crush of her power as a woman. Perhaps it was only an excuse, for I also needed the warmth of another human being. I'd established corners of my earth that belonged to me alone. She wanted and required all my corners. She expected my heart, soul, and body to become hers. Her bedroom eyes were flaring with desire.

After a luxurious bubble bath where we shared exotic fragrances of bath oil and the melting scented candles as they mingled, we tenderly patted one another's bodies dry. This began the event. The kiss, long and sensual, was the prelude. We knew our scene by heart.

Once in bed, our bodies warmed one another as we writhed. Our lips swarmed each passionate, well-mapped regions of one another's face. Her nibble of my neck trailed to my ear. Her whisper was in the form of an invitational command. "Randa, I want your intensity. Now, please don't keep me waiting."

I held her tightly in my arms. My hands skimmed the softness of her as my moist lips swept slowly to her shapely bosoms. I kissed the space between them. Tenderly, I traced my way toward her stomach. She prompted my arousal.

As if our trance was broken, I heard the pulsating ring of my cell phone. I lifted my head. "It's nearly midnight, it must be an emergency."

"Randa, let the world deal without you for a change," she instructed with a harsh annoyance.

"I can't." I stirred, trying not to move any farther than I must away from Alison. I reached the nightstand as my fingers stretched toward my phone. "Florez," I managed to rasp into my mouthpiece.

"Randa, sorry to call so late, but I knew you'd want to know about Jona Beck."

The voice was familiar. "Nevada?"

"Yes. I have a scoop for you. Enforcement is trying to sit on this as long as possible, so you've got a confidential exclusive. Jona Beck and Dr. Simone Milton are missing."

"Missing?" My mind was still foggy. "What do you mean *missing*?"

"Escaped. Dr. Milton checked in for a session early this evening. When the institution officials later did their rounds, both women had vanished. Simone Milton's vehicle is gone. And Jona Beck is listed as a fugitive."

I sat quickly. My throat constricted. "Beck left the grounds. You're saying that Simone escorted Jona out?"

"If not that, Dr. Milton is a hostage. No sign of a struggle, from what I hear. Listen, I've got to go. For now this is on the quiet. They're going to issue an APB later, so you *didn't* get this call."

"Nevada, thanks. I owe you one." I quickly began dressing.

Alison's voice sliced the air with her question, "Where the hell do you think you're going?"

"I've got to get over to *The Mirror*. I had planned to go there directly from here in the morning to work on a story, so I left my laptop there. And I have background files on my flash drives. Also the Beck audio tapes are there, too. I'm going to need it all." I was vocalizing my thoughts. "This is a major story. Confidential information. Beck just did a runner." I continued throwing my clothing on. "I'm sorry."

"Randa, we were making love. You can't leave now for some dumb story. That Jona probably wants to kill you. She could now. The story will keep until morning."

"I'll have a head start. I'll break the story before my competition even attends the news conference. And I'm not frightened."

"Randa, don't leave me like this."

"Ali, this is important. I'm sorry." I stepped into my loafers as I stood.

She threw a pillow in my direction. "Damn you. You criticize your mother for her devotion to her career. Look at you. Some lousy story comes in and you're off and running. That's your problem."

Lifting my jacket, I turned when I reach the door. "What's my problem?"

"You may have learned about things like family loyalty from the old Florez bunch, but you've never learned about complete love. Or maybe you inherited the inability to love from your mother."

My teeth clamped shut for several moments as my arms wrestled their way into my jacket. "Alison, I'm very sorry. And sadly, maybe you're correct about my emotional inadequacy."

"If you leave my bed tonight, don't bother to return."

"Maybe this is the excuse we both required to end our relationship."

By the time I reached the night's crisp darkness my anger had been released. In retrospect, I had only to admit how truly correct Alison's words were. I'd been exiled before, and I've survived. Meanwhile, my mind swirled with intentions to make this story one of best ever filed. I'd followed the story from its inception. Who better knew the workings of this criminal's mind?

I'd failed to completely find Jona Beck's soul. I hoped not to fail in finding Jona Beck the fugitive.

* * *

"Randa, you're here a little early," *The Mirror's* evening city editor, Kenny Erickson, greeted me as I approached his desk.

"I've got a tip. Need to do some background so I'll have it ready to roll."

"Going to allow me in the loop?" Kenny scratched the thinning hair on his quadrilateral-shaped head. Through lack of exercise, and his favorite German brews, he had developed a pronounced double chin, paunchy midsection, and fingers as wide as bananas. "Or are you singing another farewell lullaby to your gorgeous ex? And Marlene's will be shutting down soon, so you've come here to cry the blues. I'm frigging honored."

I sat, swinging the office chair as I pressed my legs firmly against the tile beneath. "Kenny, we're sitting on a very explosive story, so don't be a little goober. We need to hustle."

Before my eyes, his face converted to one of professionalism. His fingers gripped a red pen tightly. "Something has put lead in your pencil. You're serious?"

"As serious as I've ever been. Just stand by."

"You'd better tell me about this one."

"I haven't got time to tell you."

"Randa." His voice took a bead on me. "If you've got something, you'd better spill it."

One thing I knew about Kenny is his vow of confidentiality is solemnly taken. And he has indeed been jailed for failure to turn a source. "Okay. I just found out that Jona Beck and her court-appointed shrink are missing from the institution. No APB has been issued yet. I've been listening to the police bands. So police officials are probably going to sit on it as long as they can. They aren't even certain if Dr. Simone Milton is an accomplice, or a hostage. They'll probably avoid charges against Milton until they know. Corrections will have problems explaining their inability to keep a psychotic killer in a locked institution."

"Your plan?"

"I'll do the background now. I'll give you a prelim about what I've got now. It will be ready to roll when I call you later. I'll take a trip out to do a *follow-up* interview with Jona Beck at seven in the morning. I have a letter written weeks ago confirming my plans. I had wanted to do an updated story on Beck. No appointment set - but authorities won't know. That's my cover when I make an attempt to meet with the missing Jona. Once on the premises, I own the story."

"Nice work. You get there amidst the bustle of confusion. Police have to let you into the news. You are vigilant, noble press and all, so you promise to keep it quiet for a few hours, for the exclusive. You ferret out the information. We break the story at noon via an extra edition. Beautiful!"

"And by this afternoon, I'll have all the information on their investigation. Then I'll file my comprehensive report early this evening for the morning edition." I sketched a quick wave in his direction. "I'm working on it now," I announced as I stood.

"Don't let me detain you."

We traded grins. I hastened away. The end product was one that reporters lust after. An over-the-top exclusive. I heard my loafers tapping rapidly as I rushed to my office.

The newsroom consisted of a maze of cubicles with computer stations surrounding a bay area of circular desks where the editors performed their magic. My cubical was within shouting distance of the editor's desk.

Above my station hung an old adage: There are three kinds of news stories - The Great; The Late; and The Awful. Beneath that message was: Bless the Press.

For the next two hours I worked my way deeper into the quagmire of words. It was an in-depth encapsulation of the Jona Beck story.

Finally, at two-thirty, I had my preliminary story ready. Final edits could be made when I called in the morning. I knew I must return to my loft and attempt to shut down the great squall inside my brain. If I were to be asleep by three, I might get a couple of hours rest before being up at six. By seven I'd be on the institution's property for my *meeting* with Jona Beck.

I chuckled. If authorities had captured her by then, I would be in a world of hurt for interview questions. Blinking my leaden eyes, I considered what a colossal illusion time is. My timing would need to be perfect. And I would need to be believable.

This had cost me my relationship with Alison.

CHAPTER 3

Friday

Sweet dreams had not the time to extricate me from night's razor-sharp bites of a nightmare.

My alarm trilled. Sleep deprivation was a small price to pay for a scoop. I was known to be one of the media's most ferocious interviewers. But sadly, there are all sorts of costs. I'd forfeited the woman I loved.

Now, with a major story, I needed focus. I had often questioned my ability to live up to a war zone story. I'd been enveloped in other people's victory, defeat, beauty, and ugliness. From my vantage point of café society - the outer rim of crime, I'd done fine. I had sat pristinely and safely on the sidelines.

This seemed the point of true challenge. I probably knew more about Jona Beck - convict at large - than anyone else in the world knew about her. With the exception, perhaps, of the woman with whom she was on the lam. In my column, I had a better understanding of the killer. I knew Jona Beck well enough to have known she needed to be in restraints for the rest of her life. Something Doc Simone must not have known or believed.

So if I'd done my research, and if I knew my subject, I should be able to figure out where the escapee and accomplice, or a bad bet - hostage, had gone. Most of the places Beck might have gone were not in a safety zone. That was the perilous impact.

The prospect of my turn in the foxhole didn't excite me. All roads led to and from the where of *now*. Now there was a monumental news event.

Already showered, dressed, and ready to leave, I rushed to

the phone when Nevada returned my call. Because of the escape, she'd agreed to do a double shift. When her duty assignments paused, she finally had time to get back to me.

My plan sounded plausible to her. And I had correctly guessed that enforcement was going to keep the lid on as long as possible. She had been detailed to city duty, but requested to be assigned a tour to accompany the county and state search team.

As in other states, Colorado strongly observed jurisdictions. Often the boundaries were selfishly protected. But at times when the crime was within a county of minimally staffed enforcement, all the help offered was taken. Although Nevada's orders were still under consideration, she suspected they would agree to take all volunteers. She said there may be a possibility that she'd see me later in the morning at the institution where Jona Beck had been incarcerated.

The next phone call I half-heartedly hoped would be from Alison - wasn't. It was from Hank Richards, the photographer assigned to meet me at the institution. At twenty-six years of age, Hank had won several photojournalism awards. He was a huge black man with a giant bulbous jaw set with firm determination to take no prisoners. He was resolute. His bronze-green eyes and friendly smile reflected kindness. I briefed him on our assignment.

I had arrived on location shortly after seven. The old state institution housed those mentally handicapped prisoners convicted of brutal crimes. A pewter-colored wall with well-guarded gate surrounded dingy brick and slab cement buildings. There were patrol cars clustered at the entrance. I pointed to my press license plate on the dashboard. Although I realized most law enforcement officers were aware of my affiliation with the press, I figured it was only professional courtesy to flash my press credentials before being asked.

Slowly, dutifully, I rolled down the window. "What's the problem?"

"We've had an incident, Florez. Press isn't being admitted."

"Come on, I've got an appointment to see Jona Beck this morning." I allowed my voice to be as imploring as I dared. "Just an hour."

The tall officer traded looks with his partners "Jona Beck?" he repeated with a question.

"Follow-up interview. I've got the paperwork." I reached into my beat-up, bag. It was filled with my laptop, notebooks, and files. Inside the compartments were audio tapes, flash files, small reporter's notebooks, pens, my hand-held recorder, and a couple of granola bars. It took me a minute to retrieve a file. "Yes. Here's the letter granting permission." As hoped, they didn't attempt to find a date for the interview. If questioned, I planned to say it had been confirmed via telephone.

"Maybe we better radio Truesdale." The other officer nodded in agreement. Naturally Lieutenant Truesdale had been called in since he was Beck's arresting officer. He was assigned to the investigation. My arrival was reported to Lieutenant Frederick 'Fritz' Truesdale. Since he was so involved with the Beck case, I was certain he would bark a command to have me turned away.

Knowing the lieutenant would hear my response, I loudly asked, "Hey, what's going on here? Maybe I should call this in. It's sounding like a major story."

The thought of press descending upon this scene terrified Fritz Truesdale. Additional helicopters and handheld microphones were more than he wished to deal with now. When in a hot fury to capture, Fritz looked at reporters as viperous pests - difficult to squash, yet he realized we expected him to attempt a swat or two at us. He relented.

It took me very little time to park my car and be herded through to a spare office where Fritz Truesdale greeted me with the disdain anyone might have for a gossip monger. He motioned for me to sit opposite him. His papers and maps were scattered across the desk.

"Imagine you here today," he muttered. At thirty-five years of age, Truesdale was in 'gym-instructor' shape. His face was gaunt; his features were angular. The bridge of his nose was wide from a beating he received while he was undercover.

Beige, closely-cropped hair fringed his high forehead. Blue eyes became ice when he grimaced in my direction.

"Conducting a raid?" I quizzed.

"Florez, we've got a little problem." He paused with a gargoyle's grimness. "I consider you to be a pain in the ass, but you might just have something that could be helpful."

"Fritz, my aunt says that the butt consists of the least amount of nerve ending of any area of the body. So luckily, I must not be distressing you too badly. What's your real problem and why might you believe I could be helpful?"

"You're pretty much an authority on the Beck case, right?" he tetchily questioned.

"My interviews with Jona Beck have been thorough and in-depth. But I'd have to say that her shrink might be the true authority," I purposely disputed. "Dr. Simone Milton."

"She's not available."

"Difficult to believe she isn't available to assist with her most notorious client." I frowned. "Are you going to tell me what's going on?"

"We're trying to keep this under wraps for a while. Beck is missing. We're conducting a preliminary search. She's might be hiding on the grounds, but if not, where do you think she might have gone?"

"There's more to it than that. Your nose is growing."

"Florez, just answer the question."

"So you've got all these law officers out here because Jona Beck *may* be missing. Don't let's play around with little wooden boy impressions. If you expect me to assist, then level with me."

"We aren't planning to announce this until we've had time to check everything out. Also to explore our options. Dr. Milton and Jona Beck are missing."

"Is Dr. Milton a hostage, or an accomplice?"

"At this time we're not certain. What we know is that the doctor had a pass, used it last night, and now they're both missing."

"Security must be a little lax if they walked out of here that easily."

"Stop with your prejudicial journalism," he attacked. "We don't know the details for certain. So let's not pass judgment."

"There's a killer out there. Someone screwed up," I challenged. He wouldn't refute that there had been a huge security lapse. "Right?"

"Yes, right. This is why we wanted to keep it quiet. Until we've got the facts it's all speculation. I don't want the story leaking and causing panic. We both know I can be cooperative. Or not."

"And you want my cooperation with the big hush? Add to that, you want me to tell you where I think they might have gone? You don't want much, do you?"

"Florez, work with me. I'll give you everything I can without compromising the case. Give me your best guess where they might have gone?"

"Beck's love interest was a woman named Lucia Gomez. She hangs out at a bar called The Raven's Talon. Located downtown. A very dismal bar," I add with restraint.

"Rough dive. Leather."

"That's the place." There was a chill in remembering the sleazy S&M leather bar. Upon entering The Raven, I'd felt its enigmatic darkness. Nightmares persisted throughout the trail because of all the things I learned about the life of Jona Beck. The bar was one of them. To return and search out an escaped psycho killer promised to be no less pretty. When a past experience reoccurs, Aunt Renie claims it is like a ghost tiptoeing over one's grave.

He belched loudly. "She isn't going to take Doc Milton into a leather bar in the middle of the city."

"No. And if Simone Milton is having an affair with Jona, as rumors have it, Lucia isn't about to help them. But Lucia may want revenge." I gave a shrug, then added, "So maybe Lucia might not know squat."

"You're right. Lucia probably wouldn't help hide them. But revenge is sweet. She might be willing to turn them in," he agreed. "You've also heard the women might be having a..." he broke, rotating his hand in the air, "a thing?"

"I've heard talk. Any firm documentation?"

"So far just speculation by some of the staff."

"I take it you're more inclined to believe Dr. Milton is aiding and abetting than that she's a hostage?"

"It is early days on the investigation, but my suspicion is that the women had something going. Off the record, there's been rumors about them for some time. Add to that, no sign of a struggle."

"Back to my original question. How did they get through security?"

"Dr. Milton and Beck were in a conference room. The doc then called the guard, claiming she left some files in her car. She was only going to be a few minutes. Said she'd call the guard when she returned. The guard left the security card in the slot. It could only be reached from the outside. The guard anticipated the doc's only being away a couple minutes. The guard went behind the service desk. After twenty minutes, she returned to find the room vacant. A side emergency door had been overridden and was ajar."

He recognized my look of disbelief. I quizzed, "You're telling me that a guard failed to lock Beck down?"

"The guard thought Beck was in chains, and bolted to the floor."

"Hardware stores carry bolt and chain cutters." I issued my incredulous look.

"They trusted Dr. Milton. Guess it was common practice. She's never given them reason to doubt her."

"Until now." I looked away, frowning. "You just said that some of the employees knew about rumors. That would put doubt in my mind."

"It appears not everyone believes everything they hear. Or read," he emphasized.

"Of all people Dr. Milton should know how dangerous Jona Beck is. I don't understand it." I delved cautiously. "The doc is supposed to be intelligent."

"Love can screw up even a good mind. Your old auntie got anything to say about that?"

"Aunt Renie goes out of her way not to discuss love with me." I took a deep breath. "My grandmother says that our bodies are containers; our brains are computers; and the rest of us *is* heart. Heart equals love."

"Jez-*zus!*" he exclaimed. "That came from nowhere." He began laughing.

"Right," I agreed with a chuckle. "I'm guessing it was an assisted escape. I'll go back over my notes, tapes. See if I can come up with anything."

"You buy the affair scenario? The doc falls in love with a psycho?"

I nodded affirmatively before standing. I believed that love actually *does* make us one another's fool. This, however, I did not share with Lieutenant Truesdale. I knew when to make use of my button-down lips.

* * *

Afternoon's midsection was one of the few quiet times at Ruby's. Even the background music's lyrics were barely discernible.

"Putting a boot in?" Lanny Ventura questioned.

"Wasn't that extra edition something?" I issued my taunting question. I knew my major local TV news competitor, the colorful Lanny Ventura, planned to interrogate me. *The Mile High Mirror's* extra broke just before the press conference at noon. "I've never seen so many cameras juggling for position while we waited in front of police headquarters."

"No way of keeping gimmickry down to a minimum when the lid blows off a story." She sipped her black coffee.

Our rivalry was mixed with respect and humor. We learned about sharing a Sapphic sisterhood, and that allowed us rapport. We had crossed paths repeatedly, and in spite of our competitive natures, we'd become friends. Scooping one another became sweeter than just filing a report.

"I got the gold star on this one. I'm treating myself to a late luncheon Denver Omelet." Ruby's version incorporated onions, green pepper, ham, Cayenne pepper, and an assortment of fresh herbs with beaten eggs.

"Humph," Lanny said as her scowl intensified.

"Well, you could also have an omelet. My treat."

She had just reached her fiftieth birthday. She knew she was attractive. Her short, dark hair had become silver-streaked during the past decade. Lanny's thin frame leaned toward me. Her arms outstretched across the table. Her hands were palms down. Her eyeglasses slid down the thin bridge of her nose. Her penetrating eyes were dark and glowering in my direction.

"Remember, I've been a reporter since the earth's rocks cooled. So when you deliver your answer to me, make it good. Where did the inside info come from?"

"Coincidence. I had a follow-up interview with Beck this morning. So I had all the background information available. You might say I stumbled on the story."

"What a fortunate little messenger girl you are," she muttered. "Your exclamation smells like the state senate taking a nap." She pressed her spectacles back. "Shit!"

"Don't be a poor loser."

"I should have taken my high school counselor's recommendation. He suggested I become a streetwalker. But no, I am forced to *join* the elite pantheon of great reporters. I'm also forced to listen to a ton of drivel for every milligram of honesty. Let's hear some reality."

I laughed. "Lanny, I honestly did get lucky." A perfectly legitimate response, I thought.

"You're lucky you've got an unnamed source in the rafters."

"You're one skeptical woman," I said as I leaned back, crossing my arms tightly. "A couple thousand years ago, you wouldn't have trusted a bearded man dragging a cross down the street."

"Naturally, I'm dubious about your story about being at the right place at the right time. You're wearing that furtive smile."

I finished the last forkful of omelet, pushed the plate back, and smiled even wider. "Gotta scram. You know how rushed those of us are while attempting our climb up the ladder to become a part of the elite pantheon of great media women. Truly rushed."

"You haven't answered my question. Meet me at Marlene's tonight."

"Poor planning on the part of others doesn't call for an emergency on my part."

"Someone is carrying your water for you. You've got an insider," she shouted after me.

By the time I reached the door a new wave of flavorful grease fumes hit me. I turned. "I'll try to meet you after nine."

I heard her voice, heavy with irony. "That ought to be a revelatory encounter."

* * *

"Fuckin' pip-squeak!" Mario screamed at the kid who had just stolen an armload of magazines from Mario's newsstand. His usual wrinkled face of whey coloring converted to a crimson anger. He shook his gnarled fist. "I see that kid again and I'll kick teenage ass."

Mario's kiosk was located on one of the best newspaper stall corners in town, but he'd earned it with thirty-five years of weathering the icy Colorado winters. "Sorry that happened," I consoled.

"Kids nowadays don't put their backs into work like in my day. They steal." His short, heavyset body issued street language at its best. His fists ceased their choppy circlets in the air. Fingers splayed over the entire dome of his bald head. "If it ain't swindlers, it's out and out robbers. I'd like to see how a public hanging or two would go down." His haggard mask of a face contorted. "They need a little jail time instead of a slap on the wrist."

I felt a twitch on my face. Mario might well have been talking about my brother, Benjy. "Not all youths steal," I defended, considering Rogerio had probably never taken a penny from anyone in his entire life.

Mario turned his attention to me. "Yeah, some of 'em

might be okay. Most are grubbing little thieves."

"I guess you had a busy noon selling *Mirror* extras."

"Yeah! I tell you, we were sold out as soon as it hit the stand. Great job, kid."

"Thanks, Mario." I picked up several magazines that I knew I'll probably not have the chance to read. I tossed down twice the price. "Keep the change. It's been a good day."

"Thanks, kid. It's gonna be a slow afternoon."

"'Cause I ain't in any hurry."

* * *

After reporting back to the news office, I'd decided I'd get more research done at my loft. I needed to concentrate on the transcriptions of Beck's taped interviews. Also, I needed to go back over all my notes with precise detective work. I'd longed to probe in total solitude.

I had barely arrived at the parking area when my cell phone rang. Nevada reported that she was still at the institution's perimeter with the ongoing search. I thanked her again for her assistance. She promised to keep me informed. I expressed my gratitude by offering to take her to dinner at her first convenient moment. Presumably, a night off, or when she was rotated off owl shift. She asked if Alison might not mind. I told her our relationship had long been on a 'sizzle or fizzle' mode - and had now fizzled for good.

I leaned back against the fender of my Z, wondering about the optimism I heard in Nevada's voice when we disconnected our call.

The phone jingled before I unlocked the car's door. My father was on the other end of the line and asked me to swing by his shop for a chat. I immediately drove there wondering what might be up. He rarely phoned during business hours.

Father's auto shop was located on west Federal Boulevard. The garage itself was once a warehouse. It had been converted a decade before my father purchased it. The exterior's ancient red bricks were painted white and green with black lettering across the front. Inside there were two auto bays in the mechanic area. Adjoining was the office and a waiting room. Angie had taken it upon herself to add a woman's decorating touch or two.

Always one for appreciating bright, exuberant colors, Angie dressed in them, and naturally decorated with them. When my father objected to her use of yellow, magenta, and lime green as office colors, she countered with her line that there would be boring colors *only* at her funeral. However, when I teased that she dressed as 'splendaliciously' as a punk rocker, she indicated she plans to be buried in a very colorful costume. Maybe, she said tapping her brow, a knockoff from a Frida Kahlo dress. That made us both laugh heartily since Kahlo was the favorite artist of each of us.

As I entered the office, I heard the voices of my father and Rogerio consulting in the garage's bay area. Angie was seated on my father's huge oak desk. I slumped into a nearby office chair. "What's going on?" I questioned.

"The diva calls and your father goes sad."

"Why is my mother bothering him again?" I inquired.

"You tell me. It's your flipping lineage. I'm just glad you're like your father."

Angie played with her curls as she talked. "I got to be polite to your nutty aunt, to keep peace. Peace!" She wiggled her shoulders, allowing her low-cut cotton top to expose more of her cleavage. "She won't let up on me until her toes point to the sky," Angie ranted. "I tell her I make Paulo happy. And she clicks her tongue at me. She needs to get screwed 'til her molars melt. She needs a little action."

My smile was automatic. "I'm not sure she's ever had any."

Her laugh was mirthless. "Then your mother calls. I know she tells Paulo I'm trash. It's like being picked to death by a flock of crows."

"Angie, my mother has never said a word against you."

"High society. She just looks down her blue-blood nose at me."

"Not so," I disputed. "She was thrilled that Father found happiness with you."

"Now she can really talk. My youngest son is turning out to

be a criminal. What kind of mother can I be?"

"Angie, I'd never tell her. And my mother wouldn't judge you or Father on Benjy's actions."

"Damned kid will be racing and T-bone another car while jetting away from the cops. If he hurts anyone, I'll just die. We got us one decent kid and one kid running from the posse most of the time." She paused with her postscript. "And you."

Although I'm an afterthought, Angie had always been very accepting of me and of my closeness to my father.

"Angie, my father doesn't call her. She calls him. And she knows nothing of Benjy's escapades."

"Escapades! Stealing a car for a joyride is as near a criminal starter kit as I can think of." Her face tightened with tension. "I pick a good man for my children to copy. Benj won't go to school. Won't work."

"Maybe Rogerio and I can talk with him," I suggested.

"Rogerio has his hands full. With starting a home, a baby due any day now, and working all the hours God sends. He's got no time for a delinquent brother."

"I'll talk with Benjy again."

"You're busy with this Jona Beck thing." She paused for several moments. "Our neighbors called to tell us that they mentioned your name on one of those TV talk shows."

"I'll make time for Benjy." My brothers had always been there for me. Rogerio usually made me laugh. Benjy usually made me weep. But we all loved one another. That was the best clarity of vision my siblings offered. "I think he'll grow out of his wild ways."

Father and Rogerio entered, greeting me with kisses. "No baby yet," Rogerio reported. His hair was longer than father's but he was the spitting image of our dad. "Teresa invited the family over for a barbecue on Sunday. You'll be there?"

"Naturally," I answered. "That is, if we aren't all hanging out at the maternity ward waiting for your offspring to spring. I can't believe I'm about to become an aunt!" I sighed.

"You'll make a wonderful aunty," Rogerio encouraged. "We both think so."

"I'll try," I said weakly. While I'd hated to be known as the new generation's Aunt Renie, there was an implied responsibility for moral example. Lesbian aunt sounded much better to me than maiden aunt. Life plants dilemmas in everyone's garden, Papa Gus always said. "Father, what did you want to see me about?"

"You are to call your mother."

I acquiesced. "First thing when I get home."

"Now. I have given her my word." He took the number from the chest pocket of his shirt. "The waiting room is empty. You can telephone with complete privacy. Randa, remember my words about showing forgiveness."

"I'll call."

"Also you need to be careful because of that woman prisoner that escaped. She's very dangerous. And we're all worried she may come after you."

"Father, I'm safe. She isn't going to be taking a chance of being near me." I felt confident she was probably hidden away – frightened of being taken captive again. Although I felt safe, there were the remnants of a deeply buried chill.

* * *

As promised, I phoned my mother. I again declined her request to visit my dying grandmother. I did however agree to meet Mother tomorrow noontime at one of her favorite dining establishments, *The Wellshire Inn*. After our conversation ended as awkwardly as usual, I felt the need to activate my mind in a different direction.

I dropped by police headquarters to see if there were any new and/or relevant facts in the Beck case. There were none. That didn't surprise me. Had there been a sighting, I'd have heard it on my police radio band. Or I would have been notified by my office. The APB was in place. Also there was a media request for the public to be on the lookout for Dr. Simone Milton's late model Escalade.

Beck and Milton had vanished. Time would tell if they had outside help. Until the facts revealed themselves, my best guess was going to be that there was assistance in some way or another. My supposition required not only that I delve back into the history of Jona Beck, but also complete a new background search on Dr. Simone Milton.

I'd begin by calling on Dr. Milton's estranged husband in the morning. I had the pertinent details on Simone Milton's family, and a short list of her friends. It was a start at finding if anyone knew her whereabouts.

My fundamental belief was that any assistance the two women might have would come from Jona's camp. Simone's circle of friends was probably not the aiding and abetting kind. Jona's pals were street people who didn't give a flip about the law. They would be only too happy to collaborate with an escapee from the state mental institution

There was only one thing I knew for certain about the disappearance of Jona and Simone. *No nos invitaron a la fiesta.* They didn't invite us to the party.

* * *

"What's shaking, sexy?" Alicia greeted me as I enter Marlene's.

"I'm tired and hungry. I've been working all evening."

"Fresh pastrami sandwiches are the special tonight. And have I got a superb wine to go with it."

"Terrific," I responded. "Let's begin with wine."

I was glad that Lanny Ventura was also behind schedule. As I sipped the smooth, velvety wine, I almost hoped she wouldn't arrive. I knew she intended on cogently arguing her case. She'd shared sources with me before, she'd plead. I'd remind her that some of them were wild goose chases. We'd circle one another like a couple of sumo wrestlers. Then I'd deny her request for information. She'd order another bottle of wine, in hopes of lubricating my tongue into talking. She'd sugar the pill with whatever prized wine I desired. Like a dog with a bone, she'd work me over good. Or perhaps, more descriptively - she'd be like a dog looking for a lamppost.

By the time I'd sipped two glasses of wine and munched my way through a heaping hot sandwich, with a side of plump fries, I was feeling more relaxed. Now I longed for my bed. Giselle finished her set. She joined me.

"You're sounding as wonderful as ever," I complimented.

"And you broke a national story today. I'm honored you've come here to share your glory."

I chuckled. "Have a glass of wine and stop with the bull."

"I was right about Jona and Simone."

"So it seems. I'm guessing Simone was in collusion."

"In collusion," she repeated with a giggle. "Hell, they were *in* bed."

"That also." I turned the rim of my goblet. "Any idea where she might have gone?"

"I haven't a clue."

"The universe seems clueless." I took another sip of excellent fruity tasting red wine. It rolled down my throat. "I've been probing all the transcripts from interviews."

We watched as Lanny Ventura made her way toward us.

"More vigilante press." Giselle greeted Lanny Ventura with a double cheek kiss. "I'm due back for another set. Do let me know if you two are going to need dueling pistols."

Lanny sat opposite me. "My old pal, Gonzo. A question springs to my lips upon seeing you," she began.

"Have a drink before you start your inquisition." I grinned when she called me Gonzo. I often referred to her as a TMZ darling – blazing cameras and dripping makeup.

"I see you're gulping it down. Thirsty work, the truth. Have as much wine as your bladder can handle."

"Stein says that sentences must not have bad plumbing and must not leak. Her rule might apply to reporters, as well as syntax."

Lanny smiled back at me. "Give my ears a rest and stop with the derailments. You've got me on tenterhooks. *Who* is your source?"

"Can't it be good fortune?"

"Randa Florez, don't give me that excrement. You've got a lot of strings to your bow."

"So where do you think the fugitives are?"

Lanny poured a glass of wine from the bottle. With a pensive gesture of exasperation, she acknowledged my question slowly. "I'm not sure. They're probably still in the state. Lots of places to hide in the city. Lots more in the mountains. One thing I do know. Beck is dangerous. Even if the good doctor believes she's safe, she isn't."

"I agree. Whatever the reason for the doctor's diagnosis, Jona is not reformed by her presence. Jona's world is beyond make-believe. And worse when she gets her hands on drugs. If Simone is to fit in, her acting skills better be honed. Jona's fantasy world isn't exactly a quick rendition of French maid and wicked baron."

"Randa, during the trial I observed Jona closely. I really believe she is not only off her latch, but she's the most flawed person I've ever explored. And you've investigated her insanity more than I."

My stare was bleak. "Jona Beck's life was smudged by dark evil early on."

"Insane people are like guests on earth. They are eternal strangers even to themselves."

"That description might fit any of us." My words were reflective. "We come out the other end of each experience a slightly different person."

"Spoken like a true vintage lesbian sage. Now figure out where this season's missing fruit loop might have gone."

I lifted my glass, toasting. "To my efforts in capturing the story of the season!"

With a clank of the glass I realized how improvisational life is. For that one brief moment all problems were only petite missions to be completed.

* * *

With the melancholic elegance of midnight, I strode back to my loft. I'd anticipated a sip or two of wine, so left Garbo parked in her stall.

The few blocks I walked served two purposes. First, I wasn't driving home inebriated after having polished off half a dozen glasses of wine. And secondly, fresh air and exercise had a pronounced sobering effect. The ultimate blessing derived was that midnight in the heart of a renovated, revitalized urban village often seemed charmingly quaint. There was something very relaxing about the night's code of mystery. Often darkness tended to desensitize problems.

There were recent accusations that Denver's LoDo district was becoming synthetic. Residents living in converted warehouses enjoyed being surrounded by historic buildings with their artistic, bohemian qualities. They liked the concentration of galleries, shops, and boutiques. They disliked LoDo's recent reputation of being a party zone. Executive offices and commercialism was creeping upon those established loft dwellers. I planned on enjoying each moment, and if the ultimate convergence of progress finally enveloped my majestic Cowtown – so be it. I'd locate another outskirts area.

Glancing up into the darkness, I considered this time to be a magical time. There are a few summer stars blinking beyond the haze of clouds. When I attempted to understand the universe, I found I'm inside a very great joke. Perhaps it was mystery that made the heavens lovely enough to set to music. Perhaps the beauty traversed the underlying riddle. We were all susceptible to the earth's most frantic parody when walking alone.

Admittedly, I watched for shadows and listened for sounds that might forecast a murderous fugitive throwing herself in my path.

Being alone often created fake conflict. While I appreciated being by myself, I always longed to share life and love. Love – that other question invaded my thought. Alison hadn't issued a statement saying come back, all is forgiven. And I had no intention of holding an audition for a new lover. Love might be a primordial longing that began in the heart. Lust, I believed, started in the loins and retreats to the heart when loneliness is an alternative possibility.

I was lost to the threat that memory persists. There was a saying that a 'healed' memory is not a 'deleted' memory. The memory of love was good while it was there —while it was activated. Happiness and euphoria should energize us. It never fulfilled me entirely. My quietness made others believe I'm happy —satisfied. In its purest sense, I'm not sure I knew what happiness was all about.

I stared at the indigo-blue shadows against the building's wall. Dappled coats of light shimmered. With dream induced reverie, I watched. I wanted to admit how drastically I had changed since that night I met Jona Beck. My beliefs about life, death - and living's median strip of love and hate - had changed. The macabre life became reality. The trail of death Jona Beck was convicted of leaving behind meant the planet was an unsafe place. She'd also claimed, fictitious or not, multiple murders. All gory and gruesome, however it kept her talking into my handheld recorder.

I leaned against the door before entering my building. Often being alone hurts. Tonight, although nourished by silence, loneliness had invaded. I ached deeply with the concern I may never recover from Beck's horrific tales of slaughter.

* * *

I'd listened to a recording of one of Jona Beck's interviews earlier. She mentioned that she knew she was lesbian when in her early teens. A woman asked if she was male or female. That flashed to my own yesteryear meeting up with prejudice. I was five and lived with my father and grandparents Florez. I walked the sidewalk in front of my grandparent's home. Two little girls were there. I wanted to be their friend. They ask me what I was - a Mexican or *what?* I'd replied I didn't know. They told me I didn't look white and I didn't look as they do. So what was I, they again asked.

The world had been my enemy while living with my grandparents Randolph. At five, I realized I may never know what I am. Or who I am? Jona Beck understood what she was at an early age. She was a victim. I had not understood myself to be anything other than me - a small child questioning.

Since then I had come to know I walked between bigotry and the earth's floor. Often I walked between misery and the stars. Somehow I always felt I knew where I belonged, although not ever as completely as might have been.

My mouth tasted the wine's residual piquancy. I shivered. My spirit seemed impoverished by each twist in the road of Jona Beck's life. I had been a fractional witness to her tragedy. A continuum promised to be as tumultuous as the murder case had been. It had taken months to exorcise the grotesque, odious memories of that grizzly murder. I tried to share the killer's thoughts. Murder's bestial face never entirely left my nightmares.

Questions surrounded me. I wondered if Jona came on to Simone Milton with soft, sad vulnerability. She had tried her innocent-as-fresh-cream with me. Surely a trained psychologist could recognize Jona's ability to masquerade.

Or perhaps not. Not all women speak the language of violence. And fewer still understand the dialect of brutality.

* * *

Far beyond midnight, I attempted to quash my concerns with sleep. Answering the telephone call too brusquely, I apologized. "I'm sorry, Nevada. I thought you might be a crank call. Or worse, the news desk calling me in to work."

"I know it's late. I planned on leaving a message. I figured you might be at Alison's when you didn't respond to my earlier calls."

"I met a buddy at Marlene's. Had a sandwich and wine. I needed to unwind. And Alison is a person of the past."

"But it hurts?"

"I'm no longer certain that's the case. I'm beginning to believe that my friends, Giselle and Alicia, might have understood Alison's motives more than I had. They surmised that Alison's main draw to me was my mother."

"What's your mother got to do with it?"

"You don't know who my mother is? I figured your pal at the station informed you about my background."

"Only that you're a sister, and a crime reporter. She didn't say anything about your family. Why, is your mom in the slammer?"

"No. Not at all." I laughed at the thought.

"So what does your mother have to do with why Alison dated you?"

"My mother is an opera star. Her social standing might have appealed to Ali. Fame by association."

"My mother sings in the church choir."

I smiled. "You really didn't know that my mother is Erika Randolph?"

"I've heard of her, but I didn't know. And I don't much care. You never mentioned her. You don't seem to be close to her, so getting into her good graces in order to influence my cause with you is rather impractical."

"After everything you've done for Benjy, and tipping me to the Beck story, you're already in my good graces. Speaking of Beck, anything new on the case?"

"Numerous calls. But nothing checked."

"I'm going to be dropping by to talk with Fritz Truesdale in the morning. King of the sound bites, but he may slip and give me something."

"I'm finally getting a day off next Sunday. I was wondering if you might want to do something. We'll both need a break by then. Not that we don't need one now."

"Sunday." I quickly recalled, "I'm going to a family barbecue. But if you'd like, you're welcome."

"I don't want to barge in on strangers."

"They won't all be strangers. You've arrested one of them."

Her chuckle turned to a full laugh. "I'm probably the last person Benjy wants to see. So naturally, I'd love to attend."

I gave her the address, and we hung up. I spotted my journal. Remembering I hadn't written the events of the day, I jostled to reach the lamp. Twisting off the cap of one of my favorite collectible fountain pens took only seconds. The pen was a 1928 Waterman with an olive ripple pattern. My passion for antique fountain pens provided me with a collection of them.

I wrote my day's activities. They were concentrated, and although lucid, probably would make little sense to anyone else. I neatly scrolled ways to deceive the depression that was harbored in my soul. Trouble seemed to be lurking behind a veil of imagination.

My eyes finally shut. Perilous dreams did not.

CHAPTER 4

Saturday

By nature's design there was something lethargic about Saturday mornings. Although there was no respite from my profession, weekends were usually more relaxing than weekdays.

My day began by being thankful for having survived half a dozen goblets of wine. A dull headache disappeared after I'd eaten homemade multigrain toast with lime marmalade and coffee. Aunt Renie was a whiz at fresh-baked breads, and Mama was renowned for jellies and marmalades. My contribution was my prized blend of coffee.

I scanned my engagement calendar's Saturday listing. My agenda was to interview Dr. Simone Milton's estranged husband. From him I hoped to retrieve information about my newest subject - his wife. I intended to also drop by police HQ to talk with Lieutenant Fritz Truesdale. After lunch with my mother, I would go to *The Mirror* where I'd file an updated story on the Beck case.

Saturday night was the best time to find Lucia Gomez at The Raven's Talon. I'd be there to search for her. Although dealing with the Raven crowd would be like head-butting Pikes Peak, as a reporter my forehead was developing a robust musculature for that kind of thing. Alison described Raven as a ditchwater tavern. Even if I wouldn't locate Lucia, eavesdropping might yield a clue or two as to the whereabouts of the fugitives. Or, using the required hedge word, the fugitive and her *alleged* accomplice.

During the Jona Beck trial, I dropped by the leather bar frequently. Often to meet with Lucia, or other of Jona's friends.

I gleaned a great deal of information about Jona and her lifestyle. The establishment itself was depressing. I told Alison that a better name for the frenetic bar might be 'Club Chaos.'

I closed my date book with a snap. That thwack proved I was fully awake. And I was alive and aware of a cosmic inheritance of miniscule energy. The morning was off to a cumbrous beginning. We all lived with the mystery of what comes next. That *wonder what* might be life's main ingredient. Our uncharted paths belonged to each heartbeat.

From my family there were daily objectives. Morning usually begins life. Mama Carmina believed in greeting the morning with cheer, rather than a jeer. Papa Gus said life is a grandiose garden – with a bounty each day. Aunt Renie claimed some frivolity is fine – but too much is courting the devil.

* * *

"Simone Milton's husband doesn't know jackshit!" Lieutenant Fritz Truesdale muttered. "The guy's a prick. If he knew where his wife and Beck were, and I stress *if* he knew, he'd probably go after them. He can't be much of a man if his wife runs off with a woman."

Fritz had made me sorry I'd decided to stop by his office immediately after talking with Simone Milton's estranged husband. He leaned back against his desk chair, enjoying the fact that he had obviously perturbed me. I placed one elbow on the desk top. I rested my chin in the palm of my hand. My gaze was meant to show indifference to his remark. "Fritz, have you read Ovid?"

"Is that some kind of lesbian smut?"

"Okay, you haven't read it. In *Metamorphoses* people believe when they die they're changed into animals, trees, or maybe rivers. In that way they might achieve mortality. Or so they thought. Kind of a reincarnation thing."

"What's your point? If there is a point."

"Presuming there might be something to that concept, I can only hope you come back as a woman in your next life. It would do my heart even more good if you were to come back as a lesbian. What great copy that would make." My smile converted to a smirk.

"There's plenty of you out there, so don't go wishing I come back as a lesbian." His flickering eyes told me he believed he'd scored a point. "So you got nothing from Milton. You're here now to find out what we've dug up, right?"

I shrugged, "Right, Fritz. What have you got? If anything."

"If I knew anything, I'd be closing in on an escapee and accomplice."

I stood, picked up my tote case and nodded. "Lieutenant, this has been a delight, but I've got a beat to cover."

"Don't hurry back unless you have something to tell me."

"If you truly knew anything, you'd know your office is not my first stop when I have a scoop."

"Florez, there is one thing I know. If you get too close, you could get hurt. Beck is a danger. You're not an enforcer. Let us do the enforcing. If you get any leads, I want to know before you get involved. You'd be useless when events become shit-on-fire."

My words are playfully spoken. "When I know something, you'll be the first to know. Providing you buy the premiere issue of that day's *Mile High Mirror*."

"Get out of here. You're wasting the taxpayer's money."

It was my turn to grin. "Now that's something you seem not to need my help doing."

* * *

With an hour to spare, before meeting with my mother for lunch, I decided to hunker down in a booth at Ruby's Coffee Shop. From there I could call my office, and sip a cup of Ruby's robust coffee.

"If it isn't my sunshine," Ruby commented as she made her way to the back booth with two cups of freshly brewed coffee. She eased into the opposite seat. "Randa, girlfriend, you look like you're wound tight as a high-priced watch spring."

"It's my Hispanic roots. Latinos are always slightly

agitated," I teased.

Her laugh was clamorous. "My roots make me chill out. Like easy-listening jazz. Of course if I lost a little weight, I'd probably become ragtime."

"This is no cafe for someone wanting a diet," I said with a chuckle.

"Nope. Too much temptation. But who wants to take off pounds? Hell, honey, I like being a big woman. A heavy woman heats you in the winter and shades you in the summer." Together we laughed. She then asked, "The Jona Beck case getting you down?"

"That and the fact that I'm meeting my mother this noon." I wondered why I nourished ancient grief within my life. There was a raw lump in my throat that I had trouble swallowing away before adding, "My grandmother Randolph is seriously ill. Probably dying, actually."

"I'm sorry to hear that," Ruby spoke softly, comfortingly. She reached to pat my hand. "I know how hard I took it when I lost my granny. She was an old devil to most folks, but she was an angel to her family. Especially her grandkids. Our angel. Baked us ups so many treats, I've been a big girl since I was three-years old."

"Every child should experience that love."

"Honey, her lap was the safest place I ever been or hope to be. I'm not even that safe in my lover's arms."

Before my eyes began to tear, I rapidly blinked.

Ruby stood when the bells over the door frame jingled. "Customer."

Sipping my coffee slowly, purposely, I recalled my earliest thoughts. They were thoughts of waiting for my mother to return or thoughts of waiting for my father's visits.

Because my Grandmother Randolph was so demanding with nannies and governesses, there were many over the course of my infant and toddler years.

When my father visited, he took me back to his home with his parents for the weekends. Although loved, I was still a toddler showing up once a week for a *visit*. I garnered all the warmth I might, placing it in some imaginary emotional knapsack. It wasn't true belonging. When my mother returned from her tours, she was tired. Exhaustion and tenderness seemed not to mix.

My father always defended my mother. He would say how special her gift was to the world. Saturday afternoons he would often put on her albums, and sometimes even listen to an opera being transmitted from the Met. And he would tell me that my mother's voice was a treasure. That failed to decrease my loneliness.

I remained in the wake of those rarefied abstractions that produced my childhood. When all alone, I felt harsh reverberations of a past countervailing the future. We all wanted to connect, and needed to belong.

* * *

"I hope it isn't a breach of etiquette to order Chardonnay when I'm having tournedos," I said before sipping from the tulip stemware.

"You're free to order as you please," my mother responded. Dressed in an amethyst-colored suit, her print blouse made her attire slightly sporty, but definitely fashionable. Saturday noontime at *The Wellshire Inn* required her to be tastefully outfitted - without being ostentatious. *"Q'est-ce qu'il se passe?"* she inquired in French - what's going on.

Refusing to speak the language of *her* choice, I answered rapidly, "Nothing." Our conversation would forever remain stilted, I feared.

Glancing around at the *Wellshire's* wood paneling, stained glass, and century-old tapestries, I recalled the many times in the past when I'd dined. Housed in an English Tutor Mansion on the grounds of the *Wellshire Municipal Golf Course*, the restaurant was where the Randolph family often dined Sunday noontimes. The alternative was the *Denver Country Club*, where as a child I felt to be on display.

Erika Randolph knew egalitarian living. Although Mother made every attempt at not being a snob, she often seemed most at home with the pompous, supercilious, and absurd.

The waiter placed before me the main course of beef wrapped in bacon strips, asparagus spears flaked with dill and parsley, and baked potato with a dollop of sour cream and chives. My mother had sensibly ordered salmon and vegetables. She sipped her mineral water. She wasn't interested in eating. I recognized that anguish kept her from tasting the food.

"How is Grandmother?" I asked.

For several moments Erika Randolph gazed downward. There was strain in her face. The lighting was just right to make her eye color appear to be hyacinth blue. However behind Mother's eye color was a bleak, dull pain. And there was desolation in her voice. "The situation is extremely grim," she reported. "She has again asked for you."

"And I'm meant to pay her a conciliatory visit just because she decides she wishes to see me? I told you, I don't do pilgrimages."

"Randa, please don't be difficult. You've vilified her for no reason."

"You know better than that."

"No, I don't. Your hostility and lack of compassion shocks me. The woman is dying. Don't you understand that?"

"I understand we often remain the way our childhood has carved us."

"You're being immature. This is no time for childish precocity."

"Mother, I'm being me. And let's not blame this on childhood contrivances. I can't be expected to pay homage to her now. Not after everything that's happened. Father says I should forgive, but I can't."

"Your chivalrous father."

My gaze was one of remote neutrality until I heard her words. "Don't ever say anything against my father." I glared across the table. Finishing the wine in two gulps, I held the glass up for the waiter to see. "Another, please," I requested.

"Perhaps it wounds me that you've taken a loyalty oath to the Florez family, and resist a visit to your dying maternal grandmother."

"My only real grandmother is my *abuela.*"

"Ah, yes. Your Hispanic heritage. I find the best tutor in Europe to teach you French, and you constantly sprinkle your language with Spanish expressions. Randa, I'm well aware you favor the Florez family." Her pause lingered for many uncomfortable moments. "Might we keep this time together civil?"

My voice lacked conviction. "I apologize for upsetting you. The last days have been grueling." There was a cool wall of mistrust on both of our parts. After a deep breath, I uttered, "I'm truly sorry."

"Are you getting enough sleep?"

"Probably not. We're meant to escape lamentable events through dreams. My dreams have become monstrous."

"Do you think your editor might consider taking you off the Jona Beck story?"

Defiantly, I responded, "It's my story."

"Randa, promise me you'll back away if it becomes too much."

"It isn't just the story. I've just gone through an unpleasant breakup." We each seemed caught in the protocol of avoiding specifics.

"Alison?"

"She's been systematically extricating herself from the relationship for months. But now it's final."

"I'm terribly sorry you've been hurt, Randa."

"Eventually we all recover."

Mother closed her eyes a moment. "Not always."

* * *

After lunch I had rushed to *The Mirror* with a few ideas about how to freshen up a stale story. No sightings of Beck and Milton made a boring front page. My angle was to report on how the investigation was going. Rehashing a news event was known as a *John Garfield still dead* story. And certainly there seemed no life in the copy I'd submitted.

Mama Carmina called to invite me to stop by for dinner. I'd told her I had just finished lunch, but she insisted I drop by to pick up some hearty, healthy food for when I was hungry. She and Renie were going to play church bingo, so my 'care package' might be found in the refrigerator.

It was mid afternoon by the time I parked Garbo in front of my grandparent's home.

I arrived and checked the house. It was empty. Papa Gus spent nearly every summer Saturday afternoon puttering in his greenhouse. In the backyard a glowing citrine-colored sun cast shimmering reflections against the window panes in his greenhouse. The southern exposure side of the converted garage was a panel of windows, under a huge skylight.

I rapped on the side panel glass. "Papa Gus," I greeted my grandfather upon reaching the doorway.

Thick, silver strands swayed across his forehead as he gently thumped the rim of an upside-down clay pot to loosen the geranium's root ball. The contents dislodged as he smiled. His arms extended widely to enfold me when I entered them.

"Mama said you'd be stopping by."

"She commanded me." I corrected playfully. "Is this a new variety?" I ask about the geranium he clutched.

"Randa, this is called 'Countess of Scarborough' and its fragrance is strawberry. Here." He extended the scented pelargonium in my direction.

I sniffed several times. "Nice."

"Not luscious? You aren't a gardener. *Estas flores son de nuestros buena tierra.*"

"The flowers may be from our good earth, but even with the best soil available, I have no luck with plants." My grandfather's friendship was an inestimable gift. Each child - each grandchild, felt to be his favorite. Glancing around, I commented, "You've painted the interior of your greenhouse."

"A new coat for my hermitage. If life glistens around you, your heart will sing."

The color of the old garage had gone from a mint shade to a huskier hue of green. Inside were flowers that included hues of cinnabar, fire engine red, and pale pink. Glints of light bounced from the cluster of tools hanging on hooks and attached to a white pegboard against the wall. Two rows of cedar tables were filled with beds of newly planted cuttings. The soil bins emitted a rich fragrance of loom. Upon the top of the bins were inverted stacks of clay pots. A unique scent of terra cotta blended with soil, cedar, and fragrant blossoms to create a cloud of wondrous freshness.

After retirement from fifty years with a landscape company, my grandfather remained actively working the earth. He supplemented his retirement by selling his specialty crops of scented geraniums.

"Any luck this noon with your mother?"

The past was often an open wound. "If I don't see my grandmother, guilt is a given. That's Mother's take on it."

"Randa, your mother isn't an evil person. Forgive her for not being the way you wish her to be."

"Papa Gus, I question her love."

"Mothers and daughters always have a struggle to understand one another. We rent our children." Papa's jerrybuilt philosophy held the key to most answers. "After all these years Mama and Renie still disagree."

"Aunt Renie disagrees with most people about one thing or another. If not politics, certainly religion."

Papa Gus laughed with a robust heartiness. "It reminds me what the poet Shelley says."

"About Aunt Renie?" I playfully asked.

"About politics and religion. He says life would be better if the last king were to be strangled by the guts of the last priest."

"Don't let Renie hear that," I said before my chuckle began.

"I love my daughter, but often I think she wants to rewrite the Bible. Or maybe," he speculatively added "she only wishes heavenly ascension for an attempt at editing the good book."

We shared laughter. I paused before my spirit again dipped. "Papa, do you believe in a supreme being?"

Holding up the plant he has been caressing, he affirmed, "One who loves geraniums can't help but believe there must be a supreme landscape artist of one kind or another."

* * *

Mama Camina believed her matriarchal duty was to insure her family remained in constant contact. A note was attached to my paper bag of nourishment. It asked that I drop off a large container of leek soup to my father's house. *Sopa de porros* was Angie's favorite.

During my belletristic university days, I'd always stopped by to visit with Angie before going home to my grandparents. Angie had studied to be a hair stylist, and often volunteered to practice on me. When I'd declined, she would challenge, "You can still be a college dyke and not have such a boring head of hair."

I parked my Z in front. Benjy walked from the steps of the house. "Why don't you get the rust on your lower fenders fixed?" he bantered.

"Because the moment the car is perfectly restored, you'll steal it."

He gave me a quick hug. "So did you have lunch with the hoity-toity prima donna?"

"You sound like your mother," I teased.

"Mom has been ranting about your mother all morning," Benjy reported.

We walked up the steps. I teased, "More than she usually rants about Aunt Renie?"

"More. Aunt Renie only sprouts her flipping parables at Mom. Your mother phones her husband."

"My mother was trying to find me. That was the only reason she called Father. Besides, she thinks of their divorce as a civil one. There shouldn't be animosity."

"That idea is a dog that won't hunt."

"You might be right, Benj." When we reached the door, Benjy opened it for me.

I handed Angie the Tupperware container of soup. "You aren't playing bingo with Mama and Renie?"

"Renie has been driving me nuts. She should be a nun.

Anyway, I got to stay home and watch my family. My husband's ex-wife is chasing him down. She calls to aggravate me."

"Angie, my mother only calls to find me. I wasn't returning the calls she left on my cell phone. It's my fault."

"She should leave Paulo alone. She dumped him. Now she wants to talk to him. She may be your mother, but she's out to sabotage me."

"Of course she isn't. That's absurd." I sat on the sofa, leaning back. "Father loves you, and my mother is aware of it."

"She's alone now that she dumped the crazy conductor. The nutty molester! Now she's alone. Alone. Women alone can't be trusted. Suppose she wants your father back?"

"She doesn't. She's busy with her own schedule, and her own agenda. She's only here because my grandmother is dying."

"Another scheming white bitch! At least that conniving old *cabra* is about to take a dirt nap." Angie's emotions churned as she chewed gum violently. "So fate throws your mother in Denver. The same city as her ex-husband. She hasn't got a man, so she's going to pester my Paulo. She must want him back."

"Even if she did, it wouldn't do her any good. This is Father's family. You are the one he loves." With all of Angie's patented charm, she would fly off the handle at the slightest hint of my father being interested in my mother. Angie wouldn't believe that life's great synchronicity favored her. She was convinced that it was no coincidence that my mother arrived in Denver when my grandmother was about to die. There must be an ulterior motive involved. Angie believed her husband's first marriage was a relic my father yet savored. "I've said it a thousand time, you don't need to worry about my mother."

Benjy sat beside me. His arm went around my shoulder. "How's my favorite sister?"

"No, Benjy. You can't drive my rust bucket."

"Just around the block 'til you get done talking."

"Right!" I said with heavy sarcasm.

"Ah, come on, just for ten minutes?"

"You'll be in South Dakota in ten minutes with your penchant for speed and my super engine."

"I promise to pamper Garbo."

"Maybe tomorrow at the barbecue Rogerio will take Garbo for a spin with you. I want him to drive it to see if the accelerator is right."

"I can check it out for you now."

"Let's pass on it until tomorrow. Rogerio will undoubtedly cave in and let you drive. I've got to leave now anyway," I said. As an afterthought, I asked, "Angie, do you think Teresa and Rogerio mind my bringing a friend to their fiesta?"

"Naw," she answered. "You can even bring that stuck up *bruja,* Alison."

"Alison is no longer a part of my life."

"Who then?" questioned Benjy.

My eyebrows lifted. "I've got a real surprise for you, Benj. Trust me on that."

* * *

"No bubble-gummers allowed," the harsh voice behind the bar screamed at a group of under aged women. The barmaid redirected her attention to me. Over the booming heavy metal rock music coming from the loudspeaker, she inquired, "Now then, what's your pleasure?"

"A Coors," I ordered. The stout woman with long, bushy blonde hair nodded that she had heard my request. Her black leather skirt rode up in tight horizontal pleats. Her goldenrod-colored, high-necked silk blouse was ornamented with a spiked leather collar. From her fingertips came matching gold nails nearly as long as her fingers.

As she snapped off the beer's cap, she glanced back at the young women. "Fuckin' bunch of cherries come in here and give The Raven's Talon a bad name."

I resisted the urge to roll my eyes. "Serving minors is risky."

"Yeah. Hell, I don't run a dirty bar here."

Another urge to roll my eyes. "Of course not. Are you the

owner?"

"Nope. I'm the manager. Donna. You the heat?"

"No," I answered. "Why?"

"You look familiar."

I glanced down at my attire. Black denims, beige boots and suede vest, with black T-neck, had not passed as an S&M outfit. But it was the best my wardrobe had to offer. "I'm not a cop. Several months ago I stopped in a few times."

"Oh, yeah. I remember you now. You're that reporter. You interviewed me. I changed my hair color, and it's longer."

"Now I recall you. You didn't used to wear makeup."

"No. But my chick likes a little color," she reported with a toss of her curls. "So what brings you in again?"

She knew what. "With the escape, we're back on the Jona Beck story," I confided. I knew better than to attempt to hide my purpose. "I'm looking for Lucia Gomez."

"Haven't seen her for a week or two."

With a smile, I disputed her claim. "She's in here every weekend."

"Not since she started working up at Black Hawk."

"In a casino?"

"Yeah. She's a dealer at Winner's Palace. It just opened a few weeks ago."

"Speaking of dealers, do you know any dealers that might sell drugs to Jona?"

"She killed Bull Maynard. He was her connection. He was a mule for some L.A. gangs."

"That's old news. Where might she go now?"

"Depends what she wants. The streets are filled with suppliers."

"What was she doing?" I asked.

"In the past it was Mexican brown. Heroin. And that's expensive."

"Jona told me she once ran a stable of women to get the money for drugs. Is that right?"

"I think so." Donna's demeanor reflected that she was getting perturbed.

"Know any of the women she worked? Anyone from her old life she might have contacted?"

"Naw. Jona burns bridges."

"So who might she have called if she needed help?"

"Take a guess."

"Okay. Simone and Jona probably don't have unlimited resources. Simone's money will probably soon dry up. Particularly if Jona is back doing drugs."

"Jona was done for laying paper once."

"But she didn't have enough bad check charges to pay for the kind of habit she had."

"Probably not," Donna agreed. "She was too freaked out most of the time to have a business sense. Even without junk, she was squirrelly. Flipped out. She ran with freaks, too."

"I've met a few of the people she knew. Anyone here tonight I might not know?"

She pointed. "The gal over there by the door. She just took off her brain bucket."

I squinted toward where she's pointing. "Brain bucket?"

"Motorcycle helmet. The redhead over there."

"Her name is Vivian, isn't it?" I asked. I recalled her from last winter's series of interviews with people who knew Jona Beck. I referred to her as Vivian One-Name, or Vivian X, because no one had a last name for her. Even the police referred to her as Vivian Doe. Her past seemed invisible.

"Yeah. Not a bad looking kid."

"Kid," I repeat. I watch as Vivian moved across the barroom. She was high, and her motions seemed effortless. The dim lighting made her pale coloring even more washed out than I remembered her being. Long, carrot-colored hair fell around her shoulders. She was thin and medium tall. As she neared, I saw that drugs had started to emaciate her attractiveness. My stomach wrenched. She couldn't be much over twenty in actual years. On the streets she'd lived many high risk lifetimes. If life had assailed her, she'd cooperated to her fullest.

Strings of lighting glowed with festivity - but it reminded me of decorations for a tomb. Patrons of this bar mutilated themselves and others in bizarre games. Jona Beck told me that it was spiritual nourishment that made her a believer in sadomasochism. She called her *handiwork* creating art on flesh instead of canvas. She said we all have a death wish. She laughed with madness when telling me I should have a curiosity about death. After all, she indicted, being enamored with death was a function of my Spanish heritage.

With that memory there was a tremor. My hand tightly grasped the beer's cool bottle. I approach Vivian. "Vivian, do you remember me?"

"Should I?"

"I'm a reporter. I interviewed you last winter."

"Now I remember. About Jona."

"Any idea where she might have gone?"

"Cops already asked me. I don't know. Think I'd swallow lit firecrackers?"

"Last winter you seemed to embrace Jona as some sort of great goddess. Weren't you the newest slave in her harem before she went to the slammer?"

"I've got my own deal now."

"Vivian, she's not some underworld heroine. She's a murderer. If you're hiding her, it's not only illegal, it's dangerous." I failed to elicit a response. Not even a shrug. Vivian's glance continued to cool. "She's on the run. And she's got her psychiatrist along for the ride. Do you think Dr. Milton is safe?"

"I don't know who is safe." Her face wildly twisted into a hollow laugh. "You think you're safe? You're not. No one is."

"I know you visited Jona behind bars. Did she indicate her feelings about Simone Milton?"

"She needed a way to break out. Simone was only Jona's freedom fuck."

I leaned nearer. "She seduced Simone. But does she care about the woman? Do you think Simone is safe with Jona?"

"I told you the answer. No one is safe with no one." She gave a turbulent swat in the air. With a fleeting gleam of amusement, she added, "You want to come back to my apartment and check under my bed? Maybe I'm hiding Jona."

"You're a fool if you are hiding her."

"Want me to come to your apartment and see if I can fit under your bed?" Her giggle was from a recent hit of drugs. "Want me, lady?"

"No. I want information" I took a deep breath. With inchoate attempts to reconcile reality, I looked away. Vivian was part of the agitated, desperate living that provided Jona Beck a vehicle for murder. I handed her a card with my cell number. "If you have anything to tell me, call."

I turned and walked away. I suddenly recalled one thing Jona said at our last meeting. It had somehow terrified me. My nightmares reran her statement over and over. It was not only that she had said it, but the way she'd gloated. She told me she was the friend of sex and death - the very best friend.

On my way past Donna, I placed the bottle on the bar with a thud.

"Shit!" she yelled. "What the hell's with you?"

"I wanted to get your attention." I took out my card, dropped it on the bar, and spoke, "If you hear anything, call. I'll make it worth your call."

"You five-star stupid or what? I'd never risk going against Jona. She's all over. Her spirit is in this bar. She's standing right behind you. She's everywhere."

I muttered, "Jona is hiding from authorities. Hiding like a terrified criminal on the run. She's nowhere."

Donna's eyes glittered with a haunting stare. There was contemptuousness to her words. "You're terrified, too, Aren't you?"

I heard the door's gong as I exited. Its plangent ring accompanied me as I walked mechanically across the street. Darkness was a shroud that couldn't be shrugged. Before reaching for my car's door, I turned and spit the taste of beer and bar onto the pavement. *Tengo mal sabor de boca,* was the thought in my mind. I had very bad taste in my mouth. And perhaps a worse taste in my soul.

* * *

My loft seemed a skeletal retreat.

Even the planks of flooring echoed as I walked across them.

I showered, tossed on a toga wraparound, and then sat on my bed for nearly an hour before going to the refrigerator to rummage through the sack of provisions sent by my grandmother. I piled a plate with cookies, and then poured a glass of milk. When I returned to my bed I slid under the covers. From the nightstand, I took my journal. It was pressed to my breasts. I wanted to write, but the words were stillborn.

When the phone rang, I jumped. "Yes?" I spoke.

"Randa, I hope I didn't wake you," Nevada said.

"Not at all. I'm just sitting here."

"Are we still on for tomorrow?"

"Yes. And I told Benjy he's in for a surprise."

Nevada laughed. "I'm really looking forward to seeing you again. And meeting all your family."

"You aren't daunted by the thought of meeting a couple dozen members of the Florez family?"

"No. I can't wait. My shift ends at six in the morning, so I'll have time to sleep until noon. Like I said, I really need to get away from the job."

"I can relate to that. This Beck hunt is one of the more haunting stories I've worked on. It's like a vortex consuming my energy."

"Save some energy for me," she requested. "You sound exhausted."

"It's been a long night. I went to The Raven."

"No wonder you're spooked. Hope you didn't go alone."

"If I want answers, I can't take an army. There's a subterranean mentality that makes it difficult to break the surface. Taking a partner seems not to work in getting answers."

"Just be careful. I'm serious. Jona is dangerous and she has dangerous friends. Besides, I don't want them influencing you. I only want to use my handcuffs on criminals."

I laughed, and it felt very good. "Nevada, your cuffs won't get any wear and tear on me. I promise."

"Did The Raven inquiry yield anything?"

"Only that Lucia Gomez works in a Black Hawk casino."

"Winner's Palace."

"Why didn't you tell me?"

"I just found out about it today. I checked one of the reports. She was questioned yesterday. Knows nothing. Or so she says."

"I'm going up to Black Hawk on Monday, if she works then."

"Just a second. I'll find out her work schedule for you."

While I waited for Nevada to return to the telephone, I munched chocolate chip cookies that Mama Carmina had baked. The soup, meatloaf, veggies, and other healthy food items were yet packed away in the refrigerator. After a sip of milk, I heard the crackling sound of Nevada shuffling papers.

"Randa, she works noon until eight Monday night."

"I'll ride the shuttle bus up early afternoon. I can take my computer with me and work on the way up to Blackhawk. Maybe I can catch Lucia on a break."

"Hope you get more than we did."

"Me, too. I built up a pretty good rapport with her last winter. It might have been that we share a Hispanic culture. She seemed to trust me. Maybe she'll confide in me again."

"I hope so. Look, my break is over. I've got to scram. It's my job to pitch the bad asses in the holding tank until their lawyers spring them."

"Take care. See you tomorrow."

After disconnecting the phone, I considered what I had gleaned from the evening. The Raven was dismal and my going there was a wasted trip. I'd traipsed into the jaws of danger for nothing. Nevada gave me info on Lucia's work hours. Nevada made up for all the zeros encountered today. Nevada was on the other end of the chart from where zero begins.

With that thought I turned off the lamp on my nightstand. My eyes closed heavily, and I withdrew into sleep's seclusion.

CHAPTER 5

Sunday

Waking alone on a summer Sunday morning left a bittersweet emotion of estrangement. I showered, and then threw on beige shorts and a bright, neon, multicolored T-shirt. The bulky Sunday morning newspaper was retrieved. I unfurled it when I sat on a stool at my breakfast nook. While reading the above the fold updates on the Jona Beck escape, I sipped a mug of warm cinnamon flavored coffee and nibbled at my makeshift brunch. An English muffin had been toasted and between its crusts I've layered my grandmother's meatloaf and a slice of cheese.

My head was still thick with sleep as the newspaper was perused. The article hinted Jona's underground circuitry of friends must be involved in hiding the women. My theory was simple. Two women couldn't vanish off the face of the earth. Statements by enforcement indicated that it was only a matter of time until the women surfaced. They were confident the fugitive and accomplice or hostage would be found and apprehended. A quick resolution, a spokesperson had quoted. To me it indicated they had no viable sightings, leads, or clues. Their efforts were not entirely depleted. They asked for the public's assistance in spotting the fugitive. But they warned that Jona Beck could be armed and dangerous.

My own investigation led to the same blank page. My visit to the dark side yielded little - other than to reinforce my knowledge of danger.

Seated at my desk, I scouted several dated audio tapes that corresponded to stick flash drives. I picked files where Jona Beck discussed Dr. Simone Milton. I heard Jona's haunting, irreverent voice. Dr. Milton had called her narcissistic. That agitated Jona. I recalled there was a smirk in her eyes when she told me she may be gruesome, notorious, and brutal, but not narcissistic. She then issued a crude vomiting sound that echoed across the room. The doctor will be sorry she'd said that, Jona promised.

A small funnel of light had shone from the institution's hallway. Jona's eyes were as lucent as crystallized fruit. She related her theory of death. Her analogy explained that the body was a piece of furniture. When she killed, she searched for the soul as it exited the flesh. She hacked up armchairs, sofa, and end tables. The people she killed, she stated, had nothing except messy stuffing inside. No soul - for that was an illusion. Her glance was heavy upon mine when she related that she wished to hack anyone who dared tag her with psychiatric mumbo-jumbo.

The tape was chilling. Jona said that young women are grazing land. The older women are plowed-under fields. Dr. Simone Milton needed her body plowed by a knife.

Jona's voice was low, and sounded as if she might have been ready to detonate a very huge explosion.

I'd inquired about why she was upset with Simone. Jona's words were suddenly erotic storms. She's tempted to kill the doctor, Jona confided. She leaned near the microphone to whisper that she'd never been tempted to do anything that she hadn't actually done. The temptation dictated her spiritual outline. I recalled being glad for the mesh panel between us.

At the time I had dismissed the threat as insanity talking, or perhaps Jona's attempt to make me believe she was insane. She often said things like that. She told me she had tried to carve Bull's heart out. When she couldn't find it, she settled on carving up his balls.

How, I questioned, could one differentiate between truth and fiction when talking with such a defective human being as Jona. Her soul was deformed; her impoverished heart was callused. Her words matched the madness of her soul and heart. She was conflicted. Many, I grasped at stray thoughts, were conflicted. Most did not take it out on the world.

My crawl toward truth left me as lost as I had been last winter. But one thing had been confirmed. Dr. Simone Milton was in danger. A treacherous criminal was many lengths ahead of the posse.

Simone's background had not prepared her for a role reversal. She was a gamekeeper - she became a poacher, and was now the prey. Simone Milton obviously knew the potential brutality of the human spirit. But Jona had done a complete study in human savagery.

I immediately called Fritz's office. I left a message for him. Although he already assumed Simone Milton was endangered, this would confirm it.

There was urgency in my call to Hank Richards. I asked if he'd meet me at Ruby's in an hour.

* * *

"Kinda makes you wonder if there's not a hut outside the village," Ruby said when I sighed heavily with dejection. I sat at my favorite back booth. "Tough case. Nobody knows nothing about this Jona Beck deal. Other than the fact that her brain's driveway doesn't go all the way to the street." Ruby slid a mug of coffee toward me. "On the house, kid. You look like you've been flogged all night long."

"Thank you. And yes, I feel as though I may well have been flogged."

Ruby made her way back behind the counter to pour coffee for another patron. My thoughts seemed to die beneath chatter coming from the next booth.

"Randa," Hank Richards greeted me. "What's so important on a Sunday morning?"

"We've got to get a line on Beck. I listened to a portion of Jona's taped interview this morning. Simone Milton is in major danger."

"That's self-evident. Old news. She's riding shotgun with a deranged killer."

"I need your assistance. I have a gut feeling. Vivian One-

Name. She knows something. We need to get a recent photo of the elusive Vivian. We could publish it. Maybe we could make inquiries over the net."

"We've got old photos around the time of Jona's trial."

"She looks different. I didn't even recognize her. We need a recent shot of her."

"The authorities couldn't track her because they have no recent mug shots. So if we can get photos, maybe we could check some off-chart websites. We might reach the cult groups to find her."

"My instincts are shouting that she's involved," I muttered into my coffee mug.

"Beck is more than violent. She's cunning. That makes her first degree dangerous."

"I'm going to chase down Lucia Gomez tomorrow. We should check her chat lines. And I have one other lead. I might be able to get one of the workers out at the institution to talk with me. They've been instructed not to talk, but he's a friend of Giselle's. She called right before I left to meet you. She's already talked with him. If he knows he can trust me, maybe he'll tell me what he knows."

Hank glanced away. "He may not know anything. Randa, realistically there's only so much we can do."

"So we're supposed to sit at our computer terminals waiting patiently for something to break. Hank, I'm tired of writing reconstituted stories. Even Kenny-the-comma-chaser is hoping for action. But I want to be there when the Jona Beck story goes down. And if I'm not ahead of the story, I'll lose it to someone else."

"The spirit of adventure is a gift," he replied. "I know you're the obvious candidate in chasing down the story, but this one might not have our name on it."

"Checking sources is the less glamorous aspect of journalism, but if I dig deeply enough, something is bound to turn up."

"As long as it isn't your toes turning up in a permanent manner," he joked. "Randa, I'd be happier if we were dealing with fifteen-year old pickpockets."

"Now that, my friend," I emphasized, "*is* a chamber of horrors."

* * *

A huge buttercup sun was in the sky overhead. I hoped the family fiesta would cheer my sagging spirit.

The long, elegant nose of my Z pointed in the direction of Denver's Highland neighborhood. Highland was only ten minutes from my LoDo loft. Being near my family was important to me. It is good in case - *tengo que irme a casa.* In case I have to go home.

The *casa de* Rogerio and Teresa was a small bungalow-styled home. Upon approaching it one can tell that love lived there. It was bedecked with the spotted colors of Papa Gus geraniums. The heirlooms were blooming. Large bunches of daisies protruded over clumps of pink border flowers that surround the bronze-gray brick home.

My arms were loaded down with a case of beer. Atop the beer were two bottles of coffee-flavored liqueur. When Aunt Renie viewed the beer, she scolded, "Beer is the broth of Satan."

Pretending not to hear her words, I hoisted the case of Corona on top of the nearest picnic table. There were five tables beneath the huge oak tree's limbs. Leaves shaded a good portion of the backyard. Each table was decked out with a brightly colored tablecloth. Piles of food decorated those sturdy tables. Wafting through the air was a magnificent fragrance of corn, cilantro, freshly ground spices, and roasted chilies. Flavors echoed through various, complex sauces. My mouth watered.

Aunt Renie continued her lecture. Her words were reprimanding. "Every dog is entitled to one bite, but you miss Holy Mass every Sunday. Even your Easter duty is ignored. Your soul will burn in hell. You should be a positive influence for our Benjy. *No me parece bien su conducta.*"

"*No siempre muestra buen juicio.*" I'm not too crazy about

his conduct either. "But my going to church isn't likely to turn him around, Aunt Renie."

"You might pray for his soul."

I opened a bottle of beer and sipped. "I do."

"But not in church."

"No. Not in church."

"There is always room for another bucket in the well," Renie stated. She then was distracted a moment. She uncovered a tray of spicy tamales. The steaming corn husks crinkled.

I took another sip of Corona. I wondered if I'd adequately warned Nevada about my family. By the time Nevada arrived, I was in the thicket of family and laughter. Latino music was an undercurrent to the chatter.

There was great interest in observing Benjy's dark eyes widen when he saw Nevada at the gate. She playfully pointed her finger at him and wagged it. His smile was weak at first, but Nevada approached him with a hug.

"No warrants to execute," she said.

"Your surprise, Benj," I teased while placing my arm around her shoulder. "Glad you could make it. I was beginning to worry that you'd decided to give it a pass."

"No. I just overslept. I'm rotating back off of nights onto day shift."

Benjy politely handed Nevada a beer. "I'll drive you home," he chided.

"I live only a few blocks away. I walked in hopes your sister will offer me a ride home. But, Benj, I have an offer for you."

"An offer?" His eyes narrowed.

"Want to go on a ride along with me tomorrow?"

"Ride in a police car?"

"Sure. We can take riders. If your testicles are in good enough order to snag a vehicle and take us on a high speed chase, you ought to be brave enough to ride with the badges. Who knows, you might even want to become an enforcer," Nevada said.

Incredulously, he frowned. "I probably won't even graduate. And I'm too short."

"You'll graduate if you apply your intellect. And if you stand up straight, you'll make the height requirement."

He was quiet. I wasn't certain if her suggestion amazed him as much as it did me, but it rendered him speechless. He mumbled, "Maybe." Then he wandered across the yard.

"He'll go with me," Nevada whispered confidently to me.

I introduced Nevada to everyone, and sensed genuine affection. My family realized that while Alison had curb appeal beyond belief, there was something unattainable about her. She certainly dominated the atmosphere. They knew a scalp collector when they saw one. And they recognized that the smile touching Nevada O'Bryan's lips was legit.

Renie continued sneaking glances at Nevada. As she prepared the platters of green *chiles*, roasted pork, stuffed tortillas, cheese, and *poblano* quesadillas, and multitude of other food, she spied on my new friend.

I was glad Renie hadn't overheard Nevada's whisperings to me. "Being off owl-shift will be better for our relationship."

"Relationship?" I was taken aback.

Nevada answered me quickly, "The one we're about to begin. The love affair of our lives."

My mouth curved. "You think I look as though I might enjoy a liaison?"

Her femininity became sensitized. There was coquetry in her eyes. She had styled her hair back in a comfortable, sporty twist. I confessed that she emitted a tender side. I also admitted she was a pre-Raphaelite type beauty. Mesmeric powers were part of that charm. There was no hint of her badge.

"I think you might enjoy our liaison. You look tantalizingly wonderful."

"That's just what I was thinking about you. You look so different out of uniform." Words seemed to be stumbling from my mouth.

"I might look different, but I always feel like what I am. A cop. Don't you always feel as though you're a snoop?"

I chuckled. "As a matter of fact, yes. Right now I'm wondering where Jona Beck is hiding."

"I've been delving into the files every time I can get near a computer. I keep reading these conflicting stories. I wonder now if perhaps the detectives misinterpreted her multitude of confessions as being false. Maybe she actually has done all the things she claims in her interview statements to the investigators. Suppose she scrambled them. Carjacking and murder of one in Dallas. Strangulation of hooker in Kansas City. Suppose she interchanged dates, places, and murder victims. She enjoys creating havoc. She's a sick puppy, but she's not a stupid one. Anyway, I'm trying to pull up any match I can in the mishmash."

"The files must be jam-packed with evidence. She told me she's offed more people that I've dated." I smiled. "Where she got the idea I'm a playgirl, I don't know. But she thought I slept around a lot."

"Do you?"

"Not at all." My answer was with resolve. "My father didn't raise a sleep-around kind of woman."

"Good. My mom told me I'd get cooties if I let all the boys bonk me. As soon as I became interested in sex, she changed that to all the *women*."

My laugh exploded. "In my youth, cooties weren't mentioned, but certainly the other fears of disease were listed."

"Randa, I wonder what Jona was told."

"Her childhood was filled with abuse."

Nevada took a deep breath. "She told one detective she'd killed a guy when she was in her early teens. Hitched a ride with him from Oklahoma to Kansas City. On the way she claims she crawled in the backseat for a nap. She took the drawstring cord from her duffel bag and wrapped it around his neck as he drove. The car ended up in a ditch with the driver dead. In the report Jona said she was pissed the next day when they ruled his death a heart attack at the wheel. No credit for her first kill. Those were her words."

"Credit," I repeated. "I'm not sure if she attempts to sheath her insanity or her sanity." I paused, frowning. "You may be on to something about her confessions of the past murders. She told me she'd strangled a guy in Oklahoma that way. But she left off the first kill part. Maybe she did that so that the cops would check everything out, come up with blanks, and believe they'd been duped."

"They then drop the investigation of past killings." Nevada's glance away seemed one of worry. "I'm going to continue my investigation. One thing I know. If we close in on her without a quick capture, it will force her hand. The more trapped the escapee feels, the more chance of a killing spree. As the net draws closed, the danger increases."

"And Simone might be her next victim. The thought has occurred to me that Simone might be the only person in Jona's life who ever loved her. And Simone is in very serious trouble."

"If Jona began killing in her teens, she ought to be damned proficient at it by now."

My words drifted as they happened, "A teenager killing seems incongruous to life. Back then my greatest worry was getting my homework completed."

"My concern was getting my horse broken. We purchased some wild mustangs. Training them was a family project. It taught me patience. And maybe it taught me how to understand motive."

"So that's what makes you a dynamite cop?"

"If I can break and train wild mustangs, maybe I have a chance at turning Benjy around."

We shared a laugh before I said, "He likes you. That's a terrific start."

"I like him. *And* his older sister. That's even a better start."

* * *

Nevada's initial meeting with my family was after the arrest of my brother. Perhaps, I decided as voices lifted, her second experience would be arresting Renie and Angie for assault. My stepmother challenged Renie with an insult. It had to do with a comment about a get-out-of-purgatory-free card. Renie replied that at least she doesn't dress like a *puta.*

Angie's fists went on her hips, "Renie, your head is up your pious ass."

I knew the fracas won't end there. Luckily, Nevada saw the platter filled with dessert. She joked, "Hand over the *postres* and no one will get hurt!" Everyone laughed. The tension of the last few minutes evaporated. The *familia* fiesta continued as if Aunt Renie and Angie had not shared an unpleasant encounter. Sipping Kahlua-spiked iced coffee was an effortless pleasure. My slack eyelids reflected my contentment.

"Your '*postres*' comment came just at the right time to prevent a family disturbance call." I motioned toward the gate. "Let's go while there's peace in the village." After our goodbyes, we waved back at my family.

"They do call us peace officers."

I handed her the key to my silver Z. "Treat my wheels with the respect she deserves."

"I even drive my battered old truck with respect," Nevada replied. "And I know you're not legally impaired, but you look a little sloshy around the edges."

"I feel a little smashed."

"Good."

"Good?" I repeated.

"Yes. Booze lowers the resistance. Any great seducer knows that one by heart," she teased. "If you're a little tipsy, you might not object to staying over with me tonight."

"And?"

"And whatever," she answered as she turned the ignition key. "You might want to share breakfast in the morning. Your family sent enough provisions to get us through next autumn."

"They insist on serving acres of food from their lines of tables."

"They're wonderful. You're lucky to be a part of a loving family. My family is also terrific. I can't imagine not having their support. Especially about being lesbian. They're great about it, just like yours is."

"It isn't all sweet. Although I acknowledge a bond with them, I also know the feeling of being alone. My families, plural because of the divorce, have always been divisive in spirit and intent. There is animosity. My grandparents Randolph referred to my father as the musician turned grease monkey. My father sees his profession of auto mechanic as one of honor. He compares the understanding of an engine to the timing needed to make fine music. He has a similar reverence for purring pistons as he does for an orchestral concert. He's happiest when in a thicket of wires under a hood, or when he used to caress his guitar's strings."

"But he's become a mechanic instead of a musician. Your mother's family didn't like that, I'll bet."

"My grandparents were vehement in their opposition to my father. That included his skin color, and mine. My grandmother Randolph once told me that the reason I was never allowed to be photographed with my famous mother was because I was half Hispanic. When I questioned my mother, she denied it. She said she didn't want to make a display of me. She was protecting my childhood privacy."

"Sounds logical. But you always have your father's family."

"As a member of the Florez family I felt a slight ostracism of class difference as well. My cousins asked why I spoke in such a highbrow way. Very little idiomatic. They'd ask who I was trying to impress. If I used slang during summer break, while visiting my mother, I was quickly corrected. I tried to please everyone, and perhaps pleased no one. Not even myself. Nothing is perfect."

"Why so?"

My answer was barely audible. "At times my childhood seemed a process of dividing and re-dividing. Often until I felt to be divided into oblivion."

She inquired, "Will you stay the night?"

"Nevada, are you sure?"

"I'm attracted to you. I think you're wonderful, and," she paused, "we've both been through enough broken romances to know if it's meaningful. Also, we might scorch the sheets with our sexual encounter. Or maybe share love."

Nevada O'Bryan wasn't the kind of woman I wanted to use as a curative to my broken pride. I had been Alison's disciple.

She had only to call with a hint of carnality in her voice, and I was hers. She dumped me with great precision. There was also no wish on my part to be harmed by love.

I sighed, answering, "I'm not sure if intimacy is the right thing for either of us yet."

"Fine. Because, Randa, I've got a lot of tenacity. I'll ask again."

We both chuckled. "Spoken as a true seductress," I replied.

I leaned back into the nest of my bucket seat. Through the T-top there was a bright coin of a moon. The recently risen moon bathed my world in silvery light. A night without the seclusion and isolation provided by loneliness might be wonderful.

Our hearts remained our most singular and correct compass. It could be special.

* * *

Nevada O'Bryan lived in a two-story brick, turn-of-the-century home. It was sensitively and tastefully decorated. She's selected a combination of early-American oak furniture with an abundance of homespun antiques. There were also various textures of western, as well as southwestern memorabilia. It was a combination of eclectic, lovely hominess.

The living room was adjacent to a large formal dining room. A lawyer's bookcase was filled with works ranging from poetry to police procedure. The next room was a splendidly utilitarian, brightly colored kitchen. Upon the center island countertop were spice trays, large utensils, and a cutting board. Overhead pots and pans hung down from decorative hooks. Appliances were polished gleaming white.

After touring the main floor, we climbed the beautifully restored oak staircase. Nevada's second floor bedroom was small, simple, and very comfortable. The predominant colors were midnight blue and coral.

My yawn was an unintended combination of excellent food, drink, and a difficult day. "Long day."

She asked, "Think a shower might reawaken you?"

"I think it couldn't hurt."

"Think we might conserve water by showering together?"

There was a deliberately suspended moment. Her fingers glided across my cheek. They traced my lips. I replied, "I think it couldn't hurt."

* * *

Nevada's bathroom was purely Victoriana. An oval, forest-green shower curtain surrounded us when the warm wrap of a shower rained down our sudsy bodies. Above us hung a mammoth, sprawling fern.

Her hands reached across the spraying shower to touch my face. Her kiss was so gentle, my knee hinges wobbled. I trembled. "You're terrific," she whispered.

"I was just thinking that about you. Maybe I'm wondering why I'm experiencing such a tremendous desire for you."

"Probably," she said, "it's because you recognize that I'm scrupulously honest, undeviatingly loyal, and enormously kind. And it's fortunate for us both that we met."

"Yes. Fortunate."

Our bodies pressed nearer as our heads automatically rested on one another's shoulders. I felt her lips gently tracing my neck. I wondered if the torrents rippling through my body could ever be analyzed.

"What were you thinking?" she questioned.

"What a truly *arresting* woman you are."

Her laugh mingled with the sound of water that snapped bubbles in my ears.

After our shower, we walked across the hall to her bedroom. She carefully selected several CDs and slipped them into their trays. "I haven't got even one opera. So a little Leona Boyd, Dolly Parton, and Shakira will have to do until I get an Erika Randolph CD." She dimmed the light as we stepped onto the plush sea-blue rug at the side of her massive bed.

"I'm glad you aren't playing my mother's CDs. It would be a little creepy trying to make love with a background of her arias." We both chuckled. "I listen to very little opera. I've had an ample dose while spending summers and holidays with my mother."

Nevada's glance was penetrating. "Randa, you look as though you're about to bolt and run for cover."

"I'm just not accustomed to experiencing these kinds of emotions."

She pulled back the covers. "Want to talk about it?"

"Alison rarely told me the complete truth. All I'll ever ask of you is to always communicate honestly with me."

"I vow to always be honest with you. And do you promise to always tell me the truth?"

"Always. Truth is a journalist's Magna Carta."

As a compass needle inside my heart returned to its magnetic meridian, we resumed our embrace. The powder blue bedspread rustled like taffeta. I was swathed in the warmth of her motion. Our mutual touches seemed to be verses unraveling from a skein of love poetry. She was as authentic a woman as I'd ever met.

Through Nevada's bedroom window an amber corona of light gleamed. Her cinnamon kiss was tasted until it became part of my own. Savored, until it became an explosive carnality - my impenetrable solitude vanished.

Exhausted, we rested in one another's arms. When her eyelids closed, I watched her sleeping. It was only then I realized that she did resemble *every* softness of every woman named Margaret that I'd ever known.

My lips rested on her temple. *Te amo,* I whispered before my own sleep invaded. Drowsily, I swayed between sleep and the reality of holding her to me.

* * *

I staggered awake with the melodic burr. Quickly, I rescued the cell phone in an attempt to keep Nevada's sleep from being disturbed. I answered, "Florez."

"Thought you'd want to know," Kenny Erickson reported, "Hank Richards used one of Vivian X's photos on a few of the internet sites. He enhanced the photos with age progression and such, and there was recognition. Positive identification! Your buddy Vivian X does have a last name."

Nevada stirred awake. I mouthed the word 'sorry' to her. Into the phone I asked, "Kenny, can we be positive about this?"

"Four respondents. Different parts of the country. They came up with the same ID. The kid is an heiress from Chicago. Cut off from her family for her wild living. However she does have money from a family trust fund. Name is Clara Bernice Walters. We're rechecking the story now. I should have more on it by the time you get in this morning."

"I'll be there before seven." My clockwork punctuality was legendary. Kenny knew I'd arrive promptly at five until seven.

"Meeting at eight. The suits upstairs want to be informed about any progress we're making. They're getting impatient."

"That must mean we offered a reward for information."

"Checkbook journalism sucks," he said with a lofty tone, "but damned if it doesn't work."

"See you soon." I tossed the phone onto my pile of clothing. Glancing back at Nevada's inquiring face, I explained, "City Editor. A morning meeting."

Nevada was skeptical about my response. "Is there's something important about the Beck case?"

"Maybe. Let me check it out first."

She sat up, leaning against the bed's backboard. "Naturally, I'm curious. You're offering a reward?"

"We loaded photos of Beck's pal Vivian on the internet. We offered a reward for information. It's a form of checkbook journalism. Money for information. I guess there were responses."

She was suddenly agitated. "We're dealing with a killer here, Randa. Not scooping a story. If you have information I need to know."

"That's what I'm going to check out. Vivian claims not to have been in contact with Beck and Dr. Milton."

"Yeah, well she's one trustworthy source," Nevada said grimly. "Don't withhold information from me. I haven't withheld anything from you. And I have more to lose than you do."

"Meaning?"

"Meaning I could lose my job for leaking information to you."

"Nevada, I'm grateful to you for giving me the jump on the escape story. I don't want you to get canned because of me. Okay. Her name might be Clara Walters. Some sources claim she's from Chicago. That's it."

"Don't go on a chase to find Jona. I'll give you what I can. Just don't do anything on your own. It's a dangerous situation."

I snuggled into Nevada's hug. "I'm not the heroic, brave cop. You are. I just want to be there when it goes down. I'm a sideline kind of person."

"You're saying if you locate Jona's whereabouts, you won't attempt to interview her?"

"I'm doing the same as you, investigating. But I'm not likely to go barging onto her territory. I'm a civilian and you're a cop. I know that. After she's under lock and key, I'll do my interview. Satisfied?"

She reset her alarm for six AM. "You'll keep me informed?"

"We'll keep one another informed." We sealed the promise with a kiss.

My eyes clamped shut, but sleep eluded me. I was certain the days, perhaps weeks, ahead will be grueling. Stamina would be needed. I worried about the *suits*. I was sure they were probably considering my follow-up stories as redundantly bogus as I considered them. Although I'd continued to winnow through the Jona Beck tapes – new information didn't appear to be there. Tomorrow the hierarchy would remind me that dead-ends don't peddle papers.

Additional concerns were family in nature. My mother's insistence that I see my dying grandmother had enormous complications. My father wished me to show forgiveness. Resentment remained my sidekick. Even if I owed my mother respect, Lenora Randolph was not deserving of my esteem. She couldn't bribe my sympathies, nor could she tempt me with her accouterments of wealth. I wished I could swallow my anger away.

Another thought suddenly capsized me. My background gave me less to be bitter about than Jona Beck's past gave her. A shudder ran the length of my body. Again Jona Beck invaded my mind. If threading my way through the night's labyrinth magnified *my* animosity, what must agitate the mind of a hunted *killer*?

Suddenly I heard her voice bashing open my memories. Her words were part of her final interview with me. She spoke with arrogance, yet with a tide of anguish that only tormented memories produce. She told me she wanted to hold thoughts of her past crimes and their carnage. She remembered killing with great relish. She was only too happy to reconnoiter her bloody deeds.

Her words heaved through my mind. "I am the messenger of death," she had stated repeatedly with rabid anger. "There's a wild beast inside my heart. It hunts you all. It hunts you, Randa Florez. Machiavelli says that people are driven by self-interest. But I am driven by my suffering." Her laugh was alive with merciless rancor. "One day I'll break these chains and escape to carve the life from you all."

My strained and exhausted eyes snapped open. My heart raced. A chill rippled, and my mouth was dry. There was the afterglow of a ghost's exit.

CHAPTER 6

Monday

"Them magazine distributors are walkin' shit. If they ain't early, they're late."

Laughing with Mario was a morning tradition. "At least I'm beating the rush." I plucked the newspaper from a waist high stack.

"Yep." He rotated his stocky body around as he dug coins from his apron pockets. "And you're looking mighty happy."

"I am happy. Keep the change."

"Thanks, kid. And I hope your day continues to go great guns for you. I hope I didn't mess up your day by harping about them distributors."

"Not at all." I was used to Mario's litany of complaints.

Giant steps sped me toward Ruby's.

"What you having?" Ruby asked after I'd captured and claimed the back booth.

"Coffee for starters. I've got a full agenda today, but I'm not hungry."

"In love or in lust?"

"Ruby, I'm in luck." My grin surfaced.

"Well, at least you aren't in limbo by chasin' Alison." Her husky laugh boomed as her eyebrows lifted and bobbed. "The sweet cop?"

"Nevada. Yes."

"When I saw the two of you together, I said to myself, 'Ruby, there's a perfect match.'"

"I was only interested in getting my kid brother out of the slammer," I confided.

With her characteristic panache, she waved the pot of coffee. "Yippy, I called that one. I saw the two of you together."

"There didn't seem to be any magnetism when I first met her. Just friendship."

"And now it's hot?"

"Yes. Invigorating, energizing, electrifying, and lovely." I savored remembrances of last night. I felt elation. I shrugged. I didn't mention that romance shone upon my heart. A cargo of emotion held the soft ruffle of guitar music, and the press of Nevada's softness against my own body. It had been imprinted on my brain. I asked, "And how is your love life?"

"Not to derail me, girlfriend. You two serious?"

"She's special."

"Better order a little breakfast so you can keep up your stamina."

"Scrambled eggs, ham, and toast." My postscript was more of a concern than a comment. "I hope I don't get hurt."

Ruby thrust her huge frame upward. "She doesn't seem like the kind who goes around hurting women." The sizzle of ham and eggs as they hit the griddle was Ruby's background music. "Bet that journal you keep is getting an earful."

Grinning, I replied, "Yes." Her laugh encouraged my admission. "I wrote details in my journal."

I had written that I cherished Nevada. Love may be the elixir of life, but my background had prepared me to be a skeptic. Yesterday's romantic pagans had camouflaged themselves, and made it through my detectors. Love should be a hallowed journey of one's interior. Mine had been hit and miss.

"Well, I just bet Nevada is a good woman. She won't hurt you."

"I hadn't believed Alison would hurt me."

* * *

There was a flotsam of paper on the oak table in *The Mirror's* editorial conference room. Kenny, Hank Richards, and I lingered behind after the meeting.

"If you like the panorama of Dante's poetic nightmares, this is where to be," Hank commented. "Do the *suits* want manufactured news?"

"If it was good enough for Hearst, it should be gutter enough for us," Kenny responded. "I know management is in collusion with marketing."

"The term *paparazzi* springs to mind," I muttered. "Editorial is giving the greatest weight to the account books rather than historical tomes. The Vivian X peg seems good."

"But she may *not know crap*," Kenny stressed. "And we paid out good green to get the info. So if it doesn't pan, we've shit money."

"We're trying to uncover everything," I defended.

"When you told the suits that you refuse to write magnolia-brained stories, I thought I'd lose it," Kenny said. "Pomeroy from Advertising didn't like it."

"Pomeroy is a jerkoff," Hank said. "His wind-milling arms reminded me of a Hitler campaign speech."

"All those charlatan pricks need a day on the streets," Kenny remarked with disdain.

"Kenny," I commented, "you were nodding agreement like a pecking bird. Why didn't you just tell the poseur that his nine-hundred buck suit makes him look like a hedgehog in underwear? He knows nothing about legitimate press."

Kenny rubbed his temple. "It's our asses on the hot-seat."

Stonily, I replied, "But nobody is loafing. They want meticulous facts, but they want those facts dressed in sensationalism. We're on the trail of a callous, ruthless killer."

"That gives me an idea," Kenny leaned forward. "Randa, you worked with her. How about if in your next story you invite her to contact you? Dare her."

Hank slammed his fist down. "Kenny, you don't make a target out of your best crime reporter. Are you flipping nuts?"

"Settle back, big guy. Just a thought. Hell, you're right. We're getting desperate." Kenny instructed, "Let's just keep digging on the Vivian X background search. Now that we've got a name we can get a new character study. From Randa's perspective." Kenny rustled some pages. "The map of crime is nearly always self-centered. We have a missing psychotic killer. But who is the true Jona Beck?"

My eyes shut. I recited. "She's a sadomasochistic woman who carved her victim with surgical detail. She left her victim looking as if he'd been cleaved by a scythe. Jona Beck is seductive enough to have an accomplice. Her sadistic predilections must have appealed to Simone Milton. There must be some erotic dependence, at one level or another. Our readers know that Jona Beck is a cryptically mental mess. When entering a room she becomes impenetrable darkness. Her heart seems vacant. Her mind is filled with an ill-digested amalgam of Nietzschean ideals." I paused, breaking my thought. "Perhaps I have yet to glance into the ugliest instant of her soul. It might be fear that keeps me from knowing her soul."

"And," Kenny adds, "Jona's spirit is like chasing goblins. So is her body now."

"Because her early years of decayed home life made her a repository for pain, she works for sympathy. There were times she seemed the most pathetic human being on earth. She may have been a person from infancy - but an amalgam of abusive incidents made her into a monster. And no one was there to correct her path." My teeth squeezed down on my lower lip. "Perhaps it would help if men would keep their hands off of children."

Kenny grumbled, "We need more prison space so we can lock 'em all in the slammer for good." He grimaced. "Maybe a pedophile mass execution."

Hank vehemently stressed, "That unfortunately won't happen. So what next?"

"More Jona Becks are waiting in the wings," I answered. The moment was static, and hollow. "This job seems gargantuan."

Kenny questioned, "Where's your next stop?"

"I'm going to Black Hawk this noon. See if Lucia Gomez has any secrets she wishes to divulge." I surveyed my wristwatch. "If I want to catch the shuttle up the mountain, I need to leave now."

"Randa, one other thing. The tail we put on Vivian X got an ID on her new girlfriend. Not so much new and not so much girl," Kenny added. "She's some fairly prominent, middle-aged real estate broker working in Aurora. Her name is Elise Stuart. I'll phone you with details when I get them."

Standing, I flung my oversized pack over my shoulder. I returned to my cubical where I picked up messages. I leaned over the desk in my station. I gave a whirl to the small decorative globe at the side of my computer. To myself I said, "I wish I were in Kalgoorlie," as my index finger speared one of the continents. "Kalgoorlie, Western Australia. Kalgoorlie?" I repeated to myself and my office. "I'll bet Jona Beck is nowhere near Kalgoorlie." I walked from my office.

By the time I reached my Z in the parking lot, I'd mentally bartered to have a glass of wine upon my arrival in Black Hawk. It would be a treat for my torment.

* * *

Express buses shuttling gamblers to Black Hawk and Central City debarked on the hour. Thirty miles due west of Denver, the two former mining towns offered legalized gambling. Black Hawk was located on a spur road off the highway. One mile further, within hiking distance, was Central City.

Normally while I traveled there was a vagabond's gossamer lightness of the soul. Today, on this pilgrimage, my mind churned. During the assent up the mountains I watch the curling road that seemed a mere pin scratch on the crust of jutting rock. Around each curve was another wedge of magnificent mountains. The mountain's air was refreshingly crisp and clean. However once in the heart of Black Hawk, the scents of loam and pine resin were replaced by auto exhausts, and the smell of new construction's concrete powders, diesel fumes, and dust.

On the trip, I'd written the news story about Clara AKA Vivian. On my laptop I'd disclosed the facts that we knew. I'd e-mailed it the moment it was finished. Vivian wouldn't be pleased to have her past dredged up and exposed on the front page of the newspaper. There were times when intrusive journalism held a great deal of appeal.

I hoped the trip might yield a story that I could write on the return trip back to Denver. The mission my mind needed to focus on now was anything Lucia Gomez might reveal.

Lucia Gomez had arrived at work early. She agreed to let me buy her lunch. Our past encounters weren't joyous, but she didn't view me as the virulent press. During the trial I attributed her willingness to talk to the fact that we shared a Hispanic heritage. Now I felt to be a sounding board - a mother confessor. She jabbered about hating her job.

Lucia was seated across from me at a table in the casino restaurant. We were served prime rib sandwiches, which she ordered and I dittoed. I sipped a very mellow Ruby Cabernet between bites of the meal. Lucia's appetite was voracious. She finished her fries and some of mine. Then she ordered a slice of deep-dish peach pie with scoops of ice cream. Thankfully, she talked between bites.

She wore the standard blackjack dealer's garb of white, short-sleeved blouse with decorative tie and dark trousers. Her long, thick sable hair was pulled back in a pony tail that swayed down to the small of her back. Her black permafrost eyes had become protuberant. Her jaw was slack.

Her youth spent with Jona Beck has cost her. I realized she could tell me blood-curdling sagas of her bondage apprenticeship. She was the product of a single mother's abusive boyfriends. Lucia claimed to be a minion of the devil. Her dour face reflected that she was prone to hate. With a mouth set into a grim line, it was certain she'd recalled her dismal background. It was a wonder to me that Lucia survived childhood at all.

Jona and Lucia had a great deal in common. Both were human documents of perversity. Torture became an art form. Their adolescence honed them for brutality. Now Lucia, disciple turned apostate, tossed her napkin on the table and glared at me for my silence.

"I can't tell you where Jona is, if that's what you're getting ready to ask," she announced.

"What makes you think I'd believe that she hasn't

contacted you?"

"It's true. Why are you so interested in finding her? You aren't a cop. Does her kind of danger turn you on?" Lucia asked with a smirk.

"I wouldn't touch Jona Beck," I jousted. "With druggies there's no telling where they've been. I'm fussy about communicable disease. I'm stymied as to why her shrink would risk having sex with her. But that doesn't even scratch the surface. I doubt the S&M thing has been *cured*. I'm told sadomasochism usually sets up like stone."

"True. Not a lot of dabblers. I know I don't want to change my way of living. Even with Jona things could be okay. For a little while, she might be fine. Then she could get dangerous when she had her bouts of despondency."

"That's when the savage reprisal begins?" I questioned carefully.

"Yeah. But you can't understand her because you don't know about the excitement of our lifestyle. Mostly it's safe."

"I don't call whipping, beating, burning, and carving someone safe."

"It is mostly. A slave can always yell 'mercy' to stop the action."

"You think Maynard Jones didn't yell for mercy? Think again."

"You judge us because you've never been there. You're too proper. Too uptight. You could never stand that kind of thrill. It would offend your sweetness."

"We're not here to exchange jibes, Lucia. I won't cast aspersions if you don't." I took another sip of wine. "With less sarcasm, will you tell me the abridged version of your *lifestyle.*"

"We aren't a bunch of barbarians like you portray us."

"It's been a tough morning," I acquiesced. "I don't give a rat's ass what consenting adults do, I'm concerned that Simone Milton is going to become Jona's next victim. *No to do es miel sobre hojuelas,*" I mentioned it wasn't all fun and games.

"You're right. The doc could end up bagged. All she's got to do is get on Jona's wrong side." With a boastful lilt to her sentence, she bragged, "See, I made it because I knew how to be a good slave. Jona is the finest disciplinarian on earth. She knows how to discipline. She taught me about leather love. You know, power and pain. I learned to be obedient. She demands the best in a slave. I was her best. I'm not a slave now."

"No?"

"I'm on top now. The domineering one. I've got my own slave."

My stomach pitched but I gulped another mouthful of wine. I recognized the difficulty in explaining a foreign lifestyle. The straight world had problems understanding lesbianism. Their perception was usually a million miles from reality. They believed it begins and ends with sex. Sex was such an infinitely small part of why I'm attracted to women. There was tenderness, and understanding.

"Want to try explaining Jona's hold on women?"

"I just did. She makes sex exciting. And terrifying. Terror is her opiate."

Easing into the questions about Vivian, I'd hoped for some cooperation. But there was none. "Lucia, does it make you and Vivian upset to know that Jona is now *with* her shrink?"

"She didn't have a choice. It was her ticket to escape. You and the cops are all over me. Jona isn't calling me for a reservation to hide them. I doubt if Vivian would risk it. I don't know squat."

Lucia knew nothing. Squat or otherwise.

* * *

On my return trip back to Denver, I keyed everything I knew into my laptop. My only distractions were celebrating winners. Passengers that had a good day were louder than the losers. I had lost three dollars on the slots. However, I'd accomplished what I'd intended. Another interview with someone in Jona Beck's background was ready to be filed. And final source checks on Vivian X's identification were being concluded back at the office. If they proved legitimate, I had an exclusive.

During the Lucia interview my cell phone had been turned off. My voicemail held two messages – a phone call from the office, and another from my mother. My mother's call went unanswered. There was a selfish desire for the remainder of the afternoon and the evening to be unencumbered by her pleas to pay a visit to my dying grandmother.

There was the familiar beep indicating an incoming message on my laptop screen. In addition to confirmation that my stories had arrived, there was an urgent message. Vivian X's identity had been substantiated. All leads corroborated the fact that she was one Clara Bernice Walters. Birthplace: Chicago. Priors on drug charges in Chicago, Cincinnati, and Kansas City.

Bingo, I concluded. But the sugar topping on the *bingo* came with the next sentence. I read the updated message with joyous disbelief. Clara Bernice Walters had been followed to Elitch Gardens. She was in the company of Elise Tanya Stuart, 45, R.E. broker/owner of Stuart Property Management & Sales. Hank Richards was on his way. I was to expect his call for our meeting spot at the destination. Clara Bernice would have a photo taken. And we would have a current likeness of Vivian X!

When the bus arrived at the parking lot, I hastened to my car and barreled down a side street. Before my Z rolled onto Sheridan Boulevard the cell phone rang. "Florez."

Hank's familiar voice questioned, "You been in touch with the desk?"

"Yes. Got the message. I'm approaching Alameda. If traffic continues to cooperate, I should arrive in a few minutes."

"I'm at the gates. I've packed my tourist camera so they shouldn't be aware that they're being photographed."

"I'll wear shades and a floppy brimmed hat so Vivian won't recognize me. We'll observe for a while first. Maybe get near enough to overhear something. Then I'll approach her."

"Right. Hold on, I have an incoming call."

I heard the phone's familiar click. "What do you have?"

"It was the guy tailing them. He said they're in line to ride the Farris wheel. I know exactly where it's at. Maybe I can get a couple shots. I'll meet you there. If they move on before you get

113

there, I'll phone you."

Luck on the boulevard didn't hold. As I neared the heart of Denver my drive was a crawl. I could only hope the Farris wheel was going in slow motion the way traffic was.

* * *

"Anything happening?" I questioned.

"They've been tripping out on the Farris wheel for the past twenty minutes. Must be a favorite," Hank answered. He continued unobtrusively shooting photos. Waving as people passed, he became just another tourist with a camera. His familiar polished executive look had converted to casual. He had ditched his tie, rolled up his sleeves, and wore a baseball cap.

The Wheel, as it is called, at Elitch Gardens Amusement Park lifted into the sky, thus was easily found. I scanned the rotating basket that held Vivian and Elise Stuart. Hank handed me his camera to get a zoom angle of the women. Vivian wore a plum-colored tank top. A print scarf tied back her long hair. Her hair color seemed more carroty in daylight. She still had the remote, languid eyes of a coked-up druggie. Even her animated laughter seemed lackadaisical. When she gesticulated wildly with her arms, I sadly suspected her mind had been polluted with a recent fix.

Elise Stuart appeared nearer to mid-fifty than middle forties. She wore a yellow cotton-tee, and over that was a lightweight tapestry-designed vest. Money was obvious. Around her neck was a huge silver Indian squash blossom. It was one cluster after another of gleaming turquoise. Although she was seated, I could tell she was probably not much over five-feet tall. She was heavy, barrel-chested, and her shoulder projected a prize fighter's crouch. Her actions were raffish. Her loud laugh was heard as the wheel neared the ground. It was a sardonic booming chain of giggles. Above her jowly, swarthy complexioned face was a cap of thick, wavy salt and pepper hair. It appeared as lacquered as a decorative Chinese dragon.

When the ride stopped, they got off and began wandering. Hank was ahead of them. He turned back to me, aimed his camera as I playfully waved.

Vivian and Elise stopped to purchase cold drinks. I ordered a cup of lemonade. Listening, I realized their conversation was mundane. It did seem as though they'd known one another for some time. It was obviously not second or third date behavior.

Vivian suddenly whirled around, facing me. "Hey, I know you. You're that reporter." Her glance rotated to Hank and his snapping camera. "You're taking our picture." She gave the hissing yowl of an enraged lynx.

"Reporter!" Elise Stuart bleated her disdain. "Get the fuck away from us." Her bulky body lunged at Hank's camera. "You dumb fuck. I'll sue for defamation."

Hank moved away, protecting the camera. "Easy. Relax."

"You don't have the right to do this." Elise parried her objection. "This is outrageous."

"We have every right," I said. "Your pal here has been very elusive. To both the police and to the press. We'd like some insight on why that might be."

"Screw your insight!" Vivian clamored.

"Does the name Clara Bernice Walters ring a bell?" I quizzed.

Even her breath stopped cold with hesitation. "No," she answered regaining her composure. "No, I don't know who you're talking about."

"You should, Clara," I accused while Hank continued shooting photos.

"I'll have my lawyers pay a call on you, bitch," Elise seethed, trembling with rage. "You're that pain-in-the-ass reporter from *The Mirror*. You use one frame of me in that newspaper and you'll wish you hadn't."

"A threat?" I inquired.

Her face was white with anger. Her eyes were aflame. "Only people with single digit I.Q.s read that rag of yours."

"That's why we've got so many awards for excellence in journalism," Hank announced with a laugh.

"I'll bring a lawsuit," she threatened. Her middle finger

waved at him. "Do the words 'defamation' and 'libel' mean anything to you?"

"Does the First Amendment ring a bell with you?" I asked.

"Look, Ms. Stuart," Hank explained, "it is an invisible rule pertaining to the press. If you want to stay out of the news, don't do anything newsworthy. Or don't be in the company of anyone newsworthy, and we won't waste time on you."

"That's right," I reiterated, "Clara Bernice here is the bosom buddy of a dangerous fugitive. Front page news. For all we know she's abetting an escapee. That is news. So here we are."

"I told you, I don't know where Jona is." Her drug-enhanced gaze was attempting to focus. I'd always maintained that dope illuminated a tragedy. Vivian would probably have been a stray human even without drugs. But she was completely lost with them. She repeated, "I don't know where Jona's hiding."

Elise confronted me. "You miserable assholes have no reason to be hounding Vivian. She doesn't know anything. You're harassing her and I won't have it. Who the hell are you anyway? A goddamned flunky reporter. A nobody."

"We don't think Vivian is being entirely honest with us. *If* she is willing to shed some light on the whereabouts of Jona Beck, we'll be quietly on our way."

"I told you a million times, I don't know," Vivian screamed at me. "Leave us the hell alone."

"Let's get out of here," Elise commanded. She gave Vivian's arm a tug. "Just don't use my name or photo. I haven't got anything to do with any of this."

Hank and I watched as the women raced toward the exit. "What now?" he asked.

"Our private eye will shadow them back to Elise's base camp. They'll barricade themselves away. But it's too late. I'd call this a page one photo op."

Hank's large hand lifted and we high fived. He tapped his camera. "At least we've identified them. We've got makes on them both in living-color photos. I'm sending them to the office as we speak."

"We can have our research team check databases to see if she owns property in Colorado. From the reports it seems little Clara Walters is flush. She might have met Elise through a business deal."

"And these photos will be far more detailed than the others. Even if our PI loses them, they won't stay lost long. Someone who recognizes them will call with a sighting or knowledge of her whereabouts." Hank asked, "And no leads from Black Hawk?

"Nothing."

"I'm stopping for a burger, fries, and malt." He ejected the photo storage card. As he slipped another into the slot, he handed the filled card to me. "Would you drop this off for me in case the office needs it? I'll be there by the time the photos are ready for cropping and editing."

"I'll guard it with my life."

"Speaking of which, I thought that woman was going to deck me," he confessed. "I need to replenish a meal."

My laugh lifted. "She couldn't even reach your chin, much less deck you. But you're right, you've earned a burger." I reached for my car door's handle. "I'm not sure what I've earned, but something good, and cold. Would you please bring me a strawberry malt?"

* * *

Before the latest edition was put to bed, I'd written a recap. After which, my routine took me to a quick dinner with my grandparents, then on to Marlene's for an unwinding session. Wearily, I stared at the jewel-like color of a superb Burgundy. It reminded me of the goddess Hera. She created her supernatural red wine and called it Ambrosia. It was associated with immortality.

"You're gazing at the wine as though it's your crystal ball," Alicia said as she topped off my glass.

"Just a little preoccupied. It's been a hectic day."

"Giselle said to give you a message. Call her. She's off

tonight. Said she needs to tell you something. She left this note with her number," Alicia said as she handed the folded paper across the table.

Giselle's note and follow-up call told me the institution's employee she'd mentioned would talk with me tomorrow morning at nine. His name was Michael. He'd talked with Jona on several occasions. Giselle stated that she'd assured him that I wouldn't betray his identity. At *The Mirror*, we were known for protecting sources. The Lindley rule allowed us to use sources, and not reveal them. I'd used the shield law, but attempted to avoid it. I would protect Michael, obviously because he and Giselle had my word.

Michael could lose his job if he were caught talking with the press. It was part of the confidentiality contract that correction institution employees were required to sign when they're hired. I was to meet Michael at *The Book Boutique and Coffee Bar* on Colfax.

* * *

After a glass of wine, I contacted Nevada. I asked her if she'd like to meet me for a drink. She quickly agreed, but said she must shower first. She added that she was anxious to see me and had missed me as much as I'd missed her.

Lanny Ventura entered, motioning toward the rear booth where our meeting would be more private. "How's the world of libelous invective?" she greeted me as she quickly slid into the booth. "I need a damned double Scotch," she told Alicia. "And don't feel you must skimp for sobriety's sake. Tonight I'll take my chances. And put it on Gonzo's tab, please." She pointed in my direction.

I shrugged as I questioned, "Rough day, Ventura?"

"Oh yes. The new producer is driving me crazy with his Voltarian humor. In a world filled with tumultuous, apocalyptic events, I get sent to interview a real estate agent."

I tensed. "Real estate agent?"

"Yep. Someone saw Vivian X with a realtor." She took a

huge gulp from her drink the moment it arrived. "Thanks for the drink. Whew. And," she added as her eyes squinted in my direction, "I'm not naming names."

My grin was forced. "Gee, Ventura, I figured you'd at least share the initials with me."

"It won't do you any good. I checked it out. The realtor has never heard of Vivian X. Might have been a prank to get me off the trail."

"Then it won't hurt to divulge the name," I coaxed.

"Elise Stuart," she answered.

"For all the times you've scooped me," I teased, "And loved every minute of it - I'm loving this."

She leaned nearer. "What are you talking about?"

"Read the front page of *The Mirror* in the morning. Or our 24-hour *E-Edition*."

"Don't play coy, Gonzo. What do you have?"

"The Forth Estate is my kind of real estate." I was getting Lanny Ventura's attention. "It truly is. They say that history is life's layering. Newspapers are history's first draft."

She finished her drink. "That's right, have your laugh at my expense. They say the press is dying, but not as long as there are reporters like Randa Florez." Lanny stood, picked up her bag and muttered, "And mostly as long as there are puppies in need of paper training, the print press lives."

"Leaving so soon? I was going to spring for another drink."

"I've got to check a source."

"If it's the woman in our research department, don't bother calling her. It will only cost you a dinner and three hours of tedium. She hasn't got a clue. I haven't sent anything her way for weeks."

"How did you know I've taken her out?"

"Because she told me that she thinks you're charming. Only someone smitten with you would consider you even remotely charming."

"That's the nicest thing you've ever said to me, Florez." She winked before leaving.

I gave an exasperated sigh before spotting Nevada as she came through the doorway.

When Nevada kissed my cheek, I realized how much I'd truly missed her today. Her glance exhilarated me. While Nevada dived into a meal consisting of a magnificent Reuben, fries, and Corona, I caught her up on my day's activities.

She looked up. "Jona and Simone are cozily stashed," she surmised. "There haven't been any good leads, so it isn't like she keeps slipping her collar. It's more like she's taken her collar off, pitched it in our faces, and she's safely watching."

"Nevada, that's exactly what I'm thinking. She's reading my meager stories. She knows where we are and what we're thinking. We haven't got that luxury."

"Any feel for what Lucia knows?"

"My gut tells me she hasn't heard from Jona."

"That's what the detectives who interviewed her last also said."

"And I told you earlier when I phoned about the escapades with Vivian and her pal, Elise Stuart. That seems like another lost cause. She isn't talking."

"They gave everyone, with the exception of *The Mirror,* the slip on this afternoon's outing. And our police tail lost them when he stopped to take a piss."

"After the fact?" I chuckled. "Lanny Ventura told me she'd zeroed on the realtor."

"She may not have the photos, but I'm sure she's got the make on Stuart. Do you and Lanny really have a rivalry?"

"Friendly, yes. There is only one way she could improve her reporting. That's to be on *The Mirror's* staff."

Nevada's smile lifted. "By the way, Benjy did ride with me this afternoon. He's a good kid. He's daunted by your celebrity status in the community."

"The way I am with my mother's international fame. I've told him he's unique and special. He's got to get over comparing himself to me. Or anyone."

"It isn't always easy for an insecure kid. Did he say anything about riding on patrol with me this afternoon?"

"I didn't talk with him directly. But Angie told me he was impressed. At least until he talked with one of his buddies. His friend told Benj that there was no way he could become a cop."

Nevada frowned. "Why?"

"Claims Benjy's parents are married and that excludes him from wearing a badge."

We shared a laugh. Nevada wiped her mouth with the napkin, and then whispered, "I hope Benj does become a cop. And I hope his pal is Benjy's very first bust."

"With all the negative things I've had to say about the department over the years, I'm amazed I haven't been incarcerated the better part of *my* life."

Nevada drank a sip of water. "Speaking of the department, I do have a tidbit for you."

"Yes?"

"Fritz has been checking out the many confessions Jona Beck made over the months. Some definitely don't match, and they don't fit any form of riddle. They seem to be false statements. However, Fritz isn't so sure others are without merit. A direct transposition of crimes. A couple of them match exactly. I'd be surprised if she has only killed one human being."

"Fritz thinks her list will grow?"

"Yes. He thinks the probability is good she's killed numerous people over the years. You might want to stop by and pay Lieutenant Truesdale a visit first thing in the morning. He wants to see you. Maybe give you his list so you can examine it."

"First thing in the morning?"

Nevada chuckled. "I was telling him the theory on Jona mixing crimes, places, etc. He said that getting the worst things done first thing in the morning is best. That insures everything else is a pleasure of sorts. He considers you the worst thing."

I grimaced. "Thanks for the tip. I'll listen to my tapes to see if I've missed anything. She did her share of confessing. She confessed to a crucifixion one day. Maybe I can come up with a name or two Fritz doesn't have. If so, he should be grateful enough to share a little info."

"What a diabolic mind," Nevada teased. "I hope you're not working me the way you're working the lieutenant."

I joked, "My appetite for leads through romance is legendary. Information for sex. Actually, I've never dated anyone on the force before. If I were anxious to date someone just to find out information, I'd have gone through ten percent of the squad by now."

When we stood to leave, I gave her a hug. The hard steel butt of the gun she wore beneath her jacket jabbed my rib. I drew back to look down and saw I the clip-on holster. "You're packing?"

"With a fugitive at large we're all wearing hot guns off-duty."

"Hot?"

"Not *hot* stolen - hot as in having a live round in the chamber or a full clip. I'm not crazy about totting a gun around, believe me." There was a pause. "Are you okay with my gun?"

"Yes. It just startled me. I've never dated anyone wearing an arsenal."

"When we get to my house, I'll disarm the gun."

"And me?"

"I hope you."

"I'll be there as soon as I make a phone call to my mother. I've had a dozen calls from her."

"Better return at least one of them."

It was to be an obligatory call. I didn't want to speak with Erika Randolph. My day was going too great for dreary platitudes. And if Lenora Randolph had died, any display of grief would be a blasphemous lie. Yet I felt under siege. One's *offspring* duty should have been one of courtesy, devotion, and love. I owed my grandmother nothing.

* * *

Phone in hand, as I reached the doorway, I heard my mother's voice. "Mother, I apologize for not phoning sooner. It's been an extraordinarily busy day."

"My calls were to see if you've changed your mind about visiting your grandmother." Her voice was shaky. "Randa, it's unconscionable of you to treat a dying woman so cruelly."

"Many things in the past have been unconscionable, Mother." There was a lengthy, uncomfortable pause. Silence differed to the emptiness of a time passed. It emanated from soundless echoes of pain.

Mother despised my defiance. Her voice was harsh. "I hope you don't one day regret your action. She's slipping away from us."

"She slipped away from me when I was a child." My fist was tightly pressed against the wall. "I don't wish to see her. As I said, I'm very busy."

"She told me she needs to see you. You're too busy running after a story about some insane killer to visit your dying grandmother!"

"Yes. Yes, I am." My yawn was suppressed. There was no wish to be sad, nor be placatory.

"What difference has Jona Beck ever made in your life?"

"I once asked her why she'd gone astray. She told me *astray* is a where your heart goes when it's too frightened to go elsewhere."

"I don't understand."

"Mother, I've been there. I know the location. I've been astray in my heart. Your mother, my grandmother, was the reason for that. I'm sorry, Mother. Forgive me. It's been a difficult day."

"I'm pleading with you, Randa. Please see her."

"No," I muttered resolutely. "No."

CHAPTER 7

Tuesday

"Do you always sleep so fitfully?" Nevada asked as I woke in her arms.

My heart raced. "It must be all the events of yesterday. The tapes I listened to before we went to bed were damned grisly." Notes from the interviews were made so that I might provide Lieutenant Fritz Truesdale with some 'good faith' information. And he might be so grateful that he *might* give me his latest information, speculation, or scoop. "Jona Beck is very disturbed."

"Nothing dainty about murder – in the best of times," she kidded. "I'm the one actually picking through the blood and guts out on the street, and I slept like a baby. Are you okay?" Her arms tightened around me protectively.

"Yes. I'm fine now. And after last night's love sharing, how can one not be fine?" I pushed the hair away from her face. It streamed gently down her shoulders like a mantel of silk. My lips glided over her shoulder.

"Dreams are meant to heal. Your dreams must have been terrifying. Is anything else bothering you?"

"The skirmish with my mother. The call to her went rather badly. I allowed my voice to become loud. That's a first with my mother – talking back and doing it loudly." I sat up, and leaned against pillows. "The Florez branch shouts just to be heard over the multitude of voices," I joked. "Does your family yell at one another?"

"My sisters and I fought. Sure. But we were always told to use our 'inside' voice when things got too lively. Our 'outside' voice was for sporting events. Mostly my family jokes and teases. Like your dad's family. I guess that's why I feel at home with them."

"I'd like to meet your family one day."

"You will. On our next vacation. Hope you don't mind that I'm planning our future, but I am. They'll definitely approve of you."

"My family approves of you. You even got Aunt Renie's stamp of approval. And I'm sure if my mother were ever to get to know you, she'd think you are wonderful."

"From everything you've told me about your mom she isn't a mean-spirited person. So why the confrontation?"

"Her mother is dying. Mother insists I see her again before she dies. I might have mentioned I've been estranged from my grandparents for years." My face reflected a haze of pain. It hadn't gone unnoticed.

"What's the true hatred of your grandmother all about? When you mention her you change."

"She suffused our lives with deception. I can't - I *won't* forgive her. Her lies changed my life. Things might have been different."

"If they were, you might not have become the sensitive, decent woman you are."

"Or I might not sleep so fitfully."

She kissed the tip of my nose. "I vow to keep you safe. You'll never be alone again. Not if you don't want to be." Her arms brought me nearer against her satiny soft and warm body. "I love you, Randa Florez. I'll always keep you safe. I promise."

"We promise from what we want and we act from what we fear."

There was a pause before she replied, "Well, I fear my cupboards are bare. But I promise to take you for breakfast at The Java Brew?" Her smile was its own ballad of persuasion.

I had a reason bedecked with intuitive ardor to believe Nevada's every word.

* * *

After a buttery croissant and a steaming mug of mocha

coffee, Nevada departed for work. I remained behind in The Java Brew. A few moments were spent carefully reading the front page of *The Mirror*. My story exposing Vivian X's identity had captured the prime location, above the fold. Beside the lead article was the photo of Clara 'Vivian' Walters and Elise Stuart.

A quick glance at my watch told me it was time to scoot. There was an hour before meeting with Michael at The Book Boutique. I decided it was a perfect opportunity to pay my grandparents Florez a visit since they lived only blocks away. It was nearly seven-thirty, so there was a possibility that my Aunt Renie and Mama Carmina would be at morning Mass.

Papa Gus was puttering in his garden. I went through the back gate and into the lushness of the yard. He wore faded overalls, a straw hat, and dirt-soiled leather gloves. He was on his knees, huddled over a patch of pale pink flowers. He turned. "Randa."

"Papa Gus, I decided to stop by. I guess Mama and Renie are at church." I leaned down to hand my grandfather a nearby trowel and kiss his cheek.

"Yes. I remain in the center of my garden rather than go to church with them."

"They must know you enjoy it here more." My lips curve upward.

"If they knew how much I enjoy this, they would insist I go to church. They could nag the bark off a tree." His lined face issued a huge smile. "I'm only too happy to see them go. My geraniums don't need an audience to bloom."

"They're lovely." I crouched down to inhale the fresh fragrance. "Lovely."

Papa Gus grinned. "Emerson says that flowers are earth's way of laughing."

"I agree." I brushed a smudge of soil from his face.

"Randa, your father mentioned he's concerned about you."

"About me?"

"He realizes how important it is to your mother that you make peace with your grandmother before she dies. If you resist, it could end your relationship with your mother. Your father fears this."

My head turned from his intense stare. "Papa, I've explained to him it's useless. There's no reason for me to see her."

"I hope you'll relent. Death takes away our second chances. You need to comfort your mother. I think the term they use is 'closure' on an issue. For you, it may allow some form of forgiveness. Your father is heartbroken."

Standing, I gazed down at my grandfather. His knotted brow questioned my response. He knew I loved and respected him. "Papa, I wish I could make you understand."

"Soon it will be too late."

"I'm living my life. Lenora Randolph is no part of my life."

"She is. She's hatred in your heart."

Our gaze into one another's thoughts negotiated. "I have a meeting across town. I'd better leave now." Before I reached the gate, I turned back. For the first time I said the words, "Papa Gus, I can't do what you ask."

* * *

Michael was waiting at The Book Boutique. I'm recognized from *The Mirror's* staff photo of me. He waved me to his table. "Randa Florez," I greeted him, extending my hand.

His grip was weakly ambivalent. "I'm Michael."

"No last name? Or is that your last name?"

The man in his mid-twenties shrugged as he sat. Coils of dark curls fell over his high forehead. There was fear in his deeply set bronze eyes. "I'd rather not give my last name."

"I need you to trust me. Let's get this all out in the open. I don't need your name. I can pull up photos of every state worker at the institution. You're easy to identify," I bluffed. "I'll have a make on you in a few hours. A complete history of your life. But that's not the point. I've given my word that you'll remain an unnamed source."

"My name is Michael Adams. I could lose my job at the state institution if anyone finds out I've been talking with you.

We've been warned."

"Michael, I'm not about to give you up. That would totally ruin my reputation as a journalist. Your anonymity is safe with me. I've been threatened with incarceration before when I vowed to protect a source. And I was willing to be locked up to protect a source. I couldn't conduct business if I ratted out my sources. Besides, you're a *brother*."

Relief was obvious. "I didn't mean to be hostile. I'm a little nervous."

"Don't be on my account. Look, Giselle said you have information I might be able to use in running down Jona Beck."

"I'm not sure. I told the police everything they asked. But they only asked if I knew where she was. I'm not sure any of this will help you find out anything, but..." he began to stutter, "B-but she was going to set me up with a guy she called one of her best friends in life."

"Did you see him?"

"No. She had some very strange friends. I had joked around with her that I'm single, and I'll meet anyone. At first she told me the guy isn't into drugs and leather. Then she says he is. I back away. Hell, they have mandatory drug testing at the institution."

"Do you have a name for the guy?"

"That's why I wanted to meet you here. He has a tattoo parlor down the street. He owns it. I guess he does tattooing, piercing - things like that. Sells earrings, studs, even leather items. You know, bondage shit. It's called Scorpion Tattoo Parlor."

"And his name?"

"Eddie. No last name."

I paused as the vanilla coffees were set in front of us. "First name is fine. I can pull records on the business to acquire Eddie's full name and background. Michael, did you have any idea that Simone Milton might aid Jona in escaping?"

"None. The deal was that I could pick up on chemistry between them. Jona was working it very hard. Simone confided how her husband was trashing her big time. Jona was sympathetic. She was there. But nobody figured Dr. Milton was going to be dumb enough to try breaking Jona out."

"And you're convinced it was with Simone's consent and assistance?"

"Yep. That was one of the police's questions. I'd put money on it."

"Did you ever overhear any of Jona's conversations that might disclose a hiding location? Or a city she might want to go to?"

"When the cops ask if I knew where she might have gone, I drew a blank. Since then I've thought about it and still can't think of anything she ever said about it. And she never mentioned another city."

"How about her friends?"

"Lucia Gomez stopped visiting so often. I think they had a sort of breakup. The redhead, Vivian, was diligent in making her weekly visits. Right up to the break. I didn't hear much of anything they ever said." He took a sip of his coffee.

"How about Vivian? Did she ever mention taking a vacation, or anything like that?"

"Nope." He hesitated. "Wait a minute. Yeah, I remember after one of Vivian's visits. Jona said Vivian and her girlfriend were going *camping.* She said she wished she could go with them. She would unwind like she used to. But I think she might have meant the camping like looking for a woman. She said it sort of funny."

"Funny?"

"Like not really camping."

"Could it have been that she was stressing the camping because it might have been a mountain retreat?"

"Yeah, maybe like that. It wasn't like she was going to sleep under the stars. That's for sure. Jona isn't an outdoor person. When I told her I spent time hiking in the hills she told me people could put all that nature shit up their asses. Bugs, snakes, bears. Then she sort of shuddered. She said the thought of being outside in the forest spooked her. Imagine that."

"Imagine what?"

"Like someone who isn't afraid to go down an alley where

there are shooting galleries and pimps, and she's terrified to sleep out in a tent."

"I guess we all have our own fears." I stood, tossed money for the coffees on the table, and then pulled out my card. "Here's my card, but if you'd rather, just tell Giselle. She'll get the message to me. Thanks, Michael. I'll respect your privacy. This interview never happened. Okay?"

"Yeah. Okay."

"Will you let me know if you recall anything else? Even if you don't think it's important."

"Sure. And maybe you better have a guy with you when you visit Scorpion Tattoo Parlor. It's pretty rough."

"Think I'll need the service of a cop?" We shared a smile. I considered that I, in fact, did enjoy the services of a cop. She was the cop I was falling for in a big way.

"Just take care," Michael warned me. "She's had months to devise plots and plans. You won't see her coming for you."

* * *

Entering the Scorpion Tattoo Parlor was like a trip back into medieval times. On the back wall was a life-sized poster of a guillotine. Edward Hunter looked up from the chipped crimson counter as I tentatively stepped through the threshold.

"Eddie Hunter?"

"I'm Eddie," he introduced himself. "Will it be a tattoo or pierce today?"

Eddie Hunter was a dour man about thirty. Slim as a reed, he sported a shaved head, and had a beige curved-horn mustache over his thinly lined mouth. With arms fully tattooed, he also had rings from multiple piercing that hung from nearly all of his displayed body parts. With disdain, his icy blue eyes scrutinized me. They contained a vile, frozen expression.

We viewed one another with mutual and immediate distrust.

"I'm Randa Florez," I introduced myself while flashing my press credentials.

"Yeah? So?"

"What might you tell me about Jona Beck?"

"What makes you think I know her?"

"Come on, Eddie. I interviewed the woman for months. You're aware of that. Your name came up." From the suspicious glance, it was a given that it would be a cumbersome chat. After a restless night, I was in no mood to execute my usual bid for Miss Congeniality.

"You don't look like the type to be her girlfriend. So I suspect you're after a story."

"She's a fugitive. I'm a reporter. Figure it out for yourself."

"I just did, sweetheart."

"Has Jona Beck had any piercing or ink done lately?"

"None. Why not interrogate her sexual subordinates?"

"I have."

"Try tuning in Jona's cosmic energy," he jeered with a savage sneer.

Infierno! I silently cursed. "To hell with Jona's cosmic energy. I want to know where her physical energy is hanging out."

"You walk in here as if you're going through a million purgatories rather than having a primordial sensation. You're judgmental. I can tell. You think we're all oily little lizards residing in the gloomy abyss."

"Eddie, you haven't a clue. Your world is yours. I don't care what you do with consenting adults. Fetishes and salacious arousal aren't a crime. You are correct. I don't like having to be here, but my job takes me everywhere. And the faster you stop being a jerk and answer my questions, the quicker I can leave."

"*You* haven't a clue!" He returned behind the counter. "So leave."

"When was the last time you were in contact with Jona?"

"Before her release she phoned."

"Escape. Not release. She's escaped from a correctional mental ward."

"She called it a penalty box. She knew she'd get out. Fuck, yeah." His eyes were hard chips - wild with suppressed rage. He lowered his bass voice with visible control. "Jona is her own woman. Evil is her art form. Her fine art."

"Fine art?" My scrutiny of his face reflected doubt. "Knives, whips, and chains?"

"You don't understand the world of passion and pain. Both life and death are part of the same lottery. Pain is a part of our communal memory. As much as passion."

"I told you I don't care what consenting adults do to one another in the privacy of their own home. But my guess is that Jona is going to hurt someone badly before this is over. Maybe a person who doesn't relish being harmed."

"We all need to be harmed. Harm brings us cleansing. The spirit of life is a violent one. Are you out to save the world, baby?"

I glared at him. "We're wasting one another's time. What do you know? We both know she was a bondage aficionado. Give me some answers."

"Answers." He pointed to a body harness behind the counter. "I know a harness can cut a man's nuts off if not properly fitted. How's that for an answer?"

"Let's start again. I don't give a damn about your bondage gear. Try another flavor. When you saw her before the trial, what did she say?"

"She told me when she's executed, the State is going to fold her in half and use her ass as a bike rack."

"Why don't I just hand your name over to the authorities? I'm sure they'd love to interrogate you. They might pay you a visit here and even find a stash of illegal substances. You'll think dark humor then, pal."

"You walk in here vilifying my world - then expect me to answer your questions. My world is invisible to society except when moral snobs like you need information from someone in the S&M world. Then you'll lower yourself. You'll consider it a raw sewage stopover."

My tone was sarcastic. "I'm here doing my job. So give me one truthful response. Tell me what you really know about Jona's whereabouts. It could save her life because when they take her down, it could get ugly."

"Better get your interview with her before she's captured. She'll end up turning her face from life."

"Meaning?"

"I mean she'll waste herself."

Pinpricks ran up and down my neck and arms. "I don't think so. Beneath it all, she's an egotist."

There was silence. He pointed toward the door. "Come again, Randa Florez. I'll be glad to do a free piercing. Or a little free ink." His smile was hideous. "I've got a word for your forehead. Starts with C."

"My paper is going to give you a little free ink in the morning edition. How's that?"

"I don't read the paper. But I do know how to tattoo your face anytime you'd like."

Rarely did I dislike a human being before getting a chance to know them. Rarer still did I show my loathing. When he put out his hand to shake mine, I recoiled. I walked to the door.

"Eddie Hunter, the chances of your touching me are infinitesimal to none. However the chances of me writing about your friendship with Jona is extraordinarily gargantuan," I forewarned.

"You fucking bitch!"

"That would be me, Eddie Hunter. That would be me."

* * *

By midmorning I waited in the corridor to see Lieutenant Fritz Truesdale. When he heard I was in possession of information from several taped confessions, he quickly agreed to keep his appointment with me. Jona often bragged about many killings. I had guessed that the encounters were little more than a sick mind's overworked imagination. But there were details scattered in among her rambling discourse. I hand-picked them for Fritz to check against their new investigation of actual events.

When Lieutenant Truesdale motioned to me, I entered his office. He sat at his desk. I sat across from him. "Here's the information I have." I handed him a manila file containing tape transcripts. "Might be something you can use."

"Public duty, Florez? We all know you and your paper are the voice and conscience of the Rocky Mountains. You wouldn't expect a favor in return, would you?"

"Now that you mention it," I answered with a grin, "sure."

He opened the file and began scrutinizing it. His pen struck out three names. The other several he made checks beside. He drew asterisks in the margins by two names. I make a mental note of the process. "Je-zus! Beck has confessed to everything except corn circles and cattle mutilations." His stare finally skittered off the last page.

"The way she was chalking up her crimes, I figured she had a tremendous yearning for a lifetime of prison food."

"Well?" He looked up. "Anything else?"

"I'd love to be the recipient of your assistance in return."

"Look, Florez, we just don't have answers yet. We're still checking on several potential victims. Looks like as many as half a dozen leads might be legitimate. It's easy to pick up panhandlers, teenage street sweepers. Bump them off and who is the wiser. I'll be honest, I've been a cop for a long time, and her confessions about the killings made my skin crawl."

"I was hoping it wasn't just my sensibilities. I also shivered when I listen to her tapes."

"She has an ugly background. You can tell your readers that much. And that we're in the process of linking her to several other slayings. I'll provide you with names, dates, and places when we've got strong enough evidence. One thing I feel certain about. When we capture her, she'll be tried for numerous other murders."

"You said *when* as if you believe a capture to be probable."

"Don't quote me on this, but if we had a trail of any kind, we'd be on it. Until we make her, the best thing we can do is be ready when she does surface."

"Anything I can say about where you might be trolling for Jona?"

"She's not biting. Not even circling the boat. We've got stakeouts at all her haunts. We're tailing the people she knows."

"Not as efficiently as *The Mirror*," I jabbed.

"I was wondering when that would come up. So tell Hank his photos of Vivian X were excellent. And thanks for eventually alerting us to her whereabouts."

"First things first. The photo shoot and interview seemed a little top priority to me. Besides that, it never occurred to me that your department might lose her trail." Although 'snide' didn't become me, there were times it overcame me.

"We want this one resolved more than you do. Jona Beck is a time bomb. We'd like nothing better than to take her without incident. As time goes on, it seems it might be more and more complicated. The more freedom she tastes, the more difficult the fight is likely to be."

"I'm hearing you say she might elude you for a long, long time."

"Could be. But if we do get sight of her, look out. Hang on to your hat. And anything else that might have worked its way loose."

I grinned. "Glad to see there's the same old simpatico between us, Fritz."

"Sure, simpatico, Florez." His mouth pursed. "And time is wasting."

I stood to shake his hand. "I hope my cooperation has put me at the top of your list."

"You'll be the first to know when there's action. And Randa," he added as I neared the door, "give Officer O'Bryan my best."

"Stunned, I whirled around. "You've got me under surveillance?"

"Just give her my condolence for selecting a playgirl like you."

We both laughed. "How about if I give her *my* best and you give her *your* condolence."

* * *

Before lunch I checked my messages. Mother had not

called. Alison Pagette had phoned. I returned her call. She asked if I'd meet her for lunch. Her treat. I'm uncertain why I agreed.

We met at *La Petite Lionne*, a new restaurant in LoDo.

"You must try the curried lobster," she suggested.

"I shall," I agreed. I lowered the menu. "You're looking well." She wore a very provocatively low-cut, rose colored dress.

"Don't be so damned cold to me. We shared a very erotic life for the last few years, so you might have greeted me with a kiss on the cheek."

"Alison, first let's acknowledge the discrepancies. The few years were off and on as dictated by you. And I'm not in the mood for your games now. You wanted our affair done. It is just as *you* insisted - over."

Her lush hair covered part of her face when she leaned her head down. Her chin rested in her hand. "Randa, I've been considering us."

"There is no more *us*. At your request."

"Let's just have a nice lunch. We can go back to my condo and talk about it there," she invited. "We've both been under stress. It's time we reconsider. I know you'd like to get things back on track."

"I've met someone else."

Her back stiffened when she leaned forward. "Someone else?"

"She's very right for me."

"So what was I? Some anatomically correct interlude until the right one came along? You did profess love. Were you lying?"

"Of course not, Ali. You know how much I cared. You continued running from me until you finally got away."

"Is that how you see it?"

The pause was uncomfortable for us both. "Look, Alison, you never wanted anything with a commitment. You're like Ovid's Daphne. You told me you require your freedom."

"I've reconsidered."

"I'm sorry. It is really over this time."

"You're a bitch!" she seethed. "And don't bother asking if we can be friends. We can't. I'm not sure why I ever even gave you the time of day. It was always you and your family, your job..." Her hand flailed wildly in the air just as the waiter appeared with water. His tray tipped, toppling the glasses. Water rushed across the tablecloth. Alison moved her chair away quickly enough to avoid the water. My lap was soaked.

She hurled down her napkin and made a storming exit.

Half a dozen staff members surrounded me. Their attempt to dry my blouse and slacks was almost comedic. I reassured them that it was fine.

Before my dousing, I'd planned to return to my office to file an updated story. Instead I went directly to my loft. After tossing on dry clothing, I wrote my story about how authorities are linking Jona Beck to a number of other killings throughout the country. Also I completed a sidebar story about Eddie Hunter. If he hadn't felt well-inked before, he would now. I filed the stories via e-mail.

After exiting my loft's small office, I entered my bedroom. An additional change of clothing was quickly put together in a small tote so that I could stay over with Nevada. I would go directly from there to work in the morning.

I sat on the bed. There was a text message from my mother. Before realizing it, I had dialed her number. I apologized for not contacting her.

"Randa, it's a very difficult, emotional time for us all," Erika Randolph accepted my apology. "I understand that you're edgy over the story. And the fact that I'm in town is an added burden. Might we dine together tonight?"

"I'd like to, but I have plans. There's someone very special. She's just come into my life."

"Has your father met her?"

"Yes. And he approves," I added.

"Then I must also meet her."

"You want to meet her?" My voice trembled with a multitude of concerns. My mother had never expressed interest in meeting my friends, much less my lovers.

"Don't you think it's time we both made an effort to share

our lives with one another? I'm your mother. We were once tied together by an umbilical cord. Now, I'm treated as a stranger. I'd love for you and your friend to be my dinner guests at the Denver Country Club tonight?"

"I've got to check with her."

"Randa, give me this chance to be part of your life. Please. Shall we say around six?"

"Yes. Fine, I'll contact her. I'm sure she won't object."

"I look forward to meeting your new friend."

* * *

"Dinner with a diva at the Denver Country Club!" Nevada alliteratively exclaimed when she met my mother. She had dressed for the occasion in lovely light green pants, a matching printed blouse, with jacket. I had only worn my tan slacks, an off-white shell and linen jacket. Although my mother was clad in her usual stylish garb, she didn't embarrass me by scrutinizing my outfit.

"I'm glad to finally meet one of my daughter's friends."

"You didn't meet Alison?" Nevada inquired.

"No," my mother responded. "However, I've spoken briefly to her on the phone numerous times."

Nevada glanced over at my smile. I whispered, "Two divas at dinner is one too many. You're the first to meet my mother."

"I'm honored," she replied.

Throughout the meal conversation sparkled. It might well have been scripted, I considered, because each word seemed uniform. Entertaining stories were accompanied by laughter, and warmth.

When talking about opera, Mother's comments expressed her own vantage. "There's the perception people have about opera singers. That image alienates."

"Why so?" Nevada questioned.

Mother answered thoughtfully. "There's a prima donna snobbery expected for a star to carry off. I refer to it as the elitist syndrome. Once an operatic career has begun, it's too late to remove your shoes and walk barefoot in the grass. Decorum. One must have snob appeal." Her eyes closed for a moment.

"Your impeccable upbringing had already schooled you for that," I interjected.

"Yes," she agreed. "My growing up was very demanding, in preparation for the world of opera. In early years one is busily learning to fluently speak French, Italian, and German. Add to that the isolation required by constant rehearsals, as well as always learning new scores for one's repertoire. Well, it left little time for anything else. Then tours begin and they are very grueling."

Nevada offered, "You must like it. It's made you famous."

"Fame is ephemeral." Mother hesitated before asking. "And why did you select a career in enforcement?"

"My family has the pioneer spirit. Ranch. Cowgirls."

"Did you decided on enforcement when you were young," Mother prodded.

"Yes. Cops see a lot of societal underbelly, but sometimes we make a difference."

"I'm certain your parents are very proud of you." Mother reached to take my hand. "And I am very proud of my daughter. Mothers are the gate to a child's life. Yet we can't order the kind of human being we wish to produce. If I could have, I would have ordered Randa. Exactly as she is."

"You wouldn't change the fact that I'm lesbian?" I asked.

"Perhaps you're doing what I did. Maybe I married Paulo to spite my family." Her words were glib, but with a bite.

"Mother, homosexuality is not an elective. I'm lesbian because, not in spite."

"Of course, I didn't mean that," she derailed. "I accept you the way you are."

"The medical and scientific communities are now saying that it is coded into a person's genes," Nevada added. "And I'm going to excuse myself for a few minutes, and find a restroom."

Mother watched Nevada as she made her way through the dining area to the women's room. "I like Nevada very much," Mother said to me. "I wish you could have had the warmth provided you that her family gave her."

"I did have. I had Father and his family."

"I would have liked to provide it for you. I know I've failed you as a mother. I haven't a maternal instinct. I knew that even when you were a baby. When you were in your bassinet I felt fear. I'd gaze at you for hours, watching over you to see that you were breathing. I took breaths for you. I couldn't believe I'd given birth to another human being. You were a part of me. Now, you've grown to be a woman, and you've become a stranger. I do love you, Randa. I have never been able to convince myself of your love in return."

"How is your mother doing?" I asked, purposely changing the subject. I wouldn't argue with my mother. But I could have easily silenced her accusation. She surely could have seen the love in a young child's face – waiting for her mother to return.

"Mother is dying. Throughout the years, when my mother has had a heart episode, Father often teased that Mother owns too much expensive jewelry to ever die. But even riches aren't enough to bribe her into living." Tears began to form in my mother's eyes. She looked away.

Nevada approached the table. As she rubbed her hands together, she sensed the gloom. "Guess I'd better get back to the house. Get some sleep. I'm sure it will be another long day tomorrow."

"That's right," Mother remembered, "you've got a killer on the loose."

"And we want to capture Jona Beck soon. Before she takes another *stab* at her past profession," Nevada reported. "That's the latest gallows humor from Cop-land, U.S.A."

Laughter lifted, as did our moods. We thanked my mother and told her we must leave. Erika Randolph pleaded with me to visit my dying grandmother. And my refusal hurt us both.

* * *

I glanced at the geometric forms of Denver's skyline as my Z traveled toward Nevada's. Nevada drove since I'd indulged in two very full glasses of wine. "With you behind the wheel, we aren't likely to get a ticket. And they won't arrest you for cutting in traffic like that," I joked.

"Cops are a tight group. We need that. But we do ticket one another if the occasion warrants," she responded.

"Fritz said to give you his best."

"One of the guys at work spotted us going into Marlene's. Must have told Fritz."

"Then they're not having me tailed?"

She laughed. "You're not high on our 'harboring suspect' list."

"Tonight is terrific," I commented as I looked up through the Datsun's T-top. "The sky is loaded with stars. And my mother found you charming."

"Maybe she can tell that I'm falling in love with her prized daughter."

"At least she knows you're not influenced by her fame."

"Not when I told her I've got a sister who can yodel."

"When you said that line, my mother nearly choked laughing. Yes. My mother likes you very much."

As oncoming headlights hit the Z's long hood a glaze of silver flashed in my eyes. I considered how beautifully the evening went. Nevada said all the right things at all the right times.

"Randa, your mother loves you." There was a moment's delay before she inquired, "Why won't you see your grandmother?"

"Lenora Randolph is an awful human being. That's why. She is selfish, spoiled, controlling, prejudiced, and inconsiderate. But that only scratches the surface. She has harmed me irreparably. She has harmed my father. For that I can't forgive her."

After a gap, delaying the conversation, Nevada seemed to know it was time to change subjects. "How did your luncheon with Alison go?"

"She dumped two full glasses of water in my lap," I reported with a chuckle.

Nevada laughed. "Was she aiming to cool your sweet little heater?"

"No, she wasn't attempting to put out any fires. She was swinging her arms around."

"Assault and battery. I ought to arrest her."

"Tonight I don't want anyone in your custody except me." I leaned near to kiss her cheek. "Just give me time to figure love out. I've only experienced an epidermal kind of love before." My eyes clamped shut. "I just recalled something Jona Beck said when I asked her about love."

"What would Beck know about love?"

"I'm not certain she knows anything about love. And I've just admitted that I'm not sure I know much about love. The conversations we shared were often philosophical. For being diagnosed insane, it always amazed me when she gave a response that made me think. She was self-educated. Yet she was a quick study on the things she wanted to know. I memorized many of her more lucid comments. She said love is only a brief instant of being retrieved from the soul of loneliness."

"I say love is all that saves us from becoming Jona Beck. Do you think anyone ever loved her?"

"Simone Milton must have. She certainly loved her enough to aid and abet. She gave up any future she might have as a psychiatrist. She gave up the good life. She traded a life of respectability for being on the run with a criminal. And for her efforts Dr. Milton's prospects for a long and fruitful life aren't good. Yet another story about the betrayal of love."

"Your sadness hurts me, Randa. And yes," she said as she parked in front of her house, "I'll give you all the time you need. I'll never allow betrayal to enter our love."

CHAPTER 8

Wednesday

Saffron was the main scent that seeped throughout Angie's kitchen. She had obviously started the paella early in the morning, because by midmorning, it was saturating the house with a lovely blossom fragrance.

After leaving Nevada's home I stopped over to see how everyone was doing at my father's family. I wanted to talk with Benjy about his ride with Nevada. His day traditionally started at midmorning.

Angie greeted me with an invitation. "The paella will be done in a couple hours. I can send some along with you so Nevada can see what my signature dish tastes like.

"Nothing like your paella," I replied to Angie. "If there's time this noon, you know I'll be here."

Angie stirred the luscious smelling ingredients. "Coffee's fresh."

I poured a steaming cup of coffee for myself, and topped hers off. "Your coffee is always delicious."

"Eggshells. Sit," she directed with a point toward the table and chairs.

"Eggshells?"

"Sure. My great-grandfather worked in a restaurant. Wash eggshells clean and put them in with the fresh coffee grounds basket. Takes the bitterness out or something. The shells are like magnets. The get all the bad taste out."

"I never knew you put eggshells in the coffee. I've never seen you do it. Is that true?" I skeptically questioned.

"*Es Verdad*! Very true. I tell nobody because it doesn't sound appetizing. Putting eggshells in with fresh ground coffee. Renie would say ten million rosaries to get her hands on my coffee formula. Our secret. *Silencio, por favor.*" She sat opposite me at the round oak table. She pried, "You went to dinner with your mother last night? Paulo says the diva won't let you be."

"We had dinner with Mother. Nevada went with me."

"Now the prima donna works on your girlfriend!" She slapped the table with a tea towel she'd been carrying. "Wouldn't you know? She's getting in the act with Nevada."

"It was just a dinner. And Nevada really thinks you're terrific. She told me she liked you immediately," I praised, hoping the kudos would temper her jealousy of my mother.

"Does Nevada get along with your hoity-toity mother?"

"They seemed to relate fine with one another. I was fearful they might not. But I knew Nevada would like you immediately."

Angie smiled She reached to pat my hand. "That's because I'm not a stuffy, pompous, cold bitch who leaves my family. I stay with my family. I love you. You're like my only daughter and my only sister combined."

It was my turn to smile. "And I know you love me. Just as I love you, Angie. Nevada barely knows you and she thinks the world of you." Through Angie's eyes my mother's reserved stodginess was interpreted to be pompous. Angie was not prepared to be told that Mother laughed heartily at Nevada's comments about cop life. There was no need to report how well my mother and Nevada got along. "How is our Teresa doing?"

"Still no baby. I tell her yesterday I'm bringing her a jump rope. She's ready, but the baby has a mind of its own. I can't believe I'm going to be a grandmother."

"You'll be a wonderful *abuela.*"

"They got a surprise for you. Rogerio and Teresa," she disclosed. "But I can't tell you."

"I hate secrets," I grumbled. "Tell me."

"No."

"*Esa es una mala jugado que me hacen.*" That's a mean trick to play on me, I objected.

"Blame Rogerio and Teresa." She paused. "You think I'll

be a good grandmother? I'm not such a hot mom. I've got a lazy son still in bed?"

"I'll wake him. I wanted to chat with Benjy anyway."

"Buenos suerte!"

Good luck was not needed, for fortune smiled. My gentle wrapping on the door was met with Benjy's voice. "Come in," he yelled.

"How's it going?" I asked. I'm amazed, if not overwhelmed, when I saw he was not only up and dressed, but that his bed had been made.

"Doing fine," he answered. He leaned toward the mirror. "Nevada thinks my hair is too long. I'm going to get it cut when I get some money."

I reached in my pocket. "Here, I'll make a contribution to beautifying the community." I tossed a twenty on the dresser.

"Thanks."

"You're dressed. It's only half past nine."

"I thought I'd try making it to a couple classes of summer school. See if I like it."

"That's great, Benj. I'm proud of your effort."

His eyes met mine in the mirror's reflection "I can study hard. You think Nevada will be proud?"

"I'm sure she will." My frown of disbelief must have been conspicuous.

He explained, "Nevada, she says if I don't aim at nothing, I'll hit the mark every time. That means I'll end up nothing. I don't wanna end up nothing."

I took him in my arms. He was my kid brother and I wanted him to always feel he's someone worthy of love. "You aren't going to end up nothing. You'll grow into a fine man. Just like Father."

* * *

I'd just turned off on Speer Boulevard and was passing by Lower Downtown's Coors Field when I heard a bulletin over my police band. A triple homicide was reported. The address coming over the police band radio was located in the center of the Capital Hill area. My cell phone beeped.

"Florez," I answered. My pulse was racing. "I'm five minutes away," I reported to Kenny Erickson. "I'm on my way." I swerved into a right-hand lane, then made the right with more speed than I should have. After another turn and several blocks, I pulled up in front of an area cordoned with crime scene tape. An army of squad cars were still arriving.

This section of the city was filled with large turn-of-the-century homes. Most had been converted to multiple units of small apartments. Many were rundown; some were squalidly unkempt. The huge home where investigators and uniformed police milled, was somewhere on the scale between rundown and dilapidated.

Holding up my press pass, I rushed to the barrier where a uniformed officer blocked my way.

"I've got to see Lieutenant Truesdale," I blurted out.

"He's ankle deep in bodies at the moment, Florez."

"Look, Officer," I implored as I scanned his nameplate, "Officer Ludlow, it's important for me to talk with Truesdale. This might be connected to the Beck escape."

"Might be?" he laughed. "If it isn't, I'll eat my shorts without seasoning. It was a bloodletting in there."

"Come on, Ludlow, just radio Truesdale. It's vital that I speak with him."

Ludlow radioed, "Truesdale, Randa Florez claims you want to see her."

"Like I want a case of the hives on top of a dose of crabs," I heard him reply.

"Tell him it's important." I was adamant.

"She says it's important," Ludlow repeated.

"Okay," Truesdale blustered. "Okay. I'll have someone meet her in the entryway. No photos. No goddamn photo ops here. We're doing the dusting, bagging and tagging without media cameras. And tell her not to touch anything. We got a crime scene and I don't want to compromise the place because Florez thinks I can't live without her."

I grimaced to Ludlow, and then shrugged. An officer I'd

never seen before escorted me to an entryway. Fritz exited a door. "It's sealed," he informed me. "What's so important?"

"Fritz, you said you'd give me what you have." Within my shirt's breast pocket was my small tape recorder. I quickly pressed the record button. Then I clutched my pen and notebooks. "What do you have?"

"Triple homicide. It was a grizzly massacre."

"Jona Beck?"

"That's what we're thinking. The three victims were iced sometime late yesterday afternoon. The woman next door called us saying she hadn't been able to get any response from them?"

"Them?"

"Yes. Last name is Solomon. S-O-L-O-M-O-N." He glanced down at his notes.

"Mrs. Solomon is the landlady of this apartment house. She and husband, and son live in the ground level front apartment. Mamie, age forty-two, and Arlen, age fifty-one. Their fifteen-year old son's name is Hampton. From what we can ascertain at this reading, Jona and Simone were holed up here in the rear apartment. It has a separate entryway."

"What makes you think it was Beck?"

"Not terribly tricky. According to the neighbor Mamie and Arlen saw the front page of your paper. Recognized Vivian as the elusive woman who rented the apartment a couple of months ago. *And* they recognized Elise Stuart as the management agent that put the rental contract together. From what the neighbor said, the Solomons became suspicious. Figured they'd check the property out since Vivian seldom stopped by. At first she would rush in with bags, presumably groceries, and slip right out. Then the visits stopped the same time Vivian became front page news. Must have realized we were tailing her. But even after Vivian wasn't making her appearances, there were still sounds of muted voices, running water, that kind of thing."

"That would certainly have alerted me."

"Right. The Solomons told a neighbor that it seemed odd, and that they intended to enter the apartment. The neighbor didn't think anything more about it until this morning. Hampton

Solomon was her newspaper deliverer. No delivery. She tried to contact the Solomons. No answer."

"What about Simone Milton's vehicle?"

Fritz shook his head. "It must have been parked in the detached garage. It was part of the rental package."

"Anything else in the way of evidence that points to Beck and Milton?"

"It's gory. The M.E. is going to go bonkers trying to figure out what's what. There are blood prints all over. The trace material will verify. Off-record, I don't have a doubt in my mind."

"If all three of the Solomon's entered at the same time, how did she get a drop on them? She usually used only her trademark knife."

"She had a firearm. A couple shots were fired. Probably to make certain she'd finished them off after carving them up. A neighbor across the street heard what he thought was a car backfiring about six last night. Could have been the time when Beck began her spree. Ballistics will check it all out, but we think it might be the Lady Smith and Wesson registered to Dr. Simone Milton. How's this for a turn of events. A few years ago, Milton got the gun permit because she feared one of the loonies she was treating."

"There goes her credentials as a credible profiler." I paused while Fritz snorted a half laugh. "So Milton provides the gun?"

"My best guess is this: Jona had the firearm trained on one of them – the one that first entered. She doesn't want the other two to call the cops, so she takes the intruding one back to the Solomon apartment. They're all together then. And with a gun pointed at them. There she convinces them she only wants to escape. She's going to tie them up, and leave. Right. All three of them are gagged, bound to something or other, sprawled out and they're butchered. So much for Jona's word of honor."

"You predicted a murder spree."

"And we're off and running. Three homicides committed with malice and forethought." Fritz's face was taut. His eyes twitched with rapid blinks. His stance was beleaguered. "You probably don't want to see anything like this."

"I'm a city crime reporter."

"The forensic unit is working so I can't let you inside for fear of disrupting a crime scene. But I'll allow you to take a look from the entryway." His latex gloved hand squeezed the doorknob. It fanned back.

The room appeared splashed with blood. Its red was reminiscent of the paint used in a few of Frida Kahlo paintings. Blood had squirted like a fountain from one of the victim's pumping arterial vessel. It covered the carpeting with a rain of droplets.

"Jesus!" I murmured. One body, unidentifiable, was skewered with kitchen knives. Eyes were stark with death's luminosity. The flesh looked like an eagle pinned for taxidermy. Next to the second victim was a large smear of clotted blood. It appeared as if the victim struggled inch by inch for several yards, oozing blood like a snail secretes fluid, until death. A stench nearly gagged me. I stepped back, returning to the main entry door. "It's a little close in there."

"I'd say it is Beck's handiwork. When we say someone is considered dangerous, that's what we mean. Why didn't the Solomons immediately call us?"

"If it's a false alarm people feel foolish."

"Now they aren't feeling one damned thing," he said. "We have a media press conference scheduled in twenty minutes. Time to get ready to face those good old intrusive cameras. We'll clean up the language. We'll say things like 'brutal' killing. How do you describe this kind of high gore?"

"I describe as much as I can take by telling myself that's what I'm getting paid to do."

My entire body had the feel of being vacant – with the exception of battery acid intensely burning my stomach's lining.

I moved away from the house. I attempted to fill my lungs with clean air. After a few minutes, when my voice had untightened from the hoarseness of shock, I would phone the office. I'd give them what I had up to the moment. I'd tell them I'd be calling back after the press conference with more. When the jittery feeling in my knees subsided, I'd canvas the area for quotes from the neighborhood. Whatever I did, wherever I went, I was not likely to shake off the images I'd just encountered.

* * *

Caller ID was a wonderful thing, I mused. Sometimes events seemed perfect. It was some mystical, effortless abandon. Immediately after Fritz Truesdale's press conference, I called the office. They had just received a call from Clara 'Vivian' Walters. Vivian's conversation consists of some off-the-wall allegation about how reporter Randa Florez had ruined her life. She told the receptionist she wasn't involved. Caller ID exposed the phone number, and the phone's location was tracked to a nearly vacant building directly behind Elise Stuart's office. The complex was being offered for lease by the property management and real estate firm of Elise Stuart.

I instructed the city editor to give me the fifteen minutes to make it to the building, and an additional ten to extract an interview. Then call in authorities. A photographer was on route. That would give me ample time to set up for a shot of the police apprehending Vivian. Fritz and his buddies were hot to lay even more questions on Vivian than I had for her. And I had plenty.

I snapped the button on my recorder as I slipped it into my pocket. I exited my car and walked a cracked sidewalk to the small complex. After knocking on the door, my voice lifted, "Vivian. Vivian, I know you're there. If you don't let me in I'll call the police." When there was no response, I reached into the pocket of my jacket. By the time I'd pulled out my cell phone, the door's latch snapped.

Vivian's mane of hair was unkempt. It made her appear as crumpled as an unmade bed. Her pale eyebrows were furrowed; her eyes sunken, yet there was hatred toward me in them. She wanted to send me off to Jona for a little surgery.

Her hiss was barely audible, "You bitch. It's your fault."

"I have some questions to ask you." After carefully

inspecting the bare apartment, I pressed past her. "So where's your sugar mama?"

"Elise is trying to throw the cops off my trail. We left her apartment the minute we heard what was going down." She peered out again and then quickly clamped the door behind me. "We figured they'd be coming for me."

"So Elise carted you off to safety. Stashes you in one of her dumps. And you want to tell me what an interfering piece of junk I am, so you call my office. You lay some crap on them, and here I am. You're getting better than ever at stupidity."

"How'd you find me?"

"I've got a research team as big as Los Angeles. However, with the assist of Caller ID, the location was pulled up before you'd said your goodbyes. Now, I want some answers, or I've instructed my editor to turn you over. Question one - did you help with the escape?"

"No. I knew nothing about it."

"So Jona called after she broke out. She needed digs. You had a spare apartment. Let's see now, there's the apartment where you reside, and the one you recently rented from the Solomons. So why did you need two apartments?"

"I was..." she hesitated, thinking about how to answer my question. "My lease on the one was about to end. I figured they were about to increase the rent money. So I rented the other in case."

"Like you give a damn about rent! You're a wealthy woman, Vivian. Very wealthy. Try another story. I don't buy that one."

"I don't remember."

"I don't buy your memory lesions excuse either." I paused. "So how did she get the key?"

"She had a key to my apartment before. When we were together."

"The crimes took place at the apartment you only rented a couple of months ago."

"I gave her a key when I went to visit her."

"So why would you have given her a key to your apartment? She never had a prayer of being released? And

151

sneaking anything inside to her would have been difficult. No. You gave it to Dr. Milton as the plan was being devised."

"I just wanted her to have it. It's your fault. If you'd have left me alone none of this would have happened."

"How do you figure that?"

"The nosey landlady wouldn't have butted in. They'd all still be alive."

"If the victims would have called authorities, like advised, they'd be alive. And Jona Beck would be captured. Besides, I'm not the one pretending to be a surgeon, Vivian. I'm not the one who sprung her, and I'm not the one harboring her. Jona just murdered three people. And your story is plastic. Doll, you are pure acrylic. I'm not buying your passel of lies. Try another lie on me and I'm calling in the authorities. Where is she now?"

Vivian tottered from foot to foot. "I don't know. She didn't tell me."

"What did she tell you?" I moved strategically toward her.

"Just that there'd been a crisis."

"*Crisis*! I'd say a crisis. Now tell me." The threat in my voice was harsh.

"I'm not telling you anything more. Get out. I've answered your questions."

Sirens surrounded us. Footsteps rush toward the building. "Maybe our buddies in blue will have better luck interrogating you."

"You called the fuckin' cops!"

"That's right, I turned you. Reason one – you are lying your rotten ass off to me, and I don't appreciate that one little bit. Reason two - a change of scenery will do you a world of good. In fact, kid, it might be your only salvation."

We heard the deep, well-modulated voice announcing their entrance. "Police."

"It's Randa Florez, come on in, there aren't any weapons," I gave the all clear. When I saw one of the officers I'd known for years, I joked, "And it's a damned good thing there aren't any weapons. If there were I'm sure I would have used them on her for all the bullshit she's dispensing."

"Just so happens Lieutenant Truesdale is in a foul mood, and he *does* have a weapon," the officer replied.

They took Clara Bernice 'Vivian X' 'Vivian Doe' 'Vivian One-Name' Walters into custody. Although they were officially going to question her, she'd be hung out to dry. She was implicated in a major murder case. That was enough to bolt her inside for a while - at least until Jona Beck would be brought to justice. There would be charges of aiding and abetting. And if they did any snooping at all, there would undoubtedly be drug charges.

I called in my exclusive update for the extra that was being put to bed. In addition, it would also be used for the *E-Edition*. Just as I decided on an early lunch, my presence was being requested by Truesdale at Homicide. Verbatim from Fritz, was that I should get over to headquarters *pronto. Pronto!* His Spanish was improving.

* * *

"I didn't have time to safe-crack Vivian's secrets," I defended.

Fritz glared across his desk at me. "Randa, what if Beck would have been with Vivian?"

"She wasn't, so why the histrionics?" My grin was subtly manifested on purpose.

"She might have been. The perpetrator isn't some hit and miss, bungling purse-snatcher. We're dealing with one of the most diabolically evil, dangerous minds I've ever known. You were endangered this morning! You might have gone on the casualty list."

"My editor knew where I was going. It was all under control. A photographer was deployed. And the police."

"Eventually!"

"Did you get anything more out of Vivian?" I impatiently asked.

"She denies criminality. We're trying to keep her incarcerated, but her family has hired big-name lawyers. They'll work for bail. We want her remanded without bail."

"If they get her sprung, she's off to be Vivian X in some other metro city." I glanced at my watch. "I'd love to stay and visit, Fritz. But I have things to do."

"I want to know what Vivian told you."

"She was doing galactic travel." I stood.

"Sit back down," his tone was serious. I reeled back into the chair. "In the apartment where Jona and Simone were staying we found newspaper articles with your byline. They had been carefully clipped out."

"Maybe Jona's a fan. I did comprehensive interviews with the woman."

"Florez, she had stabbed the clippings. In a final rage before she left the apartment, she slashed all the articles you'd written. She sprinkled human blood from her victims over the paper. She viciously gashed one of your larger byline photos. I'm concerned that she may be targeting you. She might view recent material you've written as some form of betrayal."

Leaning away, I didn't feel the chair's back slats behind me. Nor did my feet feel the floor beneath me. "Betrayal. But if she wanted to harm me, she would have targeted me immediately after her initial break."

My memory switched into reverse. The manager of Raven's Talon had stated that Jona's spirit is everywhere. She said it to explain her own fear. A cool chill climbed my back. The words echoed. Jona's spirit is *everywhere*.

"Randa," Truesdale barged into my thoughts, "be very cautious."

I feigned bravery. His stare was too near to have been fooled.

* * *

By the time I arrived at Ruby's it was late afternoon. The day had been hand-delivered from hell. After my unpleasant visit with Lieutenant Fritz Truesdale, I had an even more difficult chat with *The Mirror's* esteemed editor-in-chief. Fritz had taken it upon himself to inform my editor that it would be irresponsible to keep me on the story. After a decisive loss with my editor-in-chief, I went on to argue my case in front of the publisher, and co-publisher, both of whom wanted me to step away from the Beck story.

I stood firm, contending that I had been given Kenny Erickson's word that I would never be removed from the story. It was *mine*. That promise was given me the first night I met Jona Beck. But there were now extenuating circumstances, they disputed.

Finally, I did what I'd promised myself I would never do - threatened. If they took me off the story, it would void my contract, as well as my no-compete clause. I had the word of my immediate supervisor that the story was mine. Kenny Erickson wouldn't lie for, or against. He would tell them that he gave his pledge.

Although I'd forced their surrender, they had done some serious blustering.

My case was won, but the confrontation had left me tired and hungry.

* * *

"I'll have a buffalo burger, cheese fries, chocolate malt, and whatever pie is the special of the day," I ordered. I sank back in the booth at *Ruby's*. "I'm famished."

"Your favorite fresh glazed strawberry pie *was* our special of the day, but that was hours ago," Ruby reported as she pointed to the clock. "You always come in here at noontime on Wednesdays! You're mighty late."

"Lunchtime disappeared."

"Good thing I saved you a slab." She chuckled. "And congratulations on the story in the extra."

"Thanks for saving pie for me."

Half the burger was all I could manage to get down. The mound of fries curled as they shrunk. The malt had melted down and was switched out for coffee when Ruby brought pie.

I looked up as Nevada entered. After she slipped into the booth, Ruby slid a slice of pie in front of her. "Randa wants you to try this," Ruby enticed.

Nevada's food order was inaudible. "Randa, Randa," Nevada repeated to get my attention.

"Sorry. It's been a long day."

"The Beck case took most of the day. But petty crime doesn't scoot over when there's a major case. Terrific work on locating Vivian X. But you should have called us first."

"Vivian accused me of being to blame for the Solomon murders. Said if I wouldn't have plastered her story and photo on the front page, it wouldn't have happened."

"That's a load of bull. It was Vivian's apartment. That makes her an accomplice. Bottom line - Jona Beck is responsible. Dr. Simone Milton bears a major portion of the responsibility, certainly. But not you. Not your paper."

"But I do feel some culpability. No intent, but I'd heard the rumor Beck was seducing Milton. Before the escape. I was convinced it wasn't true. And I was also convinced that there would be no way she could have escaped. If I'd reported it, maybe it wouldn't have happened."

"*Maybe* authorities would have also discounted it. You can't be accountable for her escape. Not just because you heard gossip."

My hand reached. It slid into the envelope of hers. She squeezed. "You're easy to love, Nevada."

"You, too." She sipped her coffee. "I signed up for a double shift tonight. I hate second shift, but it does beat vampire duty. I should get off after midnight. You have the key to my place, just make yourself at home. I'm assuming you'll come over."

"Yes. I think I'll spend some time at my loft first. I want to listen to more of the Beck interview tapes."

"Going to be dropping by Marlene's?"

"No. I think I'll stop by Rogerio's. He should be off work by now."

"No baby yet? Or is that what you're going to check?"

"No baby. I guess I just need to talk with my brother. We think alike."

* * *

Rogerio was working out on his back patio. Sheets of newspaper were spread on the picnic table. In the center was a sludge-encrusted small engine. He greeted me with a hug. "Sorry my hands are so dirty. I didn't smudge you, did I?"

"No. I'm fine."

"I'm fixing a motorcycle engine for a guy down the block. Moonlighting," he explained. "Babies aren't cheap. Do you have any idea what a package of disposable diapers costs?"

"A rebuilt engine and four lube jobs?" I teased.

"Exactly." His serious face looked back down at the engine. "This has seen better days."

"Me, too." My melancholia was evident, but I wished to change that. "Angie says you have a surprise for me."

"Mom and her big mouth! Well, maybe we do. But not yet." Our eyes met. "Randa, you seem preoccupied."

"Just a hectic day."

He wiped his hands on a rag. He took my hand and we walked to the swinging bench. We sat in unison. "Want to tell me what's really wrong?"

"The Beck case is ugly. Mother wants me to visit my dying grandmother. And I want time to be with Nevada." My view shifted from his concerned face upward to the spots of light visible through thick leaves. I chastised myself, "Forgive my crotchety diatribe. A good night of sleep will make me brand new."

"Randa, we love you. And soon our baby will love you. I'll always be here for you. You've always been here for me. It's family that matters most."

With family the world takes on a temporary tranquility. I'm drawn back away from the horrors of homicide, at least for the moment.

* * *

After procrastinating an hour I did laundry, cleaned the refrigerator, and vacuumed my loft. Finally, while seated at my desk, I reached into the upper desk drawer and brought out a dozen tapes. Upon their attached stickers were various dates.

Locked off in the night's corner, I relived a moment I'd sooner have forgotten. Jona's voice was chilling. For at the time, I was caught in the machinery of a madwoman's mind. A thick Plexiglas window had separated me from possible death. I looked into the icy eyes of a killer. The taped conversation began:

"Jona, do you have any regrets for your action?"

"Naw. Fuck, no. Why should I? Life gets you in its jaws and chews the hell outta you. I only did what I did to keep outta the way of everything that might hurt me."

"Maynard Jones, for instance?"

"Let's fuckin' forget him. He was nothing. You think he's anything, you're missing the point. I bet they even put the word 'nobody' on his tombstone."

"What do you want on your tombstone?"

"I want it to say that life was hard on me, but I wasn't too fuckin' easy on life either."

"Is that your philosophy?"

"How can the 'ultimate pain machine' have a philosophy?"

"Do you consider yourself to be a pain machine?"

(Raucous laughter.)

"Yeah. Yeah, I do. So does lots of people. Some I give salvation to. But most I hurt."

"You hurt some and give salvation to the others. I don't understand."

"I give salvation to the ones I murder. The ones I think are worthy - I hurt them."

"Those are the women in your circle? The ones you disciplined?"

"Not everyone deserves to die. I could decide. It was like the earth was my laboratory and people were my specimens. I don't believe in random slaughter."

"Jona, you've talked about killing dozens of people. Did you hold some kind of judicial court in your head to see if you'd save them from life?"

"Yeah, now you got it. I had influence. I will again someday. For now, I've got to stay in here and plan. That's why I'm here. It's to give me a chance to rest up before I complete my work. See, if I was free, I'd give you salvation."

"You would kill me?"

"I'd relish killing you. You and my fuckin' attorney. The courts let that dumb shit rep me because they knew he'd let 'em box me. He should die."

"And what have I done wrong?"

"You got hatred inside you. It's covered by fear. But I know it's there. Randa Florez, when I get free, I'm going to change you. Your soul."

"Why do you believe you have the right to transform a soul?"

(Reciting in textbook response.)

"*Anima* means the female soul. The legend is that Christ redeemed the male soul, but the female soul still needs to be   redeemed.   Even though the third canon of the Council of Nantes in 660 decided all women are soulless. Fuck, we all know better. I'm the female redeemer. I know what's best for all women."

"You think you know what's best for me?"

"Death is best for all of us."

My hand reached down and slapped the tape player's OFF button with such a force that it nearly rocked the desktop.

Jona's words chased themselves inside my mind. When the

phone rang, I dropped the wine I'd been sipping. It was Nevada. "Hang on a minute. I'm trying to clean up a spill while we talk."

"I haven't got much time. Look, Randa, you stay there. I'll pick you up tonight. Bring a few days change of clothing so you can stay at my house."

"Fritz told you about the murder scene?"

"He got word to me."

"I was just listening to a tape. I hadn't recalled, but she did threaten me, and her defense attorney. Said he deserved to die."

"You didn't remember someone threatening you?" she asked disbelievingly.

"It just didn't register. There were so many times Jona's responses seemed little more than wild rambling, incomprehensible fragments of thought. I was interviewing an off-the-wall wacko behind bars. I figured she would always be locked. Maybe I suppressed the threat."

"I'll call Fritz now and tell him about it. I'll also report the threat to her defense attorney. He'll probably want a copy of the tape."

"I don't see a problem with that. I'll dub one now."

"See you in half an hour." Before the receiver clicked dead, Nevada said she loved me.

* * *

"What paradoxical fate," I commented after Nevada had firmly shut and bolted her front door. "I'm running and hiding from a mad *woman*."

"You can drop me off at work in the morning and use my truck. Leave your Z in its garage. I'm certain Jona knows you drive a Z. Everyone else in Denver does."

"I've never even driven a truck. I'll get a rental car."

Her smile drifted on for several moments. "If you can parallel park a Z with its hood sticking out ten yards, I don't think a truck will hamper your style."

"I'll have a rental car dropped off here," I insisted.

Our arms wound around one another. The remainder of the

evening was retreating under love's erotic coverlet. Of all the life and death mysteries, perhaps the most relevant was located beneath the subheading of love.

CHAPTER 9

Thursday

Morning appeared before I had a chance to use night for sleep. After love-sharing, there was the tenderness of sexual contentment that should have induced sleep. It did not. We had curled into one another's haven of embraces with savory kisses and kindness. Love had exploded as if a Georgia O'Keeffe flower might have opened in one's best imagination. Yet yesterday's events were replayed each time I began to fall into sleep's cradle.

Nevada left for work early. I crawled from the bed of tangled sheets. My early morning schedule included calling an auto rental office, but first *The Mirror*.

Kenny Erickson had verified our conversation about giving his word. The Beck story was to remain mine until death do us part. I sighed with relief. But I was cautioned to keep my head down until Beck's capture.

Still not entirely convinced that Jona Beck would make an attempt on my life, I made plans to interview the Solomon's neighbors. I might have missed someone or something. I was putting together a recap story about the Solomon family that I'd promised to file later.

A bright cardinal-colored red Ford was delivered. I'd requested a beige Honda. Close enough, I muttered when I took the keys of the red bull's-eye sedan. My first stop would be The Java Brew for coffee and fresh pastry before officially beginning my day.

Morning within Java Brew's serenity provided me with essential solitude. My mind was focused on the three human beings who wouldn't be awakening. Mamie, Arlen, and

Hampton Solomon wouldn't be going about their day.

Punching numbers on my cell phone was the only escape hatch from grim memories. "Fritz, did you get the tape?"

"Thanks. Your lover-girl brought it by first thing. Amazing that Beck's defense attorney is endangered. I can understand why Jona might want to waste you, but her attorney saved her from a death sentence."

"I'm not in the mood for your gallows humor. I've just been thinking about three human beings who will never laugh again. Particularly at lame humor like that."

There was a pause. "You're right, Florez. You know how it is with cops. If we didn't have some outlet, after a while we'd jump in the graves with the victims."

Tension evaporated. "I'm just touchy this morning. So what have you got?"

"Beck is a chameleon. No sightings. And I'm telling you this first, her prints and trace materials were positive. Jona Beck and Dr. Simone Milton were there at the Solomons."

"What do you think Simone Milton's part in the killing was?"

"Probably minimal. After all, she's a shrink, not a surgeon," he said, as he began to laugh. "Sorry Randa."

My chuckle was slight, but there. "I'm getting as bad as the cops," I said to myself as much as Fritz Truesdale. "You're not exactly a treasure trove of information. Not even a possible sighting?"

"Nothing that's panned out. We're still nearer questions than answers. I do have one other thing I'll give you the exclusive on."

"I'm listening."

"One of the names on the list you gave me appears to be Beck's handiwork. She gave enough details to tie her to the case. She'd switched city names. But records show she was in Nashville at the time of the murder. Nashville is sending us what they have, but we're pretty certain there's a DNA match. Maybe she has killed dozens. She knows how to exact revenge. Listen to me, you stay tucked away."

"Fritz, before you go, thanks for alerting my employment

about impending danger to me. You can't imagine how much easier that makes my job."

"Come on, Randa. You're a pain, but we do care about your safety. I'm not sure you have the good sense to stay off the story."

"I'm still on the story. In fact, I'm on my way to interview the Solomon's neighbors."

"Florez, I'm ordering you to stay out of this."

My thumb hit my phone's OFF button. I whispered to myself, "Gee whiz, what a time for a battery failure." Pressing the button again immediately, I phoned *The Mirror* to report Beck was officially linked to an unsolved murder in Nashville. Also, that there had been evidentiary verification of Beck's presence at the murder scene. I doubted anyone was going to consider that tidbit a shocker.

* * *

After an hour spent canvassing the murder scene area and talking with neighbors living in Capital Hill, I returned to Nevada's house. I composed a quick rewrite of all information and included the new items of discovery. I e-mailed it to the office. Some little voice inside was telling me Eddie Hunter may know something. With the antagonism between us, he wasn't likely to talk freely. But if I bugged him enough, he'd at least know I hadn't believed him. The angrier he got, the longer his mouth would stay open.

I was on my way out to drop by The Scorpion Tattoo Parlor when the phone rang. Mama Carmina was panicked. She'd run out of roasted peppers. Papa Gus wandered off to play dominoes with his buddies. Renie hadn't arrived back from helping out at church. Angie was working at Father's auto shop.

I was the last in line to take Mama Carmina shopping. But I wondered if Nevada hadn't called Mama to detour my investigative reporting. I relented and agreed to take her to the weekly outdoor farmer's market.

The City Farmers' Market was a major player in my life as

a child. Although Papa Gus and everyone in my family had gardens – the market provided supplements.

Canvas-shaded stalls consisted of tables filled with produce. People milled around with bulky shopping bags. Tailing after Mama Carmina, I carried her canvas shopping bags. Those totes expanded, as they rapidly filled with fruits and veggies.

"I thought you just needed chili peppers."

"While we're here, why not get some other things on my list."

We trudged the full circle of stalls. When we finally arrive at the stall where the peppers were sold, I inhaled deeply. The scent of roasting peppers was like no other. I watched as the drum filled with chilies rotated above the flames. As chilies tumbled, there was a snap of the skins as they converted to blackened, singed, and bubbling peppers.

On the table were mounds of chilies still warm from the fire. Packed neatly in their zipper bags, the chilies came in numerous varieties. Mama Carmina picked up one packet, examined it and told me, "*Picante*. We need half a dozen of these. I'll carry them. I don't want their heat spoiling the tomatoes."

We walked back to the car.

As the ignition key turned, I ask, "Think we got enough?"

"I need to cook extra for when the baby is born," Mama explained.

"Everyone will keep Teresa's kitchen well-stocked."

"Yes, and she's so capable that she's frozen plenty. Unlike when you were born. I remember your mother had nothing prepared." She looked away. "But that was not to be our worry."

"Why?"

"Your mother had gone to her parents. She'd determined her marriage to Paulo was over."

"I hadn't realized the marriage ended so quickly after I was born." It puzzled me that no one had ever mentioned that before.

"After your mother was dismissed from the hospital, she

and her family took you away. Your father went to the hospital to visit your mother and you. You are gone. Both of you."

"You mean the Randolph's pirated me away? Father didn't know my mother wasn't returning with him?" My frown was one of dubious confusion.

Mama's eyes moistened. "No. He rushes to her parent's home and is told that you will be provided with a nurse, and all your needs will be seen to. He is told that his wife doesn't wish to see him. She is filing for divorce."

"I had no idea. Was that some kind of family secret kept from me?" I interrogated.

"I don't think you were told so you wouldn't think it was your fault."

"But I was only a baby."

"But children often blame themselves." She hesitated before adding, "That's when all the trouble began."

A wrenching spasm traveled the length of my spine. I drove the car onto the main road. My head was whirling. As though the orbiting circle of truth was tightening, I explored, "Trouble?"

"Yes. Your father goes to the Randolph mansion. He pounds the doors until the police are called to take him away. They charge him with disturbance and assaulting an officer. He spent the night in jail before we bailed him out. Your grandparents Randolph were very crafty. They knew the law. Your father's arrest set the stage for them to retain custody of you."

"And that's why I spent those early years with the Randolphs."

"Yes. It wasn't until your father had the resources, and you were old enough to decide, when we were given custody."

There was an excruciating pause before I asked, "They did love each other, didn't they?"

"Yes. With love there is always risk. And risk is often dangerous."

Our drive was completed in silence. Perhaps, I considered, it was love that often tyrannizes us as much as hatred.

* * *

Mama Carmina insisted I stay for a lunch of soft-shelled tacos. How, she asked, can I turn down her freshly baked tortillas? She uncovered a disk of dough. "It will only take a few minutes. I see your Aunt Renie is home now. Go and talk with her. She's out on the porch swing."

I went outside and sat beside my aunt. This emotional quagmire had depleted me. Loose ends of my past were flopping all over. Half-moons of sweat dampen my underarms.

Renie asked, "Is Mama upset that I wasn't here to take her shopping?"

"No."

"Good. Because I'll tell Mama that Angie should have come to take her. Angie! Her ladyship."

"Angie was working with Father. I'm sure Angie would have been glad to come over if she could have. We're all excited about the baby's arrival. You'll be a great-aunt."

Renie beamed broadly. "You should have married and had children."

"I'm lesbian and not settled down."

She grimaced before turning her head. "That's your dog to walk. You know I don't approve. The Bible says you should have children."

"I don't care what the Bible says," I erupted.

"That's obvious! The Bible's rules are written from an iron pen with a diamond point."

"Renie, please stop being a trainee saint for just a few minutes of your life. Listen to what I'm saying. I've had it with this sanctimonious crap. You pontificate about my lifestyle, and I'm fed up with it." Anger choked me. "You may want to be a martyr and kowtow to God, but my probity and moral obligation is up to me. Maybe God is only a metaphor for how we should conduct our lives. Maybe hell is just a weapon held high to threaten us. And if homosexuals are going to get battered for existing, then I'm doomed. But I'm done hearing about it. Never again."

Renie was shocked at my outburst. Trembling, she covered her face. "Such words are a sacrilege."

"Maybe I also believe I'm not a sinner. And I'm sick of being profaned by all the allegations of the righteous!"

"I'm concerned for your immortal soul!"

"Renie, it's *my* soul." My anger quelled.

She stood to stretch. "I sit too long. I've stiffened up. Age chews you up like the darkness eats sunshine." She sat again, allowing her hand to fall against mine. "I shouldn't start with you. I know it isn't really your fault. With being shoved from pillar to post, you've turned out okay. I was lucky Mama and Papa raised me."

"They raised me, too."

"You were with the Randolph family at first. What are they? Rich. God says it's easier to get a camel through the eye of a needle than to get to heaven if you've got money. That old lady Randolph beat you."

"She slapped me; shook me; terrorized me. I never said she *beat* me. But perhaps it is a very thin line." Many of those caring for Jona Beck beat her terribly. They injured her and she was hospitalized. Broken, bruised, torn, raped, and battered. That was no comparison to my ordeal. "Aunt Renie, my Grandmother Randolph inflicted pain, but she didn't injure me to the point where I needed medical attention."

"She was cruel to you. She called you a dirty Mexican."

"Yes."

"Then you begin to get settled here and your mother hauls you over to Europe. Her new husband wants to sin with you."

"He didn't want to *sin* with me. He tried to rape me. I was thirteen and he attempted to sexually assault me."

"Paulo would have killed him. He wanted to go over there, but your mother immediately sent you back. We convinced Paulo he'd only get charged with assault if he went over there. Then he might lose you forever. And he had his sons to worry about. But I tell you, if my three brothers would have gotten hold of Sanford Winton, they'd have killed him. And your rich Anglos grandparents have the nerve to look down on us."

"Aunt Renie, I don't want to talk about it anymore. I've got enough conflict with which to deal." I was caught in an undertow of hidden truths. I got up from the swing. "Tell Mama I need to get back to work. I'll call her later." I leaned down, hugging Renie in my tight embrace. "Forgive me for taking it out on you."

"Taking what out?"

"The search. I suppose searching is emblematic of youth, but I'm entering my middle years. I still haven't figured it out. But you've always been good to me. You've made a visible imprint on my life."

There was a hint at smiling. "Not visible enough for attending Mass this Sunday?"

My silence settled in. "No."

"You're forgetting Mama's lunch will be ready any minute now."

"I'm not hungry. I'm too confused to be hungry."

* * *

Vamos a dar un paseo por el parque, I suggested to Nevada we meet in the park for a walk. I figured she had an hour for her late lunch. I picked up some sandwiches and chilled bottled tea so we'd have time to share.

"Looks delicious," she said as she approached the park table.

"It's only pastrami and cheese."

"I was talking about you. I'd kiss you right now if I weren't in uniform," she teased as she sat across from me. "Are you doing okay?"

Her hand touched my arm when she reached for the bag of chips. Her fingertips felt like spun silk traversing my skin. "I'm fine. I took my grandmother to the farmers' market."

"Did you have fun?"

"Not particularly. We just loaded up on produce."

"Randa, I'm glad we're taking time together. By night we're both so stressed out from everything that's happened that it's difficult to talk." She munched a chip. "I like waking in the morning with you there."

"I feel safe with you near. I was just talking with Mama Carmina and Aunt Renie. Dredging up old times, old memories. I don't know - maybe if I just admit that the case is spooking me, I'd feel better. I've witnessed the victims of a brutal torture killing. I don't know how you deal with violence and brutality."

"You could always write the society pages."

"And you could always be a dispatcher."

"Bottom line - we're doing what we believe in. That's not always easy."

"No. I guess I lack certitude about my career decisions."

When we heard a sonic boom, I flinched. Nevada's hand covers mine. "Randa, no law says you've got to stay on this story."

"Law. I don't understand the concept of law. Not really," I admitted.

* * *

After working the remainder of the afternoon, I'd gone to another safe haven. Nevada worked late so I decided to drop by Marlene's for a glass of wine. Wine was brought to the table by Alicia without my even ordering it. "Did I look as though I need a drink that badly?"

Alicia shrugged. "The recent news events makes us all need a drink. I figured Jona Beck was on the lam and there would be little more news. But three murders!"

"Beck is a nightmare."

"And you saw where those people were killed. I could barely read your story. I don't see how you held up. *Chinga!*" she cursed. "*Ella tiene mucha malicia.*"

"We knew she is evil. Just never believed how evil. *Espere hasta que todos los hechos del caso sean concocido,*" I told her to wait until all the facts of the case are known.

"*Dime lo que quieres dicer?*" Alicia asked that I tell her what I mean.

"Jona Beck might have a trail of other murders behind her.

And I mean a long trail." I lifted the wine glass. "Thanks for recognizing it's been a rough week."

"I wanted you to be the first to try this new Zinfandel," Alicia insisted. "I need a wine review."

Inhaling its fragrance, I observed, "Excellent bouquet." It swished in my mouth. "Yes. The taste is exciting."

"I hear your love life is also getting more exciting," she indicted with a mock leer.

"News travels fast," I replied. In the background Giselle's soft, sensual voice began her set with a medley of songs from the thirties.

"Love is blind and a guide dog won't help," Alicia said. "So you're staying at Nevada's house now?"

"Mostly, yes."

"Lanny Ventura is livid."

"Why would our lady of jabs and acerbic wit be upset with my social agenda?"

"You didn't confide in her about your *novia*. She found out from another source."

"Ruby! I thought I taught my friends never to reveal a source," I said with a smile. "So what did my nemesis have to say about it?"

"Just that now she knows for certain who *your inside line* to police information is. Oh, yes. And she said to tell you, 'Shame on you.'"

I laughed out loud. "And overly eulogistic comment if ever I heard one. Did Ventura say she'll be in tonight?"

"No. She said to tell you she's working on an exclusive that will have you doing a 'bitch goddess' routine for the remainder of the summer."

"If she really had anything, she'd be here rubbing it in."

"You could be right. After she closed the bar with us last night, she's probably had her liver hanging out to dry all day long. I know she wanted to find out more about your new affair."

Thankfully my cell phone bleeped. "Florez," I answered.

"Randa," my mother addressed me with formality in her voice. "I'd like to see you. Talk with you."

"I've just settled in with a nice glass of wine in front of me. I'm at a lesbian bar, Mother. A piano lounge called Marlene's. And I haven't any intention of leaving. But feel free to drop by."

"Have you been drinking?"

"Only one. So far," I answered.

"There's so much anger in your voice."

"Answer me something."

"Yes."

"Exactly when did you leave my father?"

"After you were born." Her answer was pensive.

"That answer is vague. How about specifics?"

"I now understand why they say you're a solid interviewer."

"When I'm going for the jugular, they call me a *savage* interviewer. And they're correct. I don't want lies to slip through my net. And I'm not easily distracted. Specifics."

"Fine. It was immediately after you were born. Things seemed to disintegrate while we were still in the hospital."

"And my father had no idea you were about to take his child and leave him?"

"*Our* child. I carried you within me for nine months. I gave birth to you, Randa."

"And you had him arrested for wanting to see his own daughter."

"What has he been telling you?"

"Nothing. He's too much of a gentleman to denigrate his former wife. I don't have any other questions." I felt the scorching weight of anger as I pressed the power off.

Alicia put another glass of wine in front of me. "If you were Tinkerbelle, I'd say your light is going dim."

"If I were Tinkerbelle, I'd have used my wings to escape from my bassinet thirty-two years ago."

* * *

I was on my third goblet of wine, and Giselle had just

finished her set. She'd joined Alicia and me. Alicia glanced up at the door. She leaned and whispered to me, "*Muy guapa!* She can dock her yacht in my jetty anytime."

"Very elegant," agreed Giselle as she scrutinized the woman entering. Her eyes suddenly widened recognition before she exhaled a huge gulp of air. "Geez! It is Erika Randolph!"

As I turned, my spin strained with a twisting pressure. My breathing grabbed like ancient bellows. "Mother!" I exclaimed as she approached the table. "What are you doing here?"

"My daughter issued an invitation." She sat opposite me. "I'm Randa's mother, Erika," she introduced herself to Alicia and Giselle.

Giselle was stunned. "I only have one more set to sing before closing and it has to be in front of Erika Randolph!"

"I'm a mezzo-soprano, not a critic. And I'm certain you have a wonderful voice. My daughter thinks you do," Mother graciously replied. Giselle went to the microphone, and Alicia returned to the bar. Their gaze continued to be sealed in Mother's direction. My mother had ordered a fine champagne. "Your friends are lovely. Giselle has a certain *je ne sais quoi.* Her voice is remarkable. I'm sure being…" she paused, then continued, "Sapphic, probably hasn't helped her career."

"Mother, it wouldn't help yours if you were to be discovered here. This is a gay bar. What if a tabloid spots you? Paps would love photographing you here."

Her smile was of bemusement. "I'd deal with it. I'd deal with it because at this moment there seems not to be any other way to tell my daughter how much she means to me."

"I should never have attacked you as I did. I apologize. You really shouldn't be here."

"Are you ashamed of me?" she questioned as she lifted her champagne flute and sipped.

"Of course not I'm not. But if anyone from the press sees you here, what would you say?"

"I'll tell them I'm visiting my daughter. And I'm not ashamed of you, Randa. I'm here to tell you how much I love you."

"I'm very confused right now. I don't understand the past. I don't understand why no one told me about what went on when I was born."

"It's difficult to answer for things that happened over three decades ago. I've admitted making mistakes. Time distorts the memory. Your father and I fell in love. We were married. Then it all began to unravel." Her eyes filled with tears. "I felt the constraint of being in his loving, but demanding family. I felt suffocated."

"But why?"

"My family's reserved attitude seemed to allow space. I rebelled against the coldness. Then I was in the midst of a family so entrenched in one another that... well, I felt I was becoming them. It was as though my dreams were slipping from me. All the work I'd invested in opera was evaporating away at family functions. I was miserable. And one day I found I resented your father. As sweet as he was, his love took the energies I wanted to direct toward my career."

"Then why did you have me? Father is hardly the type to have inveigled you into having his child. So why?"

Her glance lowered. "Not all pregnancies are planned. Being Catholic, abortion was never an elective. Honestly your father was so happy about my pregnancy that I may have given birth to you in order to please him. Perhaps I was hoping a baby would change my desire to sing. But it didn't. As I've confessed to you in the past, I should never have been a mother."

"Why didn't you just hand me over to him and go?"

"It wasn't that simple. I had a very difficult delivery. The doctors expressed their concern about my being able to bear more children. That put the fear of God in my parents. I often think that if I'd been able to have another child, they would have relinquished you without a fight."

"So your parents realized I may be an end-all to their bloodline." I barked a pathetic laugh borne of discovery. It was beneath a layer of disgust. "They sequestered me like a prize brooding mare in order to continue their lineage. Maybe if they fixed me up with a nice pale, blond guy they could even get some of the Hispanic blood diluted in time. Amazing. The kicker is I'm not the grand dame of maternity. Now that is heavy irony."

"I don't care about bloodline. I care about you. Randa, no matter how my parents attempted to keep you, your father never gave up his fight for custody. When you were old enough to make a choice, I was not your choice."

"Because you left me behind with your mother. She hated me. I see why now. Not only wasn't I her cup of tea, but it was my birth that destroyed the promise of future grandchildren. That's why she really despised me."

"You say she was cruel to you. But if she were, why wasn't she cruel to me when I was a child?"

"Because you were a beautiful blonde child. I was filled with Mexican blood. She hated that. And the thought of my being her sole blood heir must have constituted a very deep disappointment. I don't know her rationale. I only know my early childhood went beyond emotional neglect. It was very near torture."

"Torture is a bit melodramatic. You had the best nannies."

"They had days off. Even as a small child I recognized your mother's loathing of me. She often grabbed my arms and violently shook me. She shook me until I feared for my life. There were times when my head ached for days after her attack. That's what they were - attacks. Then the slapping began. Not as harsh at first, but it progressed. It was only after the time she hit me so hard that my teeth dug into my lip that I told the nanny. It was explained away. Your mother said I'd fallen. Then she said all Mexicans lie."

"Why wasn't it brought to my attention until after you decided you must live with the Florez family? That did make your motives questionable."

"My treatment was the reason I wanted to live with my father. Why can't you believe me just once? Why can't you listen to what I'm saying? The physical damage inflicted by Lenora Randolph has healed. The emotional injury has ravaged me. She called me a dirty little Mexican liar. That's how she referred to me. Only a bigot says that to a kid, or to anyone. She often opened the door and told me to go back to the slums where I belonged. Try looking out at a terrifyingly strange world when you're barely past the toddler years. Hit the bricks, kid," I said before my brief laughed converted to dampened eyes. Catching a sob, I wiped my tears away with a cocktail napkin.

"You never told me that."

"She spat threats in my face often enough. If I told you, she warned I'd never see you again. I'd never see my father again. I'd be sent away. It isn't difficult to intimidate a four-year old. A five-year old. And thankfully that's as far back as I can remember."

"Because of my mother's aristocracy, she's never been a warm person, but I've never known her to be coldhearted. And I've never known her to be untruthful."

"Malice of memory."

"Randa, we can continue blaming others forever. Perhaps my mother didn't want you in her life at one time, and now you don't want her in yours. I understand your feeling of displeasure."

"Displeasure doesn't scratch the surface."

"A woman is dying. Her dying request is to see her granddaughter. It's all she asks. Your grandmother has always feared death. She's very near death at this moment. And she's not asking for her husband, her daughter, her priest, she's begging for you." Tears spilled over her eyes. She dabbed them. "You just can't be so heartless as to deny her final request."

"What makes you think I can't?"

"Because your Paulo's child."

Alicia appeared. "Ms. Randolph, I hate to bother you, but the group is getting ready for the last couple of songs. Is there any way we could get you to sing for us? Everyone would be so honored?"

"I'm terribly sorry, but I haven't rehearsed," she began.

"Mother," I interrupted, "no one here can tell the difference between perfection and just belting out a good rendition. Singing is the most important thing in your life. Sing. Sing a song for me. It's been a long time."

My mother nodded. "I'll sing one of the songs I sang to you when you were a baby." She tentatively stood at the microphone.

I listened to the lyrics of "My Funny Valentine." My moistened eyes misted over when I hear the words about smiling with my heart. At that moment I felt as near to understanding my mother as I'd ever been. Our glance merged.

Each day is Valentine's Day, was the final lyrical line. My mother had fallen in love with her art. She had then fallen in love with my father. But he was to become an interloper. Her decision had to be made. Perhaps it was only when entertaining that my mother was able to smile with her heart.

My mother's performance brought everyone to their feet. Before tabloids could be called in, we left the club. Mother decided I should not drive under the influence. I joked that it was a bad idea to get arrested by one's love interest. Mother and her chauffeured limousine would take me home. In the morning, I'd catch a ride back in with Nevada and pick up the rental car.

Once inside the spacious limousine, I viewed the amber skylight beneath the burnished bronze color of night.

When we passed the park, I knocked on the glass window to attract the limousine driver's attention. I requested that we enter, and stop when we neared my favorite fountain. "Mother, let's walk a few minutes. I can use the fresh air."

"Yes you can," Mother agreed. "At this altitude two glasses of champagne makes me giddy."

We walked for a few moments. I pointed skyward. "Look at the stars. Did you know that some of the brightest starlight comes from collapsed stars?"

Her eyes closed as she remembered. "My father used to tell me when someone dies their soul becomes a star."

"Maybe so."

"Lovely to think it might be true."

I watched the fountain sprinkling into its base. The water was streaked with spectre-colored reflections. We began our walk across the grasses back to the limousine. I stopped and suddenly requested, "Mother, take off your shoes. Let's walk barefoot in the grasses."

"Randa?" An expression of bewilderment covered her face.

"Please. You once said you wished you could walk barefoot in the grass. You can. If we don't do it now, we may never share this opportunity again."

We took off our shoes, and we walked barefoot. The grasses crinkled beneath our feet. For the next half hour, we strolled. There are few words spoken. We shared only being together. But it seemed enough.

On the drive home, she reached to cup my face in her hands. She mouthed the words, saying she loved me. I smiled. I was certain of one thing - she wanted to love me. She told me of a time when I was an infant and she'd dressed me in a pale yellow dress. Her mother insisted that she change it because the color made me look too dark. Mother said it was one of the only times she had disobeyed her formidable mother. After that the dress had disappeared. She inquired where the little yellow outfit had gone. Lenora Randolph answered that I'd outgrown it. Although my mother knew better, she also felt powerless. I felt sorrow that my mother had been raised in the turmoil of a selfish, demanding human being.

When we arrived at Nevada's I leaned to kiss my mother's cheek. "Thank you, Mother. For everything."

"Thank you. Our walk was wonderful. I love you more than you'll ever know." She hugged my neck. With that contact of our skin, for the first time in a very long time, I understood touch. It was when love allowed us to experience where one person ends and another person begins. "Perhaps you are the only perfection I've ever given to the world."

I returned her hug. "Your voice is precision. Perfection."

"Becoming a precise person leaves little time for imperfection. And perhaps that is where true life resides."

I paused, blinking away tears. "Do you believe the night has ended so quickly?" I asked.

Mother turned her head away from my vision. "Yes. Times like we shared tonight pass too quickly. However, it is a very long time until morning when one is lonely."

Kieran York

CHAPTER 10

Friday

Although inside the tender wrap of Nevada's arms, the night was spent in a very barbed cave of nightmares. Those deathly dreams replayed as if I were deep down inside a nonsensical pit from which there was no escape. I swatted shadowy phantoms. Each time I was nudged awake by terror, I contemplated my fear. I attempted to dispel panic with sensible, philosophic thought. Dreams made a mockery of reality.

My profession was to create accurate hearsay for others with my stories in *The Mirror's* corridor of columns. Sentences, paragraphs, quotations all were today's literary attempts to explain the human condition. Journalism reported the triumphs, the peril, and the flaws. The best intentioned reporter must acknowledge the fallibility of the human spirit, as well as the durability of the human heart.

Working the crime beat had inflicted the worst images of humanity upon my dreams. The temperature of pain seemed never to be normal; never neutral. It spiked the subconscious and sometimes produced intrusive horror.

According to the radio alarm's digital numerals, it was five o'clock in the morning. A large bedroom window corroborated the time with a sky as tawny as a lion's coat. Dim lighting spread across my lover's naked skin. Nevada's heartbeat ticked against mine. Her breath was warm as it fanned my shoulder.

Before sleeping, her eyes had filled with romance and mystery. She took me on a rapturous sexual odyssey. Waking, I thought of her warmth.

I jumped when her telephone rang. Sleepily, she reached for the receiver. "Repeat, please," she requested. Her eyes began to focus. "I can't believe it. Damn it to hell!" she bellowed expletives into the mouthpiece. "What time did it happen?" She reached for the lamp. Blinking rapidly when the light hit her face, she shaded her eyes. Her hand then nervously combed back through her hair. "I'll tell her. I'm on my way." She hung up.

"What?"

"Randa, I've got a message for you from Fritz. He says you're even now. He's giving you the first notification, so you can get a head start. Nevada stood, motioning for me. "We've got time for a two minute wake-up shower. I'll explain on the way."

Before we reach the bathroom, I pulled her around. "What the hell is going on?"

"Jona has just kicked a hornet's nest. She's killed a sheriff's deputy in Georgetown. Four others are dead and one is in critical condition."

"Jesus!" The oak floor boarding beneath me seems to weaken along with my knees. "I've got to phone it in."

"Come on, a quick couple of minutes under the shower will wake you. Clear your head. You can telephone your city desk on our drive downtown."

Our hasty shower was silent of words.

We rushed to Nevada's truck. She drove toward my rental car downtown. I called *The Mirror* giving them the story. I was dispatched to Georgetown where a photographer would meet me.

I reported what Nevada had told me. The murders happened less than twenty minutes ago. A fourteen-year veteran law enforcement officer was shot to death while responding to an alarm at the local convenience store. The convenience store clerk was murdered after sounding the alarm. Two customers inside the store were gunned down and killed. One male was in his late teens, and one seventeen-year old female. The male's older brother was also shot and remained in critical condition. A young mother in a parking lot had been run over and killed as Jona began her getaway. The mother's five-year old son was at her side. The boy was shaken, but physically only bruised and scratched from being thrown to the pavement. An elderly couple had just pulled their vehicle into the lot in time to see the final crime, hit and run, being committed. The shooter fired a round into their windshield. They were unharmed. The identification was positive. It was Jona Beck. She appeared to be alone.

My voice cracked when verifying the mother's death. "Five deaths," I reported to the city editor before clicking off the phone conversation.

Nevada skirted traffic with skill. "Jona Beck is smearing a trail of blood. She's been lucky until now. Her Tombstone recklessness has hit the wrong target."

Meaning?"

"Meaning you can't kill a badge without the possibility of being taken down."

"She smoked four besides a deputy," I reminded Nevada.

"Once we find her, it will probably be over. Chances are she'll be killed in a shootout. Or a suicide."

"Enforcement now wants to kill her? It's true about keeping the code. You mean even if she surrenders she'll be killed?" I asked disbelievingly.

Nevada inhaled deeply. "She's probably very dead if we get within shooting distance. You know she won't relinquish her gun without a fight."

I repeated my question. "You're saying enforcers would want to murder her?"

"Randa, I'm not telling you this right now. If a fellow officer is murdered, no one gives a damn about talking the perp down. Dainty stops. If our relationship is going to work, it's got to be totally honest. No secrets. I'm telling you something very confidential. Only one force stands between peace and total chaos. If we allow that line to be penetrated without consequence, we're inviting complete lawlessness."

There was a layer of silence. "But murder is murder."

"You can't understand. Not really. She will fire on us. Randa, people are jaded to violence. The soul of society has been bombed out by crime. Of all people, you should understand that we are at war. You see as much of it as I do."

"But I'd never kill unless it was self-defense."

"Maybe you can't see the big picture."

"Big picture?"

"If a cop had offed Jona Beck when she was standing over the body of Maynard Jones at least eight lives would have been spared. Eight innocent lives on one side of the battleground. One dirtball nut case on the other. My profession puts me on the line. I'll tell you where my priorities take me. If a brother or sister is murdered, a part of enforcement has been killed. Jona Beck doesn't deserve life. Those eight people deserved to live." Tears filled Nevada's eyes. "If she had a loaded gun aimed at me, I'd take Jona down in a millisecond, without so much as a blink backward." Nevada flushed with anger.

I glanced away, not wanting to understand what I heard. "You're excusing an execution. I don't understand." Nevada was emotionally angered by the killing, I deliberated. I was sure she wouldn't condone murdering even a cop killer.

"You needn't understand. I *do* understand. It's my badge that's a target."

"Maybe she'll turn herself in with witnesses around. She's got to know the hunt is intensifying."

"Right. We know that even if Vivian is sprung, she'll be under constant surveillance. So Jona's resources are becoming scarce."

"But she does have other friends. And she can rely on their help. None of them will dime her out."

"They may not rat on her for money, but she's got to get to them." Nevada parked in front of Marlene's near my rental car. "Be careful in Georgetown. I'll let you know if I hear anything else. I'm certain I'll be pulling a double shift."

I got out of the truck and walked around it. Touching Nevada's hand, I suddenly understood the vulnerability of loving someone in a dangerous profession. My fingers squeezed hers. "You be careful. I don't want to lose you. It's taken me years to find you. There's a word in Spanish. *Tesoro.* It means…"

"Treasure," she translated. "You're mine, too."

* * *

Georgetown was one of Colorado's historic silver mining towns. The mountain community was forty-five miles west of Denver. Its brick and board Victorian homes, old-time saloons, and shops had been refurbished, colorfully painted, and preserved to maintain a turn-of-the-century style.

On the outskirts, entering Georgetown, was a small convenience store. It was the battleground where a massacre took place an hour or two ago.

As I entered the area, the ambiance had been made somber by death. I exited my car. Police radios squawked. A knot of people had formed near the side of yellow police scene tape. One frantic woman screamed. Hair tumbled across her face as her head shook violently. She had seen the glistening blood on the pavement. Her eyes pinched shut as a gurney was wheeled toward the county coroner's vehicle.

From my vantage point there was a huge quadrant of clear sky where lines of sunlight pierced through pines. The scrim of mountain ledges crossed the horizon. Wilderness had become a sardonic travesty.

Today there were five, maybe six if the other victim died. If one assumed the death of Simone Milton to be counted – the tally went to seven deaths. Jona often told me she wanted to pay back the world. Payment in full would only end when she died, she told me during one of our taped interviews. She was amortizing the evil payback scheme.

Earth was her holding tank. Those of us who despised violence and death shared this planet with her evil. Her victims did not wish to be eternally locked in early graves. If they were now in some immortal safe zone called heaven, so be it. If not, and their caskets closed prematurely to family and friends, then Jona Beck's worst crimes would go forever unpunished.

My jaw clamped with rage. I was of the opinion humanity's malevolence remained the most obscene mystery of all.

* * *

Lanny Ventura whispered to me, "We're doing live coverage. I'm on in a couple minutes."

"You missed the witness' interviews. And you've got competition. I'll have the in-depth coverage. I just filed my scoop in our *E-Edition.* Your sound bites don't go far."

"Yeah, Gonzo," she agreed. "As we speak, a phalanx of cameras gathers for their snippet of news. I even see some of the national reporters. Damn, big shot network crews apply lots of makeup. Their cheeks are going to look like cockatiels. Buccaneering through life in Armani suits with their 'happy trails' talk. Slick as a bus station's chili con carne. All their cloying sugar sermons. My TV's mute button is worn away with use," Lanny confessed.

"Best watch your criticism of them," I teased. "You may be televising live."

"Huh. And worse yet, the paparazzi are now out in force. Too bad they don't go back to chasing starlets."

I sighed. "In the parlance of newspapers, they are the smudged ink. My lexicon is more precise. They are crap mongers. Hideous crime must intrigue them."

"This weird series of crimes must have them orgasmic." She paused, her eyes narrowed. "Speaking of sex, have you given Nevada a couple of runs around the block to see if she's worth keeping?"

"I have and she is."

"But you must have left very early this morning. You arrived before I did and I drove like a bat out of hell the minute it came over the police band." Her expression was quizzical. "By the time I arrived, you'd been here at least half an hour."

Lanny was baiting me to find out what I saw before she turned up. "I arrived only shortly before you did."

I wouldn't tell her how lengthy my report had been. I'd interviewed as many people as I could. After Hank arrived, he shot area crime scene photos. Then a report was announced about a problem nearby. Hank was deployed to a small cabin up the canyon.

It was the location of a break in just a short distance out of town. It had been unlawfully entered sometime during the night, and I was betting it was Jona's stop off. A police report told how a neighbor had called in. There was a vacant cabin's suspicious open door. Upon checking, authorities found there had been a break in. The owners were tracked down while visiting in Wyoming. They confirmed that they had several guns and ammunition. Two were semiautomatics. If the firearms weren't there, the guns and ammo had been stolen. Jona was now equipped with an arsenal.

"So what happened before I got here? I know something must have transpired. You're looking smug."

"Read it in *The Mirror*."

"I like my eyes too much to read your rag. You probably were busy with a story culled from a literary volume on sordid crime. Probably some Sherlockian masterpiece where a woman comes off her spool and ices a dozen people."

"A dozen may not be far off. The number is mounting. If Simone Milton wasn't with Jona, she might already be an additional victim."

"The doc. Hell, she offered herself up. Jesus! From shrink savior of a wayward fruitcake, to becoming the appendage of that fruitcake on a killing spree. Simone shed the layers of her prestigious background quickly, didn't she?"

"Yes. The big question is if she's still alive." I stepped back. "So much for this little convocation of ace reporters. Press conference over, story filed. My work here is finished. I've got to dash. People to see."

Lanny's visage conveyed intensity. "You're done here? You must have additional information. Don't tell me you've scooped me again!"

"Probably." After several steps and no rejoinder, I swirled back around. "Yes, maybe I did. Hooray for me."

Suddenly Lanny announced, "Lucia Gomez didn't show up for work yesterday. I know where she is. And I think she knows where Jona is hiding out."

"What else do you know?" My question prodded. "Come on, it's important."

"Listen to this noon's crime commentary."

Realizing that my face was probably Kabuki white, I glared. "Right." I couldn't be certain if she had anything or not. She bluffed with the best of them.

Lanny stretched and yawned. "Hey, I'm sorry. I just have more cooperative sources."

"Sorry! Aunt Renie says that *sorry* doesn't feed the terrier."

Lanny issued a placatory smile. "My aunt has a saying, too. 'I'm just happy as an itchy pig at a rough post,' is what my auntie would say." Her expression was a gloating smirk. It was nearly lopsided with restraint from laughter. She quickly became somber as she looked around. "God, this is awful."

"Lanny, do you believe there is a supreme being?"

"I believe only that there is a supreme pizza."

* * *

On the way back down the mountainside toward Denver I called the office. With my earphone secure, I knew my report was being transcribed as I spoke. I gave additional information for the extra edition about the stolen guns. Three handguns and a hunting rifle had been taken. Jona's prints were left behind as if they were her calling card.

A smudge of smog appeared before I reached the city's edge. It was as if my heart conked out when I reached Colfax Avenue. My stomach retched. A thin film of sweat materialized on my brow. Bloodshed unsettled me.

I felt the need to retrace my steps. On a hunch, I would begin at The Scorpion Tattoo Parlor. An interview with the self-styled idiot, Eddie Hunter, held no appeal to me. I'd just left the scene of a multiple murder. The pain gestating in my mind should have prepared me for anything. I was seeking out life's elixir among a barbarian.

Later I planned to drop by The Raven's Talon to see if I could locate Lucia Gomez. Lanny was probably attempting to throw me off the scent of any real story she might have. But checking it out was mandatory. I'd take a crown of garlic to ward off evil spirits.

* * *

"You don't want fine art on your epidermal canvas?" Eddie Hunter questioned when I entered his tattoo parlor storefront. There was a faintly perceptible tremor in his reedy voice. His lips peeled back in a tight smile.

"Eddie, you've got a smart mouth. If I didn't think you'd enjoy it, I'd belt you so hard you'd be wearing your underwear as a necklace." I paused, coughed, and pointed in the direction of his cigarette.

With a grimace, he ground it out. "You've got a fucking nerve. You come in here treating me like a social leper. Now you even object to my smoking in my own shop." He wore an absurd conical leather breastplate over a pitch black shirt.

"Nerve, yes. I also have a pretty decent sense of smell. This store reeks of filth, and urine, so why not include smoke."

"Lovely of you to stop by, bitch," he uttered nearly inaudibly. "Next time bring your own fucking air spray to rid my establishment of your arrogance."

"Do you believe in God?" I suddenly asked.

"Aw hell, God's gone missing and you think I had something to do with it." His cackle was sharp.

"Eddie, being a *guardan un secreto*," I said in Spanish, "you risk getting hassled by the cops. Your pal, Vivian, was busted for aiding and abetting. You're not far behind. The cops are going to be down here. No telling what they'll find in your back room."

"I got nothing to hide."

"Vivian didn't think they'd nab her either. She's finding herself in the accomplice category. That can mean a life sentence. Last time I checked, she's in the slammer. Saving you a place."

"Not me."

I leaned over the counter. I gave his breastplate a rough tap. "Cross swords with the cops and you'll find they have no sense of humor on this one. Jona's death tally just jumped."

Shocked eyes told he hadn't been listening to the news reports. "I'm not talking with you." His words were contemptuous. "You're fucking bonkers."

"Maybe I am. Life has suddenly become a *manicomio*. I'm here."

"Hell, you're off-the-charts, fucking nuts, lady."

"I have a very bizarre plan that might get your cooperation. Let's invite the cops in here. I'm getting desperate enough to roll around on your dirty floor so I can call the authorities and report an assault. I'm a respected member of the press. No one will doubt the validity of my little black lie. This lie will be worth my personal integrity. They can haul you off and interrogate the hell out of you. Damn it, I'm tired of seeing corpses," I lashed as I was staring him down. "If you don't say something, I swear I'll execute my plan. You probably can't afford any more negative publicity."

"Look, I don't know that much. I know about..." he bit off his word mid-sentence.

"About what? I can dial 911 faster than you can get me out of here. Answer me."

"Vivian does have a cabin or something up in the mountains somewhere."

"But we've checked building permits, addresses, property tax listings. Our research team comes up with nothing. She's not listed and her partner isn't listed."

"Maybe not." His hand formed into a fist. "Aw, fuck! I'm not going down because of some crazy bitches. Vivian bought some raw land. She had a trailer moved up there so it may not even be listed as a residence. It's very remote. But I don't know where it is."

My mind whirled. If it were remote maybe there wouldn't be resident listings of any kind. It was probably generator powered, so there weren't utilities. Well water, no hook ups. Vivian hid her identity, why not her respite. "Do you know when Vivian purchased the property or the trailer?"

"Two summers ago. I don't know exactly when. Beginning of summer, I think."

I rushed to the door. "Thanks for the info. I'm glad I don't need to dirty my clothing on your floor." I knew he would rat out the women. "You're a real prince."

"Don't tell anyone where you heard it."

"Your confidentiality is safe with me. In your case it isn't to protect you. It's because I don't give a rat's ass about you. You're a nonentity. Let's keep it that way."

I crossed the street to my rental car. After slamming the door shut, I methodically made notations. Then I called the office. I'd need a list of all trailers sold two years ago. ASAP. I'd need records from moving and transport companies that might have delivered a trailer to anywhere in the Georgetown area. ASAP. Mostly, I'd need a lucky break to find Vivian's hideout.

After hanging up, I laughed out loud envisioning my tumble across Scorpion Tattoo Parlor's grimy floor. Then my laughter stopped. I wondered if I truly would have lied by falsely accusing Eddie Hunter. I was face to face with the tangibility of my honor. Truth and the purity of truths ideal! I'd threatened to relinquish both. I savored the moment of self-examination just before vindication. It was cathartic. Then I turn on the auto's ignition. Information had been hard won.

Phase one of my sewer crawl had been productive.

* * *

Most of the afternoon was spent in my office attempting to get a fix on where Jona Beck might be hiding. Two researchers worked diligently beside me. We chased information on trailer sales and mobile home movers to no avail.

When Nevada phoned, I told her the latest. Nevada, in turn, shared that Lucia had slipped surveillance. Since Lucia Gomez was not the sharpest tack on the bulletin board, I suggested she might show up at The Raven later. After all, she didn't like missing Friday nights at the bar. The temptation for a little action might be too much for Lucia to resist. Nevada replied the cops were covering it. I argued that Lucia slithered away unnoticed from undercover – as did Vivian. Nevada instructed me to stay away from The Raven. We both knew I'd do everything I could to locate Lucia.

I told Nevada that I first planned on stopping by my father's shop. Next, I'd drop by Marlene's for a quick sandwich. I didn't mention that I'd then go on to The Raven's Talon. I'd mill around the S&M dive in search of Lucia, or anyone else who might have a clue to the whereabouts of Jona Beck. Also if anyone knew about Vivian/Clare's vacation home. There might even be a color story or two.

I knew Nevada sensed my plan when she again cautioned me about getting involved with danger.

We ended our conversation with words of love.

* * *

My father had taken a late afternoon break from under the hood of a beautifully restored antique Porsche. I told him of last night's encounter with my mother. "It seems preposterous," he stated with a glee that made his eyes sparkle. "Erika went to a gay and lesbian bar."

We sat in the waiting room adjacent his auto shop office. "As I live and breathe, it's true. Mother sang. Marlene's was rocking."

"Was it a culture shock?" he questioned. "On either side of the stage?"

"Everyone loved her. And Mother took everything in stride."

"Wait until she discovers it wasn't a paid gig," he chided playfully.

"Has Mother called you?"

"Not today. She will. Maybe she'll offer to come by the shop and perform a set for my customers." He reflected a moment. "I'm glad you had time together. Have you reconsidered seeing your grandmother?"

"Not really. She has her husband and her daughter at her side."

"She wants to see her granddaughter." Father frowned. He

rubbed his oil-stained hands on a rag he'd been twisting since I'd arrived. "Your grandmother must care about you if she's so determined to see you."

"I'm her only grandchild." I paused before asking, "Did you know that because my mother had a difficult delivery with me, it was unlikely she could have another child?"

"I don't believe she would have wanted another child."

"Did you know that she didn't want children?"

"Of course not. Children were mentioned before marriage. She gave me the impression that she longed for the family life she didn't have. Then, after she became pregnant, she withdrew. Randa, if she would have told me that she didn't want children, I would have accepted it."

"You loved her that much?"

"Yes. I wanted to believe, no matter what, our lives could blend together. She knew that our parting was inevitable. Sadly, loving doesn't come easily to Erika."

"*Muy triste.* Very sad."

"It may seem she lives with a desolate heart and austere spirit where love is concerned. But she does love you, Randa. I believe she once loved me. Maybe gullibility is a parable of youth."

"What if I take after her?"

"Love isn't instinctual to Erika. But you're naturally warm and giving."

"I felt love from my Florez branch."

"You were a natural at watching Rogerio and Benjy when they were small. You're still always there for them. They go to you with problems. You bail out Benjy. I know you helped Rogerio and Teresa with the down payment on their home. Rogerio told me you did."

"He'd have done it for me." I glanced away a moment. "Like you, he'll make a wonderful father. And Teresa will make a loving mother."

"You'll make a loving aunt."

"Yes." I wouldn't ask my father if he thought my ability to love in a complete way would finally happen. The ebullience of new love was ominous. Truth couldn't be circumvented when love was truly involved. Although love may be the favorite syllable of hope, I was frightened of uttering it. And perhaps I was most terrified of experiencing it.

However, I would become a loving aunt. Of that I was certain.

* * *

On my way to the bar, I'd stopped off at the Homicide Division. Fritz Truesdale was out. No one else had any pertinent information to divulge. So arriving at Marlene's comforted me. It was a respite.

As I was seated at Marlene's piano bar, I admitted to myself that the day had been a hell sampler.

Del Croft nodded. His trim, delicate body leaned with grace toward his piano. He seemed giddy with elation as his fingers swirled. I'd ordered a sauvignon blanc, and whatever Del wished to drink. "Thanks, sweetheart," he said. "I'm playing amusingly uplifting music because I'm about to have a conniption fit. A bad news day, huh?"

Alicia poured wine slowly. "Here you go."

I confided, "I've been gutter tromping. It was a grotesque day with ugly crime."

"That's why I brought you a great wine." She lifted the bottle so I could see the label. "And I thank you for having your mother drop by last night. She is *absolutely* divine. It's all we've been talking about. What a stellar performance your mother gave."

"Has Lanny Ventura been in this evening?"

"No. But it's early. Maybe later."

"Maybe," I responded.

"She's probably out chasing down a lead. It must be something to do with that weird Jona. I can't understand how you and Lanny can chase stories about murder all the time. It's too spooky for me." Alicia cringed. "Lanny told me about the gruesome details. The carnage! Lanny has a tough demeanor, so I can almost accept her chasing after the gory news. But you seem way too sensitive. Like maybe you should be doing the theatre reviews."

"You may be correct about my belonging in another area. There are times I hate the crime beat," I confessed to us both.

"Why did you become a crime reporter if you hate it?"

"I don't know. It's where I began. A crime reporter job was open."

"You look *so* unhappy tonight. What else is bugging you?"

Looking away, I sighed. "I'm just not anticipating my evening assignment. After I grab a bite to eat, I'm going over to The Raven."

"That *dive*?"

"I'm looking for Lucia Gomez."

Alicia ruffled her hair. "You might get sucked into some huge pagan revival."

"I'll take my crucifix."

"Why not take Nevada along for protection."

"They wouldn't talk if I had a cop at my side." I took a deep breath, and then gulped down the last mouthful of wine. "And I need to see what, if anything, Ventura might have. I don't want to lose an exclusive to Ventura because I'm wussy."

I felt a mask of solitude covering my face. For each twisted layer of evil, I come nearer to knowing the mind of a killer. The question was: had it gone from assignment to compulsion? And if so, why wasn't I notified?

* * *

"Come here often?" the familiar, well-modulated woman's voice behind me asked.

I whirled around. Looking in the face of a woman I dated many years ago, I exclaimed. "Dionne!" There was a voltage of amazement in my voice. I hadn't expected to ever see anyone I knew, much less dated, in The Raven's Talon. And Dionne Quinn was a definite shocker.

"What are you doing here, darling?" Her eyebrow lifted. Her lips framed a smile. Those smoldering hazel eyes that I'd been so smitten with in years past always seemed the key to her sensuality. Her regal face, surrounded by long, lush auburn curls had changed very little. With long, willowy limbs, a delicate sexy walk, and her air of confidence, she had been pursued by nearly everyone I knew. She sensed my amazement. "I wasn't aware you liked rough stuff."

"I'm here on assignment. Not a sadomasochistic sexual relationship."

She paused. "Ah, yes. The Jona Beck story. I was rather hoping that I'd miscalculated your inclination years ago. You're not here on a dominatrix tryout?"

"I'm not into this. To each her own, but it isn't my choice."

"You didn't expect to find Jona around here, did you?"

"Not at all. This would be the last bar she'd be. I'm looking for Lucia Gomez."

"Every cop in town is looking for Lucia. And I guess every reporter as well."

"At least me."

As if intercepting my thought, Dionne answered, "Yes. I was in this world when we dated. And I did want to go to bed with you. But after a few times out with you, I realized you weren't interested in my lifestyle. Does that answer your question?"

"I had no idea." She'd changed, I thought as I studied her. Her dress was different than when we dated. Tonight she wore a dark satiny blouse that billowed at the shoulders - rather like an Elizabethan poet's shirt. Her trousers and boots were dark leather. Around her neck was a thick gold chain. From it dangled an oversized set of dice. "A patchwork of women have made up my dating quilt, but you're correct. I am amazed."

"I always felt it was a pity that you weren't interested."

"And I'm with someone now, so it's a little late for recruiting."

She shrugged indifference. "Besides, you're looking for Lucia."

"Do you know her?"

"Not well. She isn't my type. She has leapt from obscurity to becoming famous for having been Jona's sidekick. Or slave."

"I don't suppose you know where she might be hanging out?"

"The manager, Donna, might have an idea. But as I mentioned, we never traveled in the same circle. That entire group was far too combustible for me."

"Donna said she wouldn't talk with me last time I was in. So I'm guessing if she knows, she isn't telling. And you have no other guesses?"

"If I had any idea, I'd tell you. For old time's sake."

"I appreciate that." I pulled a card from my pocket. "In case you hear anything."

She took it and then handed me one of hers. "In case you break up, or get bored."

Glancing down, I read the name, "Tyche. The Greek goddess?"

"Very good. Yes. I've taken the name. Every good dominatrix selects her appellation of choice." She lifted the dice that hung between her breasts. "Tyche is the goddess of fate. She uses dice to select sacrificial victims. Dice - oracular knucklebones, actually."

"Sounds as if it might be a good nickname for Jona."

"After all your research, don't know her *call* name?"

"I had no idea she might have been retrofitted with a new sobriquet."

Dionne laughed huskily, with sensuality. "See, I *really* could have taught you plenty."

With a good natured return laugh, I concurred, "I don't doubt that for an instant. So can you teach me Jona's nickname?"

"I'm not sure. It's kind of a bedroom thing - the names. Does Jona sport ink?"

"She has a tattoo of a container. Ancient jar or maybe it's a vase." I thought back to the tattoo on her arm. "Yes, a vase."

"A *pithos*?"

"Yes. That's right. And a small cornucopia on her hand."

Dionne smiled. "Remember your mythology? I was always impressed that you seemed to know a great deal about myths."

"Yes. It made my study of literature a little easier." I

mulled, "A cornucopia and a *pithos*. I'm stumped."

"Just a guess, but remember Pandora?"

"Sure. Of course, it wasn't really a box that was opened – unleashed. It was actually a honey vase. Pandora had a vase that was supposed to be filled with blessings, but instead held curses. And the cornucopia is a womb symbol anciently used as a vessel of death and rebirth." I searched my memory. "And if I'm not mistaken, Vivian once called her Pandy in an interview. I remember putting it down to her being stoned."

I quickly texted the news desk to begin a search on sites that listed Pandora or Pandy. While there were probably too many – at this point anything we could get would be of assistance.

After several moments, Dionne said, "It's a good bet Jona's name is Pandora."

"Thanks for the help." I suddenly blurted, "Why, Dionne?"

"Pain is life's finest indictor. Actually, fear of pain is the truest proof you're alive. I want to experience all of the most relevant aspects of life. Power, fear, pain. All the truly intense portions of living." She read my skepticism. "You don't believe that, do you?"

"I'm certain you find me sexually repressed, but I find torture depraved. For me at least. To each her own. Just not for me."

"You'll never see into your own soul." Her enigmatic smile was released.

"Isn't it a dangerous way to go soul searching?"

"Randa, restraint is the key."

"What if restrain isn't used?"

Her glance skittered. "There's a universal code word. If 'mercy' is called, it is, or should be delivered to a woman."

"Have you ever been hurt?"

She finished my question, "Badly roughed up? A time or two."

"I never really knew you, did I?"

"Would you have understood?"

"I don't understand now."

"Are you certain you wouldn't like a demonstration?" she invited playfully.

"No. Dionne, stay safe." I reached to shake her hand. She took me in her arms. I remembered the feel of her - the fit of her body against mine.

"Pity," she murmured.

My walk away from her was something we both knew I'd do. Maybe she figured it was only polite to offer.

On the way out of Raven's front door, I bumped into a woman with turbid eyes. Her snarling hair was a burnished helmet of tangles. With overt pugnacity her fist balled. She turned to me and seethed, "Incoming artillery."

Her comment seemed bewilderingly out of context. Then I saw a police cruiser slowly driving by with its spotlight beaming across the building's exterior wall. The woman issued a macabre, chilling laugh. She leered at me. Quickly, I scurried away.

The dark scowl of night followed me to my car. I coaxed enough courage to remain parked across the street from the bar for an additional ten minutes. It was dubious, but I hoped Lucia might arrive. Time allowed me a chance to nudge myself from the black blankness of a mind in shock.

To myself, I recited Dionne's final lamentation - pity. Pity my caresses wouldn't have satiated her.

* * *

My intention was to get at least a couple hours of good sleep before Nevada arrived back at her home. Clearly by the time I'd showered and tucked myself under her quilt, I was exhausted. But there were noises outside her bedroom window. Wind was blowing tree branches against the siding. Each time I heard the scrape, I popped up from bed like a piece of toast from a toaster.

My eyes shut with blinking ticks. I experienced the feel of being locked up. Jona Beck was probably not frightened. She was living her outlaw fantasy. She was very much in control, since death was at her will, and she executed it freely. With precise vengeance against humanity, she wantonly murdered. In her wake there were mourners. And there was fear.

Before falling into the narrow hole of sleep, I glanced up at the moon. It was the color of polished aluminum.

* * *

"I'm glad this Dionne person didn't convince you to select a new roost," Nevada joked. It was just after midnight when she climbed into bed and took me in her arms.

"Dionne Quinn was the very last person I'd expected to see at The Raven. Guess I should learn to read labels more carefully. Dionne has it all. She's intelligent with a terrific personality, and she is very, very luscious."

"You really must have had a thing for her."

"All the women did. I wasn't sure what it was she didn't like about me."

"You never actually made love with her?"

"We made out. We were mildly intimate, but when it got too hot, she bailed. She didn't strike me as the inhibited type, but when it came to heavy breathing, she scrammed. Women bolting from my embrace meant I'm not appealing."

Nevada murmured, "You are appealing, definitely." She paused, frowning. "Maybe there's someone in my past in that lifestyle, but I don't think so,"

"I understand Jona being in that kind of life. She had a very dark, deep scar inflicted on her heart. We're talking the rape and sodomizing of a child. But from what I gathered, Dionne's family life was wonderful. Everything about her always seemed too perfect."

"Come to find out, she's into the violence game. Fifty shades of gay. A real complicated rainbow. But thankfully, you turned down her invitation."

"She must have viewed me as a kite that would never fly." My pause was lengthy. "This happened way before Alison. Alison was into her own thing. I've come to believe she was an expert in emotional sadism."

"From everything you told me about her, she was an expert controller. Randa," she whispered in my ear, "I'm here now." We settled into a tender embrace. Her lips softly skimmed mine. Her fingertips traced my neck. I trembled. Nevada's touch was as sensual and tender as being sprinkled with blossoms.

CHAPTER 11

Saturday

Within the heart of summer one expected to be knee high in Colorado wild flowers. Instead, I was inside Denver's midsection. My limbs were leaden from lack of sleep. My mind seemed woolly. It wasn't as though I'd been plunged into exhaustion from one night's loss of sleep - but it was one week's worth of an inability to sleep. Each morning, when I finally became anchored to sleep, the alarm would ring.

The sky was hazy with a forecast for rain.

"Hey, kid," Mario greeted me. He handed me the latest copies of the three or four magazines I opted for every week. "How ya doin'?"

"Insomnia is one of my companions."

"Yeah. Hell, I couldn't sleep if I was chasin' down this murder deal. Gives me the willies just to read about it."

I folded the magazines and put them in my bag. "The killings are stealing people's friends and families. It's so sad."

"This Jona Beck is crap alright. But you been doin' a hell of a job reporting. Ventura's doin' great, too. I seen her on the news last night."

"One of the worst parts of it all is using hedge words. Jona Beck, the *alleged killer*. And the *reputed killing*. It doesn't get any more in-your-face than her crimes. She's a twisted freak."

"Crazy as a shit house rat."

With a wave I turned and walked toward *The Mirror*.

Mario's chatter had taken nearly ten minutes of my morning. There was no way of knowing for sure what part of one's day requires the healing of silence. Mornings were a time when I craved uninterrupted thought.

It must have been, I surmised, a family trait. Both of my brothers and father dislike too much gab in the morning. That always brought to mind when Angie attempted to wake Benjy one morning. He told her to leave him alone. He had to sort out his head. She screamed back he couldn't sort his head. He couldn't even sort out his underwear. It became a family joke.

* * *

Ruby put the mug of hot coffee in front of me. "I haven't seen your smile in days," she said.

My fingers were folded into a steeple beneath my chin. "I'm frustrated. I'm not locating something important."

"What are you looking for?"

"In confidence, I'm trying to get a fix on a trailer that might have been moved into the mountains two years ago. It would belong to Vivian and might very well be where Jona Beck is hiding out."

"Finding her isn't up to you. You just need to report on the crime, not come up with the criminal." Ruby's hands were firmly on her hips. "You'll do anything for an exclusive. But, honey, it's up to your girlfriend to chase after bad asses. You can't capture anyone with a pen. Even the fancy-dancy fountain pens you use. You let your girlfriend go for the danger."

I glanced back into Ruby's concerned face. "She's off duty today – at least part of the day. She'll pull one shift. So now it's up to me. Besides, when the capture goes down, I'd love to be the first on the scene."

"Not me. I don't want a thing to do with Jona Beck."

"It's as if she's playing games with us."

"Got a customer. Talk with you later." Ruby made her way back to the counter. "And tell your sweet woman 'hi' for me."

"She's due in any minute." While waiting, I thought how quickly my emotions for Nevada had intensified.

Our moral compasses seemed to coordinate – for the most part. Even though I leaned toward liberal, and she was a law and order kind of woman. However, admittedly, I remained troubled by her vehement declaration of revenge. Perhaps, I considered, it was spoken in anger about the death of the Georgetown deputy that made Nevada's statement so acrimonious. My own unwritten law about a scorched earth attitude when taking prisoners was solidly by the book.

My concerns changed course when I saw Nevada enter. She kissed my cheek, and then carefully put her shoulder bag down before sitting opposite me. She was dressed in a pair of denims and a lime-colored tank top. She looked remarkable feminine out of uniform. Just as tenderness was evinced in her face, she also moved with gentleness.

"Been waiting long?" she inquired.

"No. I've just had time for a half a cup of coffee."

Her fingers reached to bridge my own. "I've missed you. Randa, can't you take the day off? We need some time together. There's so little of it when we're both working so many hours."

"Time for young love – I was thinking about that earlier. Being near is the fragile underpinning of a relationship. But there will be time to spend together later. Later, after the story of Jona Beck's capture. We'll have a lifetime to share."

"Is that a promissory declaration?"

Words were emotional substitutes. She read my thought. "I care. We belong together." Encouragingly, she asked, "Don't you think?"

"Probably."

"Randa, there's always the fear of falling more in love with someone than they are with you."

"I remember a high adventure from mythology. The story about a maiden called Clytie. She falls for the sun-god. He didn't return her love so she was left to pine away. She turned her face toward the sun, watching him as he went through the sky each day. Day after day." My voice dwindled as I was caught in thought.

"Did Clytie ever decide she'd be better off at a singles bar?"

"No. She was changed into a flower. A sunflower."

"Randa, I promise I'll never change you into a posy. You believe me, don't you?"

"Yes." I scanned my wristwatch. "I have a staff meeting."

"I'm not seeing your deep journalistic fervor this morning."

"Naw. Not when I've got to attend a morning editorial meeting. We'll undress a few ideas and see if we want to hop in bed with any of them."

"And they call the press America's watchdog."

I stood, leaned to kiss her, and then looked into her eyes. "Nevada, I'm glad you're not on duty today. Your commander was right, you need one day off."

"I'm actually on call. We all are. I'm packing my pistol in case." She patted her left hip. From under her waistband protruded the butt of her gun. "Just in case, I have a little Sig Sauer security."

"I don't care if you've got an assault rifle. Be careful. And if you hear anything, please let me know."

"You'll be the first to know. And if you get any solid leads, let Fritz know immediately. Remember my lecture on leaving the dangerous stuff to the badges."

"I'll keep the law informed. Sig Sauer, Smith & Wesson, or Heckler & Koch. Just be careful." I was amused a moment. "Did you know that the Smith-Corona Corporation was a branch of Smith and Wesson?"

"Yes, and IBM is an offshoot of the Patriot Missile."

I chided, "Fun stuff. Comparing our various utensils. I'm at home in front of a computer terminal, and you're at home with weapons."

"Take care. I love you, my sweet high-tech goddess."

Her words followed me to the door. I turned and said, "And I love you, my goddess of weaponry." Her eyes were filled with loving concern. My own eyes misted for a moment. "I'll try to get off early."

* * *

"What are you pissed about?" Kenny questioned. "You got front page, top of fold byline, and you're chasing your tail over Lanny Ventura's interview with Lucia Gomez. The story was only a rehash of what you reported earlier this week. Lucia still claims to know nothing."

"But Ventura made a big deal out of it," I stressed. "*Big flipping deal*! They reported it as an exclusive unearthed by Ventura!"

"Relax!" Kenny attempted to calm me. "You'll hit the finish line before she does."

"You heard the hierarchy in our meeting. They made their point. This is the biggest case in years. Decades."

"Trust your shit detector. That's my advice. Ventura had Lucia Gomez stashed. You did all you could. Checked your sources. She sent you on a wild goose chase. So frigging what? You've sent her on enough of them."

"My Aunt Renie would say that a person can always find plenty of free cheese in a mousetrap."

"Florez, yesterday was Ventura's day. Today will be yours. Remember, payback's a bitch. Pick up your boobs and go on."

I began the walk to my office. Under my breath, just loud enough for Kenny to hear I muttered, "Ventura could kiss my ass if I wanted TV makeup smudges on my derrière."

* * *

Seated in front of my video terminal and wearing headphones, I requested, "Wait a minute, not so fast." Information was being scrawled into my notebook. "Just give me the general directions," I requested. "You can phone me when you get the exact location pinned down. I'm on my way up to Georgetown to check it out. At least I'll be in the vicinity when we get directives."

After replacing the phone receiver, I stared down at my tasseled loafers. It was only midmorning and exhaustion was setting in. My lack of rest would make driving to Georgetown infinitely more difficult. I reported to the day's editor-in-chief that one of our researchers came up with a mobile home dealer who recalled towing a unit up to a remote location outside of Georgetown. The name Vivian Walters didn't ring a bell, but the woman did have red hair. He remembered approximately where he relocated the mobile home. He was currently looking up his records. He knew one thing - it was difficult to locate even with exact directions given by the owner.

With a toss of my light weight blazer over one shoulder, and my large shoulder bag and daypack over the other, I rapidly signed out and was on my way.

Optimism was guarded when it came to obtaining an exact location. If the lead fizzled out, I'd have made the trip for nothing. There were hidden areas in more mountains than I cared to consider. Experience had taught that driving winding mountain roads was tough. At times there were no major landmarks. One might search the back county forever and not find Vivian's hideout. The source had mentioned the word *secluded* multiple times.

There was an ominous feel to the day. Clouds hung like gray cotton batting. The weather prediction was for showers in the city, and storms in the high country. By the time I reached for the rental car's door handle, I was convinced the angry nacreous skies were cursed.

* * *

Nevada chastised me for taking off into the wilderness without her. But, I argued, she was taking a day off from a long week of punishing double shifts. She deserved a rest. And, I stressed, I was only going to check it out. If it looked like a make on the property, I agreed to call her immediately after calling authorities.

Although I stressed it was probably another false lead, Nevada insisted she was on her way. I was to call her when I had updated information. The wild goose chase argument did little good. She countered, even if it wasn't Vivian's, we could meet up and grab a late lunch together in Georgetown.

Passing through Georgetown, I saw the dirt road where the mover thought the trailer might have been hauled. I drove the rental car onto the road's shoulder and awaited the research team's additional directions. I took the time to slip a tiny voice-activated tape recorder into my pocket.

Across the horizon mountains lifted. Adjacent was a steep wall of rock. Mist-enshrouded pools of vapor rose from the base of the meadow. Vision was difficult as the fog-veiled skies became denser. There was a shimmer from flecks of rain. A shiver went through my body. It was both from the coolness, and the scene's eerie gloom.

I phoned Nevada to tell her my exact location. I also told her I was awaiting directions. She was on the outskirts of Denver. "This is probably just an empty chase," I grumbled. "Lanny Ventura probably paid this mobile home hauler to set me up."

Nevada began to talk, but the signal was lost.

"Nevada, I'm losing you."

She repeated, "We ought to call in additional badges."

"I don't want authorities barging in on some innocent citizens enjoying their weekend trip. Isn't there a law about wasting police officer's time?"

"Yes. Obstruction. But if it is the location where Beck is hiding, it's only prudent that we get some backup."

"You're my backup. Listen, I'll ring you when there are details. I'm getting an incoming call."

Her voice was fading in and out. "I'm driving without sparing the horse. Let me know."

Quickly, I answered the call. The source had come through with exact directions. I jotted them down. After a failed attempt to call Nevada, impatience overwhelmed me. In the mountains there were areas where cell phones simply wouldn't connect. Waiting seemed out of the question. My plan was simple. I'd locate the mobile home, scope it out, and if it looked remotely as if it could be hiding the fugitive, I'd call Nevada, and emergency backup.

My instincts told me that even if Jona had been there, by now she'd be cleared out. She knew the authorities were using Georgetown as ground zero. Just as the crime in Denver forced her to relocate, I believed she had again hit the road.

Driving up the circular gravel road taxed the engine of my rental car. Beneath its tires was the crunching of stones. As I passed by wisps of steam, I turned on the windshield wipers. The woods were dappled with pepper-colored shadows. I checked my instructions, and then took a sharp right.

Before me was another road, and beyond that a wizened string of smoke came from a faraway cabin. It was dwarfed by distance. I saw no sign of a mobile home. Around another curve, and my foot hit the brake. Beyond was Vivian's mobile home as described by the moving company. The blue skirting had been described on the moving order forms. It was hemmed in - concealed by numerous huge spruce and overgrowth. Approximately fifty yards away, between me and the mobile home, was an unattached garage.

After pulling off to the side of the road, I again attempted to phone Nevada - to no avail. The trailer looked completely vacant. But from a distance of nearly two hundred yards, and with the misty conditions, it was difficult to tell for certain. No vehicles were in sight, but if Jona was hiding out in the trailer, she would have undoubtedly parked the vehicle in the garage. And, I noted, the garage door had a row of windows facing me.

I called the office, confirming I'd found the trailer and fine-tuned the directions. They'd been in touch with Nevada, and had relayed the message to her. Before the phone's connection cut out completely, the dispatcher said they'd also contacted local authorities.

Slowly, I exited the car. It was obscured from the trailer's line of sight. There was enough brush and cover for me to make it safely to the garage. Once there, I could take a quick peek to see if Simone Milton's Escalade was inside. My walk was cautious. There was but one glance back at the comfort zone of the rental car.

I clicked the 'ON' button of my voice-activated tape recorder.

Rain glinted as it sprayed to earth. Carefully, I moved toward the garage. As I walked the dampness of creased earth beneath me, my loafers sloshed. The crush of pebbles and my breath, heavy with the air's moistness, were the only other sounds. Even the usual forest sounds of birds and scampering animals were missing. Wildlife had taken cover from the storm.

Stepping over an outstretched limb in my path, I slipped on a lichen patch. It was tangled like mop strings against the graying, decayed bark. I regained my footing. Clumps of moss on a large boulder were intensely green. It did my heart good to think that at least one living thing was enjoying the rain.

By the time I reach the garage's edge, soggy loam beneath my feet was making traction difficult. My knees shivered. For a moment they locked as I press up against the pane of glass. Inside was the auto that had been driven by Jona Beck. My plan was now to return to the car where I could safely attempt to contact Nevada, and authorities with the news. They should be arriving soon, I surmised.

Sensing something on my right, I whirled around. Terror squeezed the air from my lungs. My gasp was barely audible. I was staring down the bore of a gun. Jona's menacing smile became a sneer of savagery. I opened my mouth, but my voice shriveled. My heart pounded so hard it ached.

Jona's bony index finger stabbed in the direction of the mobile home. I quailed at the thought of entering the trailer with her. I'd seen her victims. Fear became a drug as my mind entered a surreal area of shock. If death sent an echo of life, I'd heard its call. *Muy pelgroso*, I said to my own silence. Very dangerous, indeed.

Tentatively, I walked toward the mobile home.

* * *

Beneath a low deck of stony, gray clouds, tendrils of fog billowed. The sky began to leak as an impatient sieve might. By the time we reached the door, a curtain of rain was falling. It was too late to run.

My self-admonition to stay calm seemed useless. My chin quivered. Jona's reflection in the trailer door's window was terrifying. She had aged since last we met. Her frail face was more freckled, presumably from the sun. Her skeletal cheeks were seamed with lines. And her lynx eyes were vessels destitute of emotion. They reflected a truth I'd failed to notice before. Her heart was dead. Somewhere along the way, her heart had expired. I was now a prisoner of that emptiness where the worn away heart once resided.

Jona's tense, pugnacious swagger was contained. Her fingers tightly pinched the wooden stock of a .357 Magnum. The gun's pewter blue metal snout glistened. Our glances met in the trailer pane's reflection.

"Get in," she ordered. Fanning back the door created a loud snap. When I began to turn toward her, her hand stuck my back. "Move, I said," she screamed at me with contemptuous censure.

By the time I was through the door, I realized thoughts were tumbling incoherently. *Eventually* Nevada would find the mobile home. The authorities would arrive, *eventually*. But this trailer was difficult to find. Reviewing the option of time forced me to realize, I must keep her talking. Her attention span was brief.

My walk was threading through debris on the floor. Cluttered with empty cans, torn and discarded junk food bags, and assorted garbage, the floor was a maze. I stepped over fangs of glass shard from a picture frame. Inside there was a scratched photo of Vivian on a huge motorcycle. Low light bathed the room with drabness. My eyes were slowly adjusted to it.

Squinting at first, my eyes focused. I recoiled. I swallowed a fist of panic that lodged in my bronchial passage. Chills uncontrollably rippled down my spine. Bunched against a door, with one arm lifted upward, Dr. Simone Milton was roped to a doorknob with a tightly knotted red silk scarf. The cloth reached the floor as if it was a silken puddle. Simone's crumpled body had become a toppled human statue, unable to move.

She had been unmercifully tortured. I winced when I recognize the slash marks were letters being formed. Beneath a thatch of matted hair, Simone's face was hardened into a mask of pain. The cords of veins along her temple were swollen. Her sunken eyes were in a semi-somnolent state.

Simone blankly gazed up at me. Her clothing was blood soaked. The flesh on her arms and legs had been carved upon. Skin hung like dripping red feathers. Alive, barely, she angled stiffly toward me. Her head rolled as she moved. She flinched.

Pain, and perhaps fear, destroyed her whisper. It left behind only patches of breathing.

My mind clamored. The grotesque scene angered me. To Jona I accused, "Wearing your colors is costly. Why the brutality against someone you professed to love?"

"She fuckin' ampted me. She turned on me."

"When? When she saw that you're not some poor pathetic psychotic in need of rescue? When she realized you're nothing but a cold-blooded murderer? Your mind is made up of evil intent and she and her arrogant diagnosis had pegged you as sick soul. But when she presaged the end and saw you leave a trail of death behind you, she knew what you are. And was that when she turned on you?"

"She thinks I'm bats. But I'm the fuckin' road gladiator."

"It's understandable from your past you might wish to make war with the world. But why her? She wanted to help you."

"I told you. She says I'm bonkers!" Jona was agitated. Her eyes squinted. "But now she's damaged goods. Who cares? She's so old that she's gone to seed. Look at her. Five and a half feet of wasted time. Not exactly your hot hootchie mama. Naw. Not for me." There was haughtiness in Jona's words. "I deserve better."

"She was a classy, intelligent woman. Look what you've done to her."

Jona slammed her fist against a wall "She was a fake. Like the rest of them. Like putting lipstick on a fuckin' donkey. She thought she was better than me. She isn't better. She knows that now."

"She loved you. Look how you've repaid that love. Your love cost her everything."

Jona answered with an icy grunt.

My words struck with anger. I was incensed by having viewed those lifeless bodies she'd left in her wake. "You really don't care. You kill randomly. Needlessly. Even the most ferocious beast kills for food or territory. That makes you worse than a beast. What kind of human being are you?"

"You fuckin' tell me. You're the bullshit authority. I watched you talking on the newscasts. They made a big deal about you bein' the only one who I'd talk with. I got you national TV guys chasing to find out what I'd told you. You had network coverage. I did that for you. 'Cause you're a sister. I talked with you."

"You're not my sister. And I certainly didn't enjoy running from the tabloid press." I look up at the ceiling light that spilled its low wattage dimness. "And I don't know what makes you tick."

"You know me better than anyone. I told you more."

"I interviewed you. How does one human being understand another, if one of them is twisted?"

"Twisted!" she raged. "See, you and your crappy news reports are on their side. You've fucking turned on me, too. Now you're gonna pay."

"You'd better pull that trigger. This is as near to a compromising position as I get. No ropes. No atrocious pagan sacrifice. I'll fight you to the death." *Guerra a muerta,* I said to myself with determination.

"I got the gun. I give the orders."

With the brief pause, I watched as she formed her plans. Stall, I lecture myself. "Jona, just tell me why you've become a monster. Help me to understand."

"Bad genetics." She smirked. "Yeah. That's it. Bad genetics are to blame. It isn't demonic apparitions. It's just plain bad genetics. Not some ego trip like that bitch over there claims. She's the ego hag."

Glancing across the room at Dr. Simone Milton, my mind manufactured snippets of thought. There was always vulnerability where love was concerned. Simone appeared to be in a comatose state. Danger had been at her side for the past week and a half. She was now buried beneath pain. The only sound was the sonorous cadence of her raggedy breath.

I pointed in her direction. "Jona, Simone loved you. If she doesn't get medical attention, she'll die. Do one decent thing in your life. Let me call to get her help."

"She never loved me. *She* was egotistical enough to think

she could cure me. Reform me. Redeem me. She's supposed to be so fuckin' smart. A doctor! I outsmarted her and her titles and degrees. Me. I'm not so batty after all."

"Jona, if you're not batty, then you're evil. You've set Sapphics back centuries. Women are supposed to be the kind, maternal gender. Jona, I understand that your past was very sad. Very lonely. It made your soul hermetic. But think about being kind just once. A woman risked everything she is. Everything she has. She did it for you."

"Fuckin' shut up about the bitch!" Jona screamed. "Maybe I cared something for her. But she ended up hating me like everyone else."

"I don't think she hates you. I don't hate you."

"Yeah, you do. You're just saying you don't so I won't take my time killing you. But you hate me."

I reached within my soul for courage. There was a hovering of doom. I felt it. Jona's captured prey was without territory. "Jona," I began slowly, "Jona, if you kill me, there won't be anyone to write about your story - perpetuate you. Isn't that what you want – an accurate report of your life?"

"Didn't you do that with your newspaper articles?"

"I didn't capture what you're really about. You need to tell me." Above all, I couldn't allow her to sense my fear. After the knowledge she'd stabbed my newspaper photo, there was an acute awareness that she intended to kill me. The doctor had obviously diagnosed her as being egocentric. Jona's response to that might be used to my advantage. "I can tell the world about you - the way you want the world to know you."

"Like when you say I distorted reality?"

"At the time I wrote that, I believed it to be true." My voice was tremulous as I continued, "Jona, everyone distorts reality. Everyone has his or her own vantage point." Just as journalism classes taught the classic way of handling a source with confidence, I attempt to become part of Jona's conspiracy. "I understand how your early years were filled with terror. That kind of childhood tends to make anyone distort reality." Nudge, but don't bully, I pulled from one of the reporter's rules. "Tell me what you think about life?"

"Life sucks." She laughed with hollowness.

"My grandfather is a philosopher. He quotes Thoreau's words about how a person should live life deliberately. That's a pretty good line."

"I got a low bullshit threshold," she warned. "So don't tell me about all that crap." As an afterthought, she asked, "You believe in a hereafter?" Her question was menacing.

"I've asked the question often lately. Of myself. And of others. Maybe there is no shorthand version of an answer. But there must be some reason for the journey of life."

"Birth is a death sentence."

"Part of life is that no one has any guarantees. My maternal grandmother is dying. She's going into the box very soon. But if you murder me, now, I'll precede my dying grandmother to the grave. No one knows the future. Do you believe in something after death?"

"Maybe it's all darkness. Like sleep. I'll know soon. I can't run forever. But I ain't letting them take me alive. You know. It'll be a do-it-yourself job. I don't want to go back to that institution for the criminally insane. All the fuckin' nuts." She gave a toss to the ruff of hair that fell over her forehead.

"You'll kill yourself rather than return?"

"Yeah. You don't approve of suicide. I can tell the way you're looking at me."

"I believe your life is up to you, and so is your death."

"You and your compassion." Jona's face was grim.

"I hope I'm a compassionate person. I was raised to have empathy." There were several blank moments. I saw her eyes darting. I had to change the course quickly. "You said I know all about you. But I don't. I met a person from my past in The Raven. She said you had a secret name. I didn't know that about you. Pandora, right?"

"Yeah." She gave a cocky smile. "Yeah, that's right. Now you know. Took you long enough to figure it out."

"Did you pick the name because you relate to it? Or did you become Pandora by unleashing a curse on humanity? You have opened a *pithos*."

Her motion was one of total swagger. "Yeah. Everyone knows me now."

"And I'm the best one to write about your world. About you. But I can't do that if you kill me."

"Fuck you." She was through with mythological and metaphysical queries. My hope fragmented. She wasn't going to allow me to stand there talking all day. I sensed her aggressive agitation building. "You're all wrong about me."

"Jona, give it up. Just put the gun down. Let me call for help. Life is important. We're living at the center of our lives as each moment passes. And I'm asking you to dispense mercy for Simone and for me. I'm pleading for your mercy. Your restraint and your mercy. My life depends on your decision. You're right, it's only a matter of time. The authorities are going to be here soon."

Her voice was metallic. It had not resonated fear until she said, "They're coming for me. Maybe I oughtta comb my hair. I wanna look piss-elegant for the cops." Her eyes suddenly froze when the door was kicked open. Jona took aim toward the doorway.

"Police!" Nevada's gun was trained on Jona. "Don't move! Not even a tremble. I see your trigger finger flinch, and I'll blow your head off."

The two women braced for a standoff. There was the great silence of facing death.

"You didn't even wear your riot helmet," Jona chided Nevada.

"I don't need it. I've got you directly in my line of fire. My aim is excellent, my reflexes legendary, my weapon has a hair trigger, and I'm feeling a hell of an advantage."

"Fuckin' cop. Smart ass, fuckin' cop!" Jona ranted. "I got aim on you, too. And I'm mad as a cut snake. That gives me the advantage."

Nevada's eyes narrowed. "Give it up. Drop your weapon."

"Fuck you. Fuck you all."

Nevada cool demeanor, and controlled voice didn't expose her fear, but fear must have been there. "I know you're not about to be retrofitted with decency, but Jona, it is over. Do the right thing. Give it up before anyone else is hurt. I don't want to shoot you."

Simone stirred. Her plea came in a low hypnotic monotone. "Jona, listen to her. It's over."

"Shut up, bitch," Jona spat. "Let me think."

The moment was still. I felt the lethal ticking. There were words inside I wanted to say, but they were stillborn with panic. All our lives were on the line, but Nevada would take the first bullet. My jaw clamped tightly.

"There's nowhere to go, Jona," Nevada coaxed. "Just drop your weapon. No one will get hurt. Do this one good thing."

"Our bodies," Jona said as she reflected, "are containers. So what if I die. People are like machines anyway. We all are."

"No, Jona," Nevada disputed. "We're more than machines. Each human being has a very complicated nature. Your nature is so complex that no one can read you. Maybe you can't even read what you're all about. But let that bad stop now."

"Naw. I don't give myself up. They'll never let me out."

"Maybe they will one day," Nevada tempered her words. "Maybe you'll improve."

"The fuckin' doctors don't help me," her voice surged.

"Maybe you'll be able to help yourself get better," Nevada said.

"Yes," I affirmed. "Jona, please listen to reason. There is always hope. I know you've had a rough life." Her expression registered. She was thinking about having sat on the hard bench of existence when she was a child. She was considering the theft of her childhood innocence. I attempted to reach her. "But in spite of it all, there must be some goodness in you. Please."

Confusion was scrawled on her face. "Yeah. Maybe I can pull a few years. Rehabilitate. Get help. You know, get real help. Not some bitch trying to make me into her little pal."

"That's right," I continued her thoughts. "It might work out fine. But you've got to cooperate with the authorities. You've got to drop your gun."

"Naw. I can't. You see, there's gonna be new charges. When I was on trial before, eleven wanted the death sentence.

In court I sat there all well behaved. Never said a word. And sure enough, there was one juror stupid enough to keep me from death row. That candy assed juror helped me. I escaped and killed a bunch more people. I lost track how many. But my next jury might see through me. Death. I wanna be in control of my death. Not them."

"Just drop the gun," Nevada ordered.

"Drop your own fuckin' gun," Jona mimicked. "You bitch pig!"

Nevada's eyes became fury-enraged. I'd never seen their dark anger before. She carefully sited those eyes on her targets. "While you're deciding what to do, Jona, I'm taking charge. Randa, I want you to untie Dr. Milton. Then take her outside. Get into your vehicle. Start the engine. If there is a showdown and Jona gets lucky, I want you at a safe distance. Backup is on its way."

"I can't leave you," I argued.

Nevada's stern voice hammered. "That was not a request. It was an official order. Do it *now*."

My walk to Simone's side was methodical. I didn't want to surprise anyone with a quick motion. My hands quivered as they worked to unloop the scarf. It was tightly bound. I reached for a small knife at her side. When the blade touched between the scarf and Simone's wrist, she flinched. Her hand slid free. I cautiously lifted Simone into my arms, then up to her feet. She weakly staggered, leaning against my body for support. By the time we reached the door, I was damp from Simone's oozing blood. Warmth radiated from her blood-caked body. It was the only clue that she was not a moving cadaver.

We made it through the forest colonnade. Once on the path, I rushed, dragging her to the car. I quickly pressed her limp body into the backseat. By the time I reached the driver's side, I heard her blurting sobs that broke through her contorting face.

I got into the car. I wanted to scream at her. I wanted her to shut up. I looked at the surrounding sentinel pines. We were safe from Jona. But my lover wasn't.

"I didn't want it to turn out like this," Simone whined. "We were going to escape to remote Canada – the backcountry. Live off the land. Together."

"You had to know there was a risk," I said bitterly.

"I've had time to peer into my soul. I honestly believed she was making progress." Her words were said with slow conviction, but with a docility that led me to believe otherwise. "I never wanted anyone harmed."

"Who the hell do you think you are, the lunacy commissioner? You unchained a convicted killer on the world. Multiple deaths later, you tell me you didn't want anyone harmed."

"I thought I was in love with her. I wanted to make her well. I pitied her. I believed in her recovery."

"Is that why you selected your profession? You have some propensity for loonies? Is that what you're telling me?" I raged. "The woman I love is in there. You and your psychobabble! I'm not even trained, and I sensed, yes *sensed* how dangerous she is."

Her hands limply lifted to her face. She cringed as she wept. "Being wrong was my darkest fear."

Blood smears across her cheeks appeared to be war paint. I glanced away. "Maybe you'll be on the lucky side of life and they won't execute you for your complicity in the murders. They'll just let you rot in prison with people nearly as dangerous as Jona." I wanted to recite the victims by name, age, and detail, but I wanted something else even more. I wanted quiet.

"I deserve execution." Her eyes were lusterless. "My being implicated makes it all so much worse. I'm a doctor."

"You might have missed your golden opportunity to save her. You've really spun gold into straw on this one, *Doctor* Milton."

Her attention receded. Mine, too. I wished to be more compassionate. I wished to tell her that it wasn't all her fault. That she'd suffered enough. I couldn't. Her own ego would topple her. She should have said *mercy* to her lover.

And my lover was risking her life. My eyes closed for many moments. I turned to glance back into Simone's distraught expression. Her mouth trembled. She asked, "Can you forgive me?"

"Forgiveness is not my strongest attribute. I'm fed up with people making mistakes that impact other people's lives. Then they wanted their evil deeds to be absolved. Excused." I suddenly realized I was talking about Lenora Randolph. My words were meant for my estranged grandmother. When Simone's lips moved, I quickly interrupted. "Don't. Don't say another word."

My spirit was as depleted as the doctor's body.

* * *

It had been less than a few minutes, but seemed like hours. Waiting for police backup; waiting for the confrontation to end; waiting to know if Nevada would survive - the waiting mauled my brain. Although we faced the unknown each day, direct peril was different. It was more ferocious.

My head suddenly snapped upward. There was no sound in the world that truly imitated the sound of a discharging weapon. The popping blast was unmistakably gunfire. I tightly clamped the steering wheel. For several anxious moments my heart ached with anticipation.

Every inclination was to run to Nevada. Her instructions were clear. I sat still. If Jona had shot Nevada, I could do little to help. My becoming Jona's hostage again would endanger the lives of authorities that would soon be here. I cautioned myself to remain in the vehicle. I was to wait for what I hoped would be Jona's surrender without incident.

"Randa," a shout was finally heard.

It was Nevada's voice. My race from the car to the mobile home's door was a sprint of exhilaration. Nevada was alive. And she would not have called to me if she were not the survivor. She would never endanger me.

My fingers trembled as they reached for the door's handle. Inside Jona was crumpled on the floor. Blood gushed from her temple area. There was splattered blood near the entrance wound. Intermingled were dots of gunpowder residue. I glanced at Nevada. Her right hand and arm were also speckled with blood, and with powder peppering. She saw I'd noticed her hand. She wiped it quickly on her blouse.

Nevada said, "Good thing I convinced your office to give me the directions they relayed. They were worried about you."

"I was detained from calling them again. You saved my life." I moved into her arms. The stench of gun powder was strong - pungently strong. "Thank you." I glanced down at Jona.

"She's dead."

"What happened?"

"It was self-inflicted. She ate her gun."

I lifted Nevada's arm. I touch the tattooing residue. "Or did you feed it to her?"

Nevada pulled her arm away with force. Her protest was defiant. "She said she was going to move her hand, but that I was in no danger. She took her finger from the trigger. She lowered her firearm. Then she turned it on herself. I tried to get to her. To grab the gun. But I was too late. That's why my hand and arm are bloodied and peppered."

In my attempt to calculate, I realized one thing. That was only one possibility. "When she moved her hand, she could have been moving it to kill you. I think your first reflex might have been to defend yourself by firing. But this head wound is at close range. Self-inflicted gunshot wound?"

"I told you what happened. I would have shot if the gun would have been aimed at me. She only wanted to shoot herself. You heard her say she wanted to be in control of her life. And death. She was."

"Tell me again," I requested.

"Randa, I told you. I have tattooing because I reached for the gun just as she turned it and discharged it. That's all." She saw skepticism in my eyes. "*If* I'd wanted to kill her, I could have rapidly snapped the trigger at any time."

"You might have been killed by the discharge of an errant bullet. But if you would have talked her down, and she'd dropped her gun, you could have retrieved it. Then the gun at close range would have made certain that she died."

"I'm an expert markswoman. My aim was between her eyes. That's where the bullet would have struck if I had intended to kill her." Her words sounded rehearsed. "*If.*"

"Certainty is within arm's length. And suicide doesn't require you go up before review when an officer's firearm is discharged. No questions."

"Randa, Jona murdered a cop. She's murdered innocent citizens by the score. She had a gun pointed at me. Do you honestly think my concern is that I might face a review board? Enforcement will back me, no matter. Evidence will show that I did not kill her. Because of your life events, you find trusting difficult. I've told you what happened. But maybe you'll always have doubts."

"Maybe. I can't have a relationship without truth."

"And I can't have a relationship without trust."

"Am I supposed to trust regardless?"

"The way you're interrogating me is as if you want to give the liberal press more damned garbage than the gullible reader can swallow. You can't make up a scenario. I told you what happened."

"I want the truth. It's my profession."

"The truth is Jona Beck wanted to kill, and in the end, she wanted to die. That's the truth and we both know it. There's your truth."

"We promised never to lie to one another. None of this is adding up. You wanted to get me out of here. Away from danger. Was that for my protection or because you didn't want eyewitnesses?"

"It was for *your* safety. You know that. If she got off a lucky shot, you would have been next. I wanted you out for your protection. That's my job. To protect citizens. And believe me, my greatest concern was to save one citizen. You."

"When I left, Jona was nearly talked down. I could tell she was becoming more and more convinced she needed to give herself up."

I searched Nevada's face for clues, twitches, blinks, or anything to answer my question.

There was a pause before Nevada disputed my suspicion. "You only thought she was ready to fold. She was erratic."

"Nevada, we can't have anything like this between us. You need to tell me the truth."

"Regardless of how it went down, you're the press. If I tell you it was suicide, that's what you report. Everything is neat and simple. You've got the story."

My shoulders sagged. "I want the truth. I'll take myself off the damned story. I want for us to be able to always share the truth. We promised one another that."

She blanched. "I wasn't standing here when I promised. I was moralizing from a best scenario vantage point."

"If I were to require honesty, as your lover, could you give it to me?"

"Don't you understand, there will always be areas of confidentiality that separates us? We are in professions requiring confidentiality. We aren't likely to ever forget you're press and I'm police. I just now got that. There will always be sources you can't give up. And there will be police matters I can't and won't divulge. We've got to give one another understanding. Empathy. My parent's favorite saying is a good marriage requires two forgiving people."

"This is about death. And being honest about it. As your lover, I would require knowing your life, Nevada."

"As your lover, I wouldn't want you implicated. Can't you see I have no way of answering your question? If I tell you I *was* involved, you become an accessory. I tell you no, and you obviously don't believe me anyway." She remained unflinchingly stanch with her answers. "Randa, I'm in love with you. I have done nothing wrong in the eyes of a Creator or in the eyes of the law. All I can ask is that you trust my judgment."

I glanced back at Jona's body. An implosive incident at the frontal head area had left the remnants of tissue and bone particles. They dripped down her face. Her right temple area was torn open as was the back of her head where the bullet exited. With an instinctual reporter's curiosity I guessed at how it might have been.

One: Just as Nevada stated, Jona had lifted the gun to her

own temple and discharged a death bullet. Nevada had rushed to stop that from happening, and had been splattered, and tattooed. It would have meant that she would have risked her own life if Jona had turned her gun back around to kill Nevada. Nevada knew that danger increased each moment they were at a standoff. Jona had multiple times stated that she would never be taken alive. Nevada believed that and allowed her to move her gun to shoot herself.

Two: Nevada O'Bryan fired the bullet. She talked Jona into dropping her weapon. She moved near the disarmed Jona, picked up the weapon, decided on the best angle to make it appear to be suicide. She then fired. She sanitized the gun handle and trigger. She copied Jona's prints on the weapon, and then called me. There was adequate time to have performed those tasks.

I questioned if Nevada might have pulled the trigger for her own reasons. This bloody episode of Jona's rampage would never happen again. No one could every spring Jona Beck from a mental facility or release her from prison. No technicality of the law would ever free her.

The pain pavilion had been shut down. And that was what Nevada had just related her job to be about - protecting the innocent. Jona massacred a police officer, as well as others. I wondered if in Nevada's eyes that justified a death sentence. I believed if she didn't kill Jona she wanted the mad fugitive dead. But my *beliefs* wouldn't make it to court. The public would be fine with the headline: Jona Beck Kills Self in Police Standoff.

I questioned, "What were her final words?"

"She said she wanted to be able to love, but that she was better at hate."

For the first time I felt nearer understanding Beck than ever before. The rage she *always* felt was similar to the way most of us *sometimes* feel.

* * *

It was nearly midnight as I sat in *The Mirror's* office. The carpeted cubicle, with its earth hues, and neutrality, offered respite from a day like no other in my life. My cubical seemed cramped. Everything might have fallen in at any moment. Walls, photos, the small globe at my terminal desk, everything might have collapsed on me. Perhaps the claustrophobic emotion came from being inside the nucleus of confusion. Events had irrevocably altered my perspective of this story.

Giving the globe a good spin, I whispered, "I wish I were in…" I pointed, and then quickly inspected the city I'd selected. It was Naples, Italy. I spoke only phrases of Italian. Naples was not Denver, and I wished I were there.

I returned to the thoughts of the day. I recapped. My first story, for the extra edition was a quickly drafted thumbnail of the day's events. It was little more than a montage of my memories. Now, I took another look. This outline would be the first installment of an in-depth, three-part article. Above all, I did not wish to romanticize the violence. Braggadocio and machismo need not apply. The day had provided all the hoopla I could manage.

I recalled waiting with Simone until an ambulance took her away. I gleaned as much information on her condition as I might from the medical attendants. She was responding to the medication they had administered. They would save her. Save her, I mused, for her trial as an accessory, or possible accomplice. There would be a long list of charges. The escape, cluding, and nearly everything that Jona would have been charged with now landed on Simone.

By the time Simone's first responder medical team had shut down my questions, there was a crescent of official vehicles that had arrived. Although I made every effort to mentally note events, I remain certain there were things that would surface years down the road. The day was the most tortuously challenging in memory.

Naturally, I'd been questioned by the local sheriff's department. My answers were clinically brief. They confirmed everything Officer Nevada O'Bryan had stated. I had also mentioned that in my final conversation with Jona Beck, she had discussed not being taken alive. Her words were - I quoted - 'a do-it-yourself' job. End quote. That would indeed bolster and corroborate Nevada's statements. Not that speaking on her behalf was necessary.

She had become an immediate champion on site, and later of her unit. Lieutenant Fritz Truesdale, along with the captain, met her when we arrived back in the city. There was a hearty, long, photo-op handshake for Truesdale's hero. He mentioned pride in her cool, reserved handling of the event. He boasted of her heroism in the line of duty.

I concurred. She entered a field of danger to save lives. And she *had* saved two lives. Had she not entered, I would have become a victim.

On my return trip to Denver, I was driven in one of *The Mirror's* all-terrain vehicles. The rental car would be impounded as part of the investigation. Another staff reporter and a photographer assisted with the story that I was phoning in to the City Desk. I experienced the first relief of the day when I finished the story by saying the traditional 'thirty' - reporter's jargon for ending a story.

With my preliminary story filed, I quickly phoned my family, telling them I was fine, and urging them not to come to headquarters to meet me. I'd call them in the morning with details. Another grueling hour or two of testimony was needed by the Denver Police Department. I planned then to take quick trip home for a shower and change of clothing, after which I would scurry back to my newspaper office.

One image, of many, I couldn't shake was my return back from Georgetown to Denver. I recalled looking out of the vehicle's window at the road that was a thin scar carved around a mountain peak. Upon that rock-studded hill, Jona Beck died. She had played with death for her final time. She had strayed from all that makes us human. She'd stray no more.

I remained traumatized after returning to the vital soul of Denver - its center. The Metro desk was fueled with questions, comments, with the frenetic pre-deadline fever that happens when a story like this one goes down. The images tugged me back.

I recalled when my hand reached into my pocket and I found the small voice-activated recorder. I had taped the entire event. I knew then my three-part story was to be completely accurate.

I had not mentioned the recorder to authorities. Even though it was used in my profession, it might have been viewed as an eavesdropping instrument. Anything that intercepted oral communication was subject to Public Law 90-351. For that reason, and because I'd questioned Nevada about the death of Jona, the tape would remain deep-sixed in my personal files. The police had more than enough to answer their questions.

Alone in my office, before concluding the first installment, I listened to the tape for accuracy. I needn't have. Most of what I had written was verbatim. Tomorrow morning I'd finish the other two parts of the story. I pressed the key that sent my first part of the story to the city desk terminal.

I was weary. I was hungry. Although one of the editors had earlier ordered take-out sandwiches, I had only played with mine while working.

My thirst for a good glass of wine was immeasurably strong. But I dared not go out of the building earlier this evening, and before I'd clear-headedly written the installment. The press would be haunting me for a week or two, I feared. And now, as the midnight hour struck, I still wished I were sipping a glass of fine Zinfandel. Or a brandy might be lovely.

My watch read ten after midnight. I slipped the recorder, a disk, and some notes into my pack. By the time I stood, my cell phone rang. I answer, "Nevada?"

"Yes. Are you okay?"

"Not really."

"Miss you. Are you coming home?" she questioned.

"I'm going home to my loft. I think it's better until I sort everything out." My words were strained. "I love you, Nevada. I'm very confused. Give me time."

"Can we meet for a drink?"

"Not tonight. It's late, and I'm spent."

"Randa, we've got to talk. You want a confession to

something I can't give you. You've got to learn to trust me. I need to know that."

"I'm empty now. I've got nothing to say. I've talked. I've written. And there isn't anything left in me. In the morning, maybe. I need time."

"I wish I could see you. Be with you. My heart hurts with love of you. Please?"

Tears seeped from my eyes. As they dripped, they moistened my face. "Another time when I understand my own doubts," I whispered into the receiver, then disconnected. Within the vault of grief I resided. Perhaps the solemnity of a soul in turmoil continued forever. Perhaps, I considered on my walk to the elevator, I would never fully recover.

Introspection about Nevada and my barely-incubated love had brought me to terms with my true fear. There was a moment when I thought *forever love* with Nevada might have existed.

More than anything in the world – I wanted to believe in Nevada. She deserved my trust. I somehow knew that much. Why was it I needed to prove her words to my heart?

CHAPTER 12

Sunday

The night's sleep seemed as perilously difficult as yesterday had been. Dreams were reruns. I woke in my unkempt loft's bed of loneliness. I was frightened. My adrenaline turned on like a spigot of high octane anxiety. I coaxed another hour of sleep.

By nine Sunday morning I was seated at the breakfast nook. Before me was piled a mountain of rolled newspapers. They'd been delivered earlier. Although eager to read press reaction to yesterday's events, I was more interested in a cup of coffee.

Self-evaluation was never without purpose. It was seldom without pain. In only a fortnight, my life had journeyed through the geography of the soul. The terrain I'd covered included both triumph and tragedy.

The Mirror's truth was a banner. JONA BECK KILLS SELF. The subheading was: *Mirror's* Crime Reporter Randa Florez Captured by Crazed Killer. The first installment of my personal account was on the left side of the front page, top of crease headline. On the right was my exclusive report of the day's events. Beneath that there was a follow-up story by another staff reporter about the victims. The savage campaign of Jona Beck's terror was recounted. I only gave a cursory glance at the huge bulk of Denver's Sunday paper. Then I tossed it aside.

After a sip of hot coffee, I unfold pages of the national papers. Their perspective differed greatly from local accounts. The headlines were gargantuan: ERIKA RANDOLPH'S DAUGHTER HELD CAPTIVE BY FUGATIVE. They didn't realize the greater truth. I was actually *Paulo Florez's daughter*.

I did realize the error, and I strongly objected.

My eyes pressed shut. A dart of pain stabbed through me. I suddenly wondered why I'd endangered myself and the woman I loved. Both lives were nearly taken yesterday. Also, why was I chasing horrendous crime and criminals?

My fingers trembled when I attempted to grip my coffee cup.

* * *

One of LoDo loft dweller's main concerns was parking space. Most garage space was located away from the building. In my case, I was about a block away. I planned to leg it to my Z.

Before exiting my building, I saw shadows moving in front of the doorway. The paparazzi was thickly entrenched outside. Their cameras appeared tethered to them. The Jona Beck trial brought a similar crush last time. But it was mild in comparison. It was a brief badgering and a slight mauling. But this was frightening because there were a couple dozen frenzied reporters – paps mostly. I moved away from the entry. A race to the back doorway was unencumbered. As the door opened, I experienced a great shoving from the other side. Before I knew it, I was in the midst of a camera crew. Microphones were being thrust in my face. Tabloid reporters were coaching a headline.

"Randa, were you frightened?" A background voice asked.

"Of course." I battled my way through the crowd. "The round from a gun's chamber can easily find a target when only a blink away." I was in the custody of their tightening circle. "I'd rather not talk about it now."

"Come on, give us a break. We're just doing our job. You can appreciate that, you're a reporter." The jeering voice was contemptuous.

My own was irascible. "Same church, but different pew," I challenged. There was an opening behind me. I stepped back, took a side-step, and then made break for it. There was a scurry of footsteps clacking as I turned the corner. My race to an adjacent alley was successful. I ducked behind a dumpster. The pursuers passed by. My head dug back against the brick wall behind me. My chest was pounding. When they got to the end of the block and saw I was nowhere in sight, they'd return. They passed me for a second time.

When they were out of sight, I came out of hiding. With every morsel of energy my legs beneath me pounded asphalt. My run left me gasping for breath when I reached the underground parking area. I quickly slid the entry card into its slot. I was safe.

There was the wobble of exhaustion as I unlocked Garbo's door. I leaned back in the bucket seat for many moments. Then slowly I pulled down the visor to examine my eyes. Around my weary eyes were spider webs of previously unnoticed lines. It was indeed a somber revelation. I'd grown older. With a wan smile of defiance, I admitted that after yesterday's escape from death, it was a pleasure to age.

I had never felt this reverential about life.

Passing by the street wild with paparazzi left a trace of achievement. For the time being, I'd eluded them. In my rearview mirror, I saw them scurrying to their mobile units when my Z passed. *Daban vueltas bailando el vals.* They were dancing round and round. And I was on my way to a decompression zone.

* * *

"You're looking like crap on a crutch!" Ruby chided. "Guess I nearly lost a couple patrons yesterday."

"Yes. It's been a tough twenty-four hours," I replied. I sank down on a stool at the counter. My elbows hit the countertop with the thud of something toppling. Ruby placed a mug of coffee in front of me. "Thanks."

"You're lucky you didn't get popped. Nevada, too."

"If she hadn't appeared, I'm certain Jona was planning to ice me."

"So why aren't you with Nevada now?"

My fingernails traced a mar on the knotty-pine counter top.

"I need time."

"Whatever floats your boat. From all reports, she saved your ass."

"I did the reporting. It's accurate. No retractions. She came in with gun drawn. She did save my ass."

"Your ungrateful ass? She's called several times to see if you were here."

"I'm not here."

"Maybe your heart ain't here, but you sure as hell are. Randa, just cut the crap. It's me, Ruby. Ruby is the passion stone. I know about these things. Tell me what's wrong with you."

"I'm not sure."

Ruby leaned nearer. "Yeah, you are." Ruby's insight was on the mark, as usual.

"I'm uncertain what my emotions mean. I need time to locate the reasons. Yesterday Jona Beck used a gun as a .38 caliper tongue depressor." I tentatively paused. "Now it's too late to ever again search her meaning. I'd wanted to believe people are less than the best thing they do, and better than the worst. Maybe I wanted her redemption. Contrition. I never witnessed even a sliver of true remorse."

"I could have told you Jona wasn't about to be sorry. She isn't the type. If she was gonna be sorry, she'da never done any of the killings."

Amused by her slant, I said, "Common sense prevails. Your wisdom prevails."

"In the newspaper you called Jona a human question mark."

"Jona Beck's naked insanity and morbid renegade qualities made her good copy. She executed contempt with Gothic contours of revenge. In her words, she wanted to pay the fuckers back."

"She was evil. She wasn't born. She was developed in a test tube by the devil. Randa, lotsa people have it bad when they're kids. They don't go out killing."

"But what intricate detail makes the difference?"

"Maybe none of us know. For instance, you looked happy when you and Nevada hooked up. You sure you want to risk losing her by needing space?"

"Some events are very complicated. Love is always complicated. Nevada deserves more than my uncertainty."

"She knows and accepts that you reporters live in your own parameters stretching around you. Anyone chasin' crime is bound to get lost. You and Lanny get all dubious about things you know can't be lined up."

"As journalists we need to see all the sides. Be objective."

"Randa, you aren't being objective now. You're gonna end up letting a first rate filly bolt out of the paddock because you're exploring yourself? Because all that space you need is spinning your objectivity? Do you think Nevada would ever do anything wrong?"

"Sometimes life is sad." *Muy triste*, I said to myself. "Maybe I'm just exhausted."

"Maybe," she repeated. "Maybe. Maybe you just gotta let life take to you where you need to be."

Ruby put down an empty coffee cup next to me. "I'm betting Nevada will be checking for you here." She turned the cup's handle and put it on the other side. "Attention to detail. I always remember which of my customers are left-handed, so I can get it right for 'em."

Suddenly I reached for her arm. It occurred to me. "Thank you, Ruby." Before I could answer the question on her face about why I was thanking her, my cell phone rang.

It was my mother calling. She said it was an emergency. The doctor didn't expect my grandmother to live through the day. My mother begged me to see her. A dying request, Erika Randolph emoted.

A harrowing experience can't help but create changes within us. I realized that when I finally agreed to see my dying grandmother. This was perhaps not out of a magnanimous gesture, but rather so that my own pain might become one of lower wattage. How intricate our layers of love and hate truly were.

"Ruby, I've got to go. I'll explain later. Just *thanks*."

* * *

Usually childhood memories shrink with age.

Memoires de la famille were just as I'd left them. My drive through the gates was tentatively made. The winding circular drive led to the *mansion's* entrance. Its Italianate stone exterior remained hauntingly unfriendly - stately. Even in summer's noontime pale gold heat there was a dark coolness coming from the shade of the columnar blue spruce.

The chime of the doorbell hadn't changed. I cringed, just as I had done when I was a child. Because of a court order restraining my father from entering, I was taken from his arms at the gate by a staff member. As I grew older, I would walk from my father's protective custody to the door, stand on my tiptoes, and ring that very same bell. And I would despise the sound of those chimes, as I did now.

A precisely tailored butler ushered me inside. He called me Miss Randa. I correct him. Just Randa, please, I spoke. He smiled knowingly. I was, after all, the prodigal granddaughter. With decorum he shepherded me to the study.

As was the rest of the palatial home, the study was filled with luxurious woods, exotic marble tabletops, and lavish elegance. My grandparents basked in the extravagance of wealth. My own egalitarianism relegated me to a station other than this.

A glance around the room produced recollections. Renaissance, fifteenth-and-sixteenth century Italian and French artwork surrounded me. Often the paintings had become trails leading a small girl's imagination away from loneliness.

Inhaling, I realize the floral bouquet was also lodged in my memory. I glanced down at the rose-packed vase. There was the scent of fine pipe tobacco, aged leather, and books. And behind me was the expensive aftershave that belonged to my grandfather. I turned.

"Sir," I greeted him, extending my hand.

His melting gaze watered for a moment. Then he opened

his arms and took me into them. His memorably rich timbered voice whispered, "Randa, thank you for being here. For better or worse, you have inherited your grandmother and me."

When we parted, I studied my debonair grandfather. Years had been added to him, but there was still his chevalier image with its lofty brow, well-groomed thick gray hair and mustache, and proud carriage.

His strained face was one of sorrow. Beneath his eyes were reddened flesh pillows - sagging tributes to his pain. He was losing the wife he had adored for over five and a half decades.

My emotions wavered. I was in pain for him. He'd been kind to me. If there was blame, it was that he sided with my grandmother. As did my own mother. They sided with her, and in doing so, it was against me. I realized that I should forgive him for placing his loyalty where he believed it most appropriately belonged. Although based on Lenora Randolph's lie, a lie that doomed me to additional heartache, he had no way of knowing the truth.

Hesitantly, I began, "I came because my father requested I be here for my mother's sake."

"On behalf of my family, please thank your father."

"I shall, sir."

With the grace of aristocracy, my grandfather's arm reached up toward the door. "Shall we?"

"Yes." We both know the urgency. Lenora Randolph's candle was burning low. It was soon to be extinguished by a supreme being, or a spent clockwork heart.

* * *

Timothy Randolph and I passed though the long, richly paneled hallway. My steps slowed when reaching a Regency table with an elegantly painted porcelain vase. I closed my eyes for a moment remembering its link to my past. I once ran past it, bumping the table. My grandmother thought the vase might fall. She threatened to send me away to a house where naughty children are locked up. I experienced the same chill as when I was small and frightened. Then I plodded on, after my grandfather. He gave the bedroom door a staccato knock before we entered.

Lenora Randolph's colossal ego mixed with incremental death was an incongruous blend. She slept. She wore a peach-colored dressing gown. Around her wax-pale face was a plastic loop providing oxygen. Her eyes were hollow, her jowl a series of wrinkled folds, her cheeks withered, and she was colored with death's mask of soot-hued clay. The wheeze of her breathing was irregular as her energy became depleted. Her soul was escaping.

My mother stood next to the brass bed's sculptured head post. Across from the bed was a square beveled mirror. In it was my reflection. My heart constricted with anger and contempt. I attempted to hide the ripples of rage as I moved toward my mother's side.

Erika Randolph's blue eyes were reflecting the incandescent light of a hanging crystal chandelier. Her ash-blonde hair was upswept in a delicate crown. Her serene beauty was an every-changing garment. She wore weariness.

"You're here," she said. "Yesterday was one of the worst days of my life. When the reports were issued, I feared I'd lost you."

"As I told you last night when I called, I'm okay."

"Deep down I was confident you'd survive."

"Why so?"

"Because my prayers needed to be answered. Not all of them can be." Through blurred tears, she glanced down at her mother. "Thank you for being here for my mother and for me."

"Father has been encouraging me to be supportive of you."

My statement stung her. "My request meant nothing to you?" she questioned with a thin, pain-pinched voice.

My silence was an edict of anger. I grappled with fierce hatred, yet cautioned myself about compassion. I should possess a melancholy soul, rather than the Homeric wrath of scathing. A ferocious rancor burned my stomach. Remaining were memories of my grandmother's volatile temper. The kaleidoscopic shift in her personality, and the endless vitriolic invectives were a part of my early childhood.

My mother leaned down, whispering, "Mother, Randa is here. You wanted to see her."

Lenora Randolph's eyes drowsily flickered - then opened. A torrent of repentant tears flooded them. Her weak voice began, "I'm sorry, Randa. So very sorry." Her arms shakily outstretched, but not with the arrogant deceit she so often used to give an impression of caring for me in front of others. Once, with feline grace, her arms expanded like a Delphic priestess welcoming me. Then those same arms would shake me, thrash me, and threaten me.

"I've come." Cringing slightly, I reached for her hand. It was cool. Although shrunken, it enveloped mine.

There was a moment's silence before she spoke again. "I am so very sorry," she repeated. "I ask your forgiveness. Can you find it in your heart to forgive me?"

My mother's face blanched. "Mother," she asked, "what do you mean 'forgive' you?"

After a cough my grandmother answered, "Randa didn't lie. I lied about my treatment of her."

"No, Mother," she argued. "You've always maintained you never harmed Randa. That she'd lied."

"It was my lie. I mistreated…" she broke coughing. "It was more than mistreating. I was unmerciful to Randa. Brutal. I've got to confess these terrible things I did. She wasn't lying when she told you the names I called her." Her eyes shut. "She didn't lie about the beatings. I was angry. I was frightened you might throw your life way. I wanted to create a rift between you and all the Florez family. Randa is a Florez. I lied so that you might go on with your art. And with your life."

"Opera is a part of my life." My mother's eyes flared. "My daughter *is* my life. And you made me mistrust her. All these years I've doubted her. All because of you." She stepped back. "My *God*!"

"I believed it was in your best interest. Please understand that I lived vicariously through your fame. Paulo threatened that. Then Randa. I couldn't batter the true object of my hatred. I loathed Paulo. I wanted to harm him and couldn't. So I took it out on Randa."

As if suddenly struck, my mother gasped. She recoiled from the direction of her mother. The truth was being absorbed slowly. She became aware of the extent of harm done to me. She also realized I'd told the truth about Sanford Winton trying to rape me. Her body trembled. Our eyes traded glances so painful to one another that we looked away.

My grandmother's grasp of my hand tightened. "Please, I implore you to forgive me. I know I'm dying. I have no right to ask this of you, but I beg your forgiveness. I beg you to forgive me before I die."

It was with yesterday's events in mind that I shook my head affirmatively to her request. I also knew what it was like to be caught in death's net. My grandmother would certainly be devoured by her own mortality. Her shallow breathing presaged her end.

"I forgive you." My words were clearly spoken. Solemnly spoken.

Erika Randolph screamed, "Mother, what you've done is unforgivable. You've torn me away from a man I loved. Paulo Florez requested that Randa see you. The man you hate so! Randa isn't here because I wanted her to be. She isn't here at your behest. She is here because of Paulo Florez. He raised your granddaughter to become the fine woman standing before you. The truthful woman. The woman that forgives you. You've ripped apart my relationship with him and with my daughter. And my sin was that I allowed you to do that."

"I loved you too much," my grandmother defended. Her eyes blinked with the realization that she was sinking rapidly. She sputtered, and then repeated, "I love you so very much."

"What you're about isn't *love*. You didn't trust me enough to make my own determination about love. It isn't any wonder I'm still searching love's meaning. Paulo and the Florez family gave Randa love. Love I wasn't able to show her."

"I was doing it for your career."

"Mother, you were doing it for your own selfish purposes of controlling me. That was your ulterior motive - you. *You!*

Coddled by your own family. Spoiled by your adoring husband. You needed my total devotion. Even if the price was my future. My daughter. And at this moment, I hate you."

"Please…"

"It is unpardonable," my mother spat. She rushed toward the doorway. Turning back, her words were anger-charged. "Mother, I trusted you. I can never forgive you for this - this travesty. I can never forgive myself for my part. As a mother I should have protected Randa from you. I should have believed her. I should have known that she is Paulo's daughter. She is honorable. These are the traits she inherited from Paulo. Certainly not from you or from me. When I should have stood by her, I didn't. When I should have believed her, I didn't." Tears streamed her face as she exited down the hall.

I followed, past my grandfather, behind my mother. I pulled her around to face me. "Mother, she's finally done the right thing. She might have died leaving this deceit between us. She would have continued her legacy of being perfect in your eyes. She didn't do that. It took courage for her to confess and humiliate herself."

Mother took me in her arms, holding me so tightly it was difficult to breathe. "Don't you see what she did to both of us? All the mistrust? All the years it has cost us?"

"Does it matter now?" I asked. "The entire ledger of her life came down to one moment. She has finally vindicated me."

"But I sided with *her*! And you might have forgiven her, but how can I expect you to forgive me for misjudging you? For allowing her to ruin our relationship?"

"Yesterday it was very nearly too late to retrieve our relationship. I might have died. Today it could have been too late. Death might have stolen the truth. But it isn't too late now, Mother."

Her trickling tears gave way to a gush. She began to loudly sob against my shoulder. Her usual stoical demeanor was lost to the moment. "Oh, my God! What have I done? How can you forgive my actions?"

"The same way you'll forgive her." For the first time in nearly thirty years I felt my heart thaw. "You're my mother.

She's yours. She needs you now."

* * *

After being swarmed at the door of my Florez grandparents, I hugged Papa Gus and Mama Carmina. Both Papa and Mama wept. Aunt Renie, sobbing profusely, crossed herself several times. Her hands reached upward toward heaven. I knew what she meant, for yesterday was a very close shave.

"*Dios provida,*" Renie told me God will provide. "Randa, you go to church. The crazy girl is dead, and you are saved," Renie stated with another rapid-fire crossing of her head, chest, and shoulders. "*Dios le bendiga!*" She pounded her heart, as if restarting it.

"God bless you, too," I repeated with a fleeting smile. "But now it's all over and I just want to think about my family."

Papa Gus sat on the sofa beside me. He patted my arm. "You were very brave. Nevada was very brave."

"Yes, she was." my word hurt me to say. "Yes."

"And she's helping our Benjy," Mama interjected. "He's talking about working with some police program. He wants to be a police officer."

I paused. "Being a cop or a crime reporter can change one's heart."

"Nevada isn't frightened. And she has a good heart," Papa stated. "She showed her mettle yesterday. The article you wrote about her, it shows she's a hero."

"I wrote what I witnessed. She's a fine, decent person," I agreed. "However, I'm not seeing her any longer."

Mama and Papa traded conspiratorial glances. Mama frowned. "She mentioned that to Benjy when he called her today. But, why?"

"I'm just not ready for being near. I'm not able to love. Or trust." I looked away.

"What's wrong?" Papa Gus asked.

"I've just left my Grandmother Randolph's bedside."

Renie sat to attention. "That old *culebra!*"

"Yes," I replied. "The old snake. Mother called earlier and said she was approaching death. I went. I talked with her. She begged for forgiveness for lying and for the violence. Now my mother knows I've been telling the truth all these years."

"*Quiere tu mucho a su madre, no?*" Papa questions.

"Yes. I do love my mother very much. But she's been a better daughter than a mother. Mother phoned just moments ago telling me Lenora Randolph died shortly after I left."

Ever pious Renie crossed herself again. Slowly, for it was in respect to the dead. "At least the old woman repented. At least she finally came clean," Renie said. She would be pushing beads for the soul of Lenora Randolph. "At least she has confessed her sin. Her lies about you are no more."

I agreed. "She paid a precious price. And forced what family she had to pay a portion of that price."

"The price has made you stronger," Mama said with conviction.

"She asked my forgiveness."

"And?" Papa inquired.

"And I forgave her. Time passed her by. Any love I might have had for her had passed us both by." I paused before tears began to seep lines down my cheeks. Words clogged in my throat as I explained, "At first I thought I was forgiving her for my father. My mother. All of you. But that was wrong. In the end I forgave her for myself."

* * *

The Florez household had quieted. Although not wanting to face a 'sin and repent' diatribe with Aunt Renie, I did welcome a moment on the porch before I left.

"When you were a child and you would take my hand and we would walk to the store, I would pretend that you were my daughter." Her eyes filled.

"Aunt Renie, I love you."

Her eyes dulled a moment. "You are always going to be with women?"

"I'm always going to be who I am."

"Randa, you know I think you're wonderful. Even if I go on at you."

My smile was hesitant. "I must know, Aunt Renie. I do believe there's something very wonderful inside of me. I'm looking to find that authentic, trusting person."

She stated with the stall of a lonely heartache, "Life moves on different rails."

"To different countries of the heart. But the passport is the same."

Her glance was soulful, yet sullen. She had finally accepted me completely. She kissed the center of my forehead.

* * *

Deciding I'd rather not face the paparazzi, I elected not to return to my loft straight away. The sun was westering by the time I reached Marlene's.

Entering brought embraces from Alicia and Giselle. "Easy does it," I said with a laugh.

"You might have been heaving up sod!" Giselle exclaimed. "Your news stories in the paper were great. You're being called the champion of investigative reporters by the national press."

"Congratulations!" Alicia squeezed my hand. "Great work."

"Enough platitudes delivered for now," I said with a degree of pride mixed with embarrassment. "Just bring on the booze."

"My finest bottle of wine, on the house," Alicia promised. She pointed in the direction of the corner. "Lanny has been awaiting your arrival. I think she wants to tell you that the entire event of yesterday was just a lucky hunch on your part."

I shook my head, as I made my way back. I slung my body into the booth. Lanny Ventura was across from me. Although Lanny was slightly inebriated, she wouldn't slur or totter. "I knew you couldn't resist coming in here to gloat," was her opening speech of welcome.

"About what?" I teased.

"Your story. Congrats on terrific work."

"I hear you think I was just lucky."

She stood, and then came to my side of the booth. She reached down and gave me a tight sisterly hug. "I think," she said while taking her seat opposite me, "that the entire city is lucky to have you as a reporter. That's what I think. And you're damned lucky you didn't get your sweet ass blown away. Glad you're safe."

"Safe from everyone except the tabloid press. They're stationed outside my loft."

"The vagabond inquisitors are getting you down?"

"And it isn't over. My mother called. My grandmother died."

"Erika Randolph's life is true opera this week. Her daughter nearly bought the farm. Her mother did. Anyway, I'm sorry about your grandmother."

"My grandmother's death will rate a small story in legit press, but the paparazzi will love it. They relish the death of a celebrity and, or, family. The subject of their scrutiny isn't likely to object from the depths of a grave."

"When will your grandmother be planted?"

"The funeral is Wednesday."

"So the gutter press hounds your mother and you until then. It can't be any more difficult than being nabbed by Jona Beck."

"The funeral will be a circus. My grandparents knew everyone in Denver."

"And there will be your mother's fans."

Alicia set down glasses in front of us. She poured. "My best."

"Thanks," I responded, lifting the goblet in a toast. A sip confirmed it was indeed a superb vintage. "It is the epitome of mellow. Heaven."

"Yeah," Lanny agreed. "Mellow heaven. When we finish the bottle, we'll have another. Keep 'em coming. Pass glasses to your piano player, singer, and you have some. Just keep our crystal filled. Put it on my tab."

"You've got it," Alicia said. She left for the wine cellar.

"A rather extravagant celebratory gesture," I commented.

"You did *good!*"

"Thanks."

She inquired, "Did you see your grandmother before she checked?"

"Yes. I finally relented."

"And?"

"She said I'm a Florez. She was very nearly accurate. And finally truthful."

"Very nearly?" Lanny's analytical lance sharpened.

"There are times I wonder where I belong. Often I relate to words more than human beings. I'm uncertain how that can be." I took another sip.

"Life, like love, is a great dichotomy. You had quite an ordeal yesterday. In the midst of that kind of turbulence, it's no damned wonder you're confronting doubt."

"Time passes quicker than split infinity. And I'm still searching my territory. I'm not certain of complete acceptance from the Anglo world, nor from the Hispanic world." I felt somehow disenfranchised. "When I was four, I remember my grandmother Randolph taking my hand as we crossed the street. She pulled me behind her, half dragging me. On the sidewalk there was a woman. She asked if I was the *maid's* daughter."

I closed my eyes, recalling back to that moment. My grandmother shook her head affirmatively. When we arrived home, she was livid. I was so frightened when she led me to my bedroom. Then she shook me, threw me onto the bed, and turned out the light as she closed the door behind her. It was late afternoon. She didn't open the door until after my grandfather had left for work the next morning. Before the nanny had arrived. I had wet my underwear. She called me a filthy, stinking Mexican. I wondered when prejudice might end.

I took a deep breath. "My grandmother hated my being her daughter's child. My mother had dirtied herself by becoming my father's wife. And I was the end product of that debased, shameful union." My glance was away from Lanny's penetrating stare.

"What about the Florez family?"

"I'm certainly included. I mean, I'm not an outcast. But

acceptance is a difficult commodity to measure. My youngest brother says it's easier for me because I have Anglo blood. Lighter skin. Everyone else probably agrees, and won't say so. Being half and half isn't easier. It's a division of camps. How can that ever be easy?"

Lanny topped off our wine glasses. "That's why I'm so arrogant. I guess I always had too much approval. There were lots of relatives around to give support. I was their gene duplicate. Their DNA copy. There was totally subjective, biased approval." She gulped a mouthful of wine. "That's also what must have made me such a righteous, opinionated shrew," she observed with trenchant wit.

"How can a family get all the ingredients right for children?"

"I don't know. I do know what you get when you don't get any of the ingredients right. You get Jona Beck." She paused. "Want to talk about it? Off the record."

"I did talk on record in this morning's edition."

"No. I mean the part that's so painful for you right now."

"There is always some unknown vacancy left behind by violence."

"You and Nevada. Are you two casualties?"

"Yes." I took a sip of wine. "Probably."

"I don't understand it. You should be falling into your hero's arms." Lanny waited a moment for my response. "Maybe there's more to the story."

I tried on a frown. "For instance?"

"It hasn't escaped my breadth of curiosity there are certain possibilities. Jona was a cop killer. One way or another, she probably wasn't going to leave there alive."

"Speculation."

"I'm not suggesting your story wasn't accurate. Just that you might have quashed a detail or two." She peered over her eyeglasses at me.

"You know my stance on cleansing stories."

"You're reverential about accuracy." Her mouth curved in a vague half smile. "What I'm questioning is your instantaneous break with Nevada."

"Look, I wasn't there when Jona Beck died." My anger lifted. "It is just exactly as I wrote. Jona talked about suicide before she died, and when I interviewed her last year. Even Eddie Hunter claimed she'd never be taken alive. I quoted them both verbatim. It'll be a do-it-yourself-job, Jona had said."

"But maybe you doubt Nevada. You may believe she helped, encouraged Jona. It's plausible. After all, most police experience absolute burnout at one time or another. Maybe her's happened when her lover was about to become a deadly killer's next victim. Between that, and the unwritten law of always covering your fellow officer's back. Particularly in death. It might even have made Nevada angry enough to off Jona."

"Absolute speculation. Our profession makes us jaded. But that doesn't excuse either of us for speculation. I believe it was exactly as Nevada related it. And evidence proves it."

"Your lips are tightening to a line."

My smile was weak and fraudulent. "Your agile imagination wants more of a story than there is." I considered the blood splatter that was on Nevada's right arm. There was the fact that the stippling spray was on the upper part of her right hand. Nevada wouldn't have allowed her gun out of her hand. Her left hand was tightly wrapping her gun's handle when I entered the trailer. Detectives on scene saw what I saw, and knew that Nevada had not shot Jona.

"You weren't exactly in the romance-testing stage of your relationship. You were both hoping for more. Something went on."

"Lanny, we have professions that oppose one another. I foresaw the difficulties. That's all. And as for what we would have liked, yes we held hope. Hope may be little more than dreams gone astray."

"So you're going to hold out. Not going to give me your morning headline?"

"Lanny, there is no story beyond the fact that the press and police belong in separate beds."

"Not that I would ever use any of this speculation.

244

Especially from an 'off the record' source." Lanny sighed. "I know what I'd do if I were in you. I'd give Nevada a pass for her occupation not meeting your standards."

"It isn't Nevada's problem." I paused. "And if I understood love, I would ask her to give me a pass."

"So, my wild, 'adverb-ish' speculation isn't a story. Now I go back to the station empty-handed."

"Lanny, I do have a scoop for you. I'm considering a change of occupation. I'm thinking about how nice it would be to work as a well-mannered columnist."

"Bullshit!" She laughed hardily. "Gonzo, you can't fake me out."

"Well, you had your chance at *finally* breaking a major story. But tomorrow it may not be relevant. I might not be front-page news. Just like a year from now few people will remember the tragedy of yesterday."

Lanny frowned as she sipped wine. "There will be a flock of new tragedies. Actually, since laws were going to be changed years ago when Columbine happened, it's gotten worse. Multiple murders have increased. We've changed the name *tragedy*. It's now so common that it's become an incident."

"So a decade from now Jona's rampaging incident will only be another crime statistic. If recalled at all, they'll ask, what was the name of that dyke that went on a killing spree?"

"But the Jona Beck story has changed you."

My blinking increased. "It has."

When my cell phone rang, Lanny chuckled. "Don't tell me you're off on another story?"

"Can't you take it, Ventura?" I listened to the quick announcement, then disconnected. "Got to rush," I said as I stood.

"Going to keep me in suspense?"

"They've just taken my sister-in-law to the hospital. I'm about to become an aunt."

"I'll get in touch with the society editor immediately."

My words were suddenly robust. "Well then, there's your scoop of the day."

* * *

"Patrolling my car?" I asked. A uniformed Nevada was beneath the shaft of a lamplight. She leaned against her squad car. It was parked strategically behind mine.

"Randa, we owe it to one another to talk. Please?"

By the time I'd opened my Z's car door, she had approached me. "I'm in a hurry. And there isn't anything to discuss at this time."

Her fingers combed through her hair. "You owe me an explanation." Her eyes appeared desolate.

"Not now."

"You've been drinking. I could use the breathalyzer and take you in."

"Look, don't play stupid games. You know I haven't had that much to drink. Teresa is about to deliver my first niece or nephew. I've got to get to the hospital."

"Follow me," she quickly instructed. "I'll give you an escort."

"A police escort isn't going to make a difference in how I feel."

She lifted my chin. Our eyes read one another's message. "No. I suppose not. But I can hold out hope."

"Nevada, maybe you do deserve to know what I'm feeling. I've lived with a lie most of my life."

"You can't live with doubt?"

"I can't give my love without my heart having an ability to trust. Events touch lives in ways we can't even begin to understand. You need to be trusted. I know you told me the truth. But I should have trusted you. You deserve that."

"If I gave up my profession?"

"You'd be miserable."

Nevada acknowledged, "I understand. I know when to say goodbye."

I touched her arm. "Still offering an escort?"

"Yes. And a friendship. Sometimes those convert into relationships. Maybe you need time."

"Time gives everyone a chance to work through their own meaning." She gave me a hug. There was warmth that ran the length of my body. I pulled away. My voice was more nonchalant than my heart. "I'm not sure why I'm in a hurry to get to the maternity ward. As Aunt Renie says, in hospital situations, I'm as useful as a bent nail."

Nevada's full, rich laugh filled the night air. "You never would have made an enforcer."

"But you make a terrific one."

"I love you, Randa."

"I'm not asking you to wait for me to become a trusting, loving person. Love might take us in separate directions. And you deserve the best love."

"I'll be waiting. Randa, for me there is no love better than yours. Yours is the best."

"But I doubted you."

"And now you don't."

It was my turn to murmur a quick yes. Life seemed garbled for a moment. Then I slid into the driver's seat and started Garbo's engine.

Nevada drove out in front of me. I saw the patrol car's roof lights begin blinking. When we got to the intersection, Nevada hit's the siren.

When we arrived at the hospital, I pulled into a parking space. I got out and I walked toward Nevada's vehicle. She uttered, "I still have some of your belongings at my house."

"I'll pick them up later," I replied with a chuckle.

"I can't believe you don't love me any longer," she said.

"We touched magic together. We faced death together. I'll always love you. I'll always wish things might have been different."

"And I'll always believe they can be."

"Always?" I questioned

"A normal life span ought to do. Well?"

"Nevada, all bets are off if one person can't trust another. I'm broken. From childhood my trust mechanism wasn't nurtured. There's a glitch inside me. I need to fix it."

"But you can always trust me."

"Dido should never have trusted Cupid."

"And Othello should have trusted Desdemona."

"Shakespeare?"

"I love the bard. There's so much we don't know about one another. So much I want to know about you, and I want you to know about me. We didn't have time. And we may never have the chance to know."

I silently turned. I then walked away toward the hospital's entrance. When I glanced back, she was still there watching me. I assumed she would remain until I was safely inside. But I didn't check to make certain once I reached the huge glass doors. Many of life's intricacies were far too excruciating.

The people who knew me – my family, friends – they guessed I might be throwing away the best woman I was likely to ever met. I also knew that.

* * *

Our journey through calendar pages might be the timing that comprises life, but there was so much more involved in each blank agenda space. One day becomes a child's birth date. A Sapphic scrivener becomes an aunt. A child was born to Rogerio and Teresa Florez at exactly one minute after midnight. Along with a new day, this child - a girl, began a new generation.

Father and Angie beamed with pride. I was elated. And when we were allowed to enter Teresa's hospital room, we viewed the baby. She was in Rogerio's arms. Tears filled my eyes. My arms wrapped around my brother and his child.

"She's lovely," I commented when the blanket was pulled away from her face. She was tiny, thin, and had a massive amount of dark hair sticking out from beneath her little cap. And there was such beauty in her face. "She's beautiful. Beautiful!"

"Yes. She is a beauty like her mommy," Rogerio agreed.

"Our surprise," Teresa said, "has to do with you. You want to say, Rog?"

"Our daughter's name is Pilar Randa Florez." He glimpsed from his child to me. "After her Aunt Randa."

My father laughed as he explained, "They transposed your first and middle name so that little Pilar won't be taken for her Aunt Randa by angry criminals."

"I don't have that many enemies," I disputed through my tears.

"And today you have one more fan," Rogerio said. "Want to hold your namesake?"

My reach extended toward the baby. Pilar was placed in the basket of my arms. My cheek lowered until I felt the tickle of hair that drooped across her forehead. Her skin was blossom soft. "I'm so honored," I told them. "More honored than I've ever been."

Angie joked, "*Tia* Randa, even more honored than with all your prizes and awards?"

"There's no comparison. This is the greatest honor of my life. Thank you both. Teresa, are you doing okay?" I asked.

Teresa's smile was huge. She appeared weary, but totally content. "Wonderful. Our child is healthy, and we'll try to make her happy."

Father's arm went around my shoulder. "Yes. It's every parent's wish to make their children happy." I felt his squeeze and knew he was talking directly to me. "Some parents don't know exactly how to find the secret of giving a child the happiness that every child deserves. But it doesn't mean the parent doesn't want the best for the child. It only means their way of trying might not have been the best."

Our glances connected. I knew he'd talked with Mother. "I'm aware of that now."

I felt the squirm of Pilar within the bundle I held.

Father said, "Good. Good." He observed, "Your little niece is strong, just as you were when you were a baby." With a somber glance in my direction, his eyes watered. Although he didn't elaborate, I realized he had missed out on my immediate infancy. He was robbed when I was taken away from him at birth. He hadn't witnessed those months before a court allowed him access to me. But he must have known I needed to garner strength to face my ordeal with the Randolph family.

As if there was suddenly a snap of knowing, I understood my father's integrity. Through it all, he hadn't allowed himself to affix blame. He wanted my heart to find peace, and my soul to locate serenity. It was at that moment I finished examining the inside of my own question. The important answer was that I'd always belonged. And I was gratified beyond words.

Perhaps trust would now become part of my soul's wealth.

EPILOGUE

The Following Wednesday

On the day they buried my grandmother it had been nearly a fortnight since Jona Beck's escape. Under cloud-filled skies, Lenora Randolph was laid to rest. The cemetery's earth had been jabbed, scooped, hollowed, and groomed.

There were, I noted, a huge multitude of mourners. The funeral had been a media event. Not only my mother's fame drew the press, but also my recent notoriety.

This was the first time I could recall being driven through the great gates of the Randolph mansion and seeing the structure as a respite. We were safe from the media's intrusion. And even though it had been only days since my grandmother's death, it was as though the home was free of her onerousness.

Erika Randolph entered the family home at her father's side. He was bereaved. He wore a mutinied expression throughout church and graveside services. Entering the home, he displayed more grief. His face was a testimonial to his loss, as well as his awareness of what his wife had been capable of perpetrating on her own child, and her grandchild. But we were children no longer.

The grand dining salon's long table was dressed with white linen, huge silver epergnes heavy with floral arrangements, crystal candelabras with flaming candles, and a multitude of epicurean delights.

Guests milled offering their sympathy. My mother had gone to change her clothing. She detested dark colors. My grandfather lifted a glass of wine from the tray that was being passed. He handed it to me with chivalrous decorum, and then took a glass for himself.

"Thank you, sir," I said.

His sip was taken as if there was no taste of the fine wine. "With all my heart, I wish I would have known what happened all those years ago. Have you told your father that my wife made us live with a lie she perpetuated for all these years?"

"No, sir. There was no need. My father knew I was telling the truth."

"Of course." His eyes filled nearly to brimming. "I am so very sorry."

"It's in the past now," I replied.

"I regret I haven't been able to know you."

"And I you, sir."

"Perhaps the future will bring us together. I'd very much like the opportunity to get to know my only grandchild."

"I'd like that as well, sir."

"The lessons in life are so late. So late. Stone memorials. Ruins. I regret my treatment of you, Randa."

"As I said, and meant - it's all in the past."

"And what is in your future?"

"I've taken a leave of absence from the newspaper. The events of last week have made me think about so many things. Perhaps I'll travel. Twirl a globe and point." I demonstrated with my index finger. "Where I point, I go."

"Yes. Time away is certainly well-earned after your ordeal."

"I need time to contemplate. I may not want to continue in my profession as a crime reporter. Maybe I might make a fine columnist. Perhaps a poet," I confessed with a half-hidden smile.

"Whatever you do, I'm confident it will be done with the best you have to give. You've become a fine woman."

"I've had excellent examples."

"Of course. Paulo and the Florez family have done a superb job in raising you. They've taught the things I would have liked to have shared with you. Honor." He looked away. There was more pain in his declaration than I had ever before heard in a human voice. "I so regret what we've missed."

I touched his arm. I was glad when my mother appeared at

my side. She wore a silk wheat-shaded blazer with cream-hued blouse and straight skirt. The scarf around her neck was the color of summer wildflowers. She smiled, and then spoke, "Father, I'd like to borrow your granddaughter for a few moments. We'll return after I show Mother's sunroom to Randa."

Mother took my hand as together we walked the great hallway. When we got to the sunroom, I slowed. It was not where Lenora Randolph's only grandchild was allowed.

The door fanned back and I entered. There was an entire wall of paneled windows on the easterly side. The brightly painted canary-colored room housed a white wicker daybed, desk, and a rocking chair. Plants profusely lifted. On the wall were small photos of my mother's many opening nights - her achievements. In the center was a large painting of my mother, and one of me. Its likeness had been taken from the photo used a couple of years ago with my articles and bylines.

"She had your portrait painted to go on the wall next to mine."

"I don't understand. She was ashamed of me," I exclaimed. "Why this?"

"Perhaps she wanted to love you. Maybe she didn't know how. Maybe she recognized her love too late."

"I thought it was only people like Jona Beck who don't know how to love?"

"Many of us need to be taught."

"Mother."

"Randa, allow me to finish. The package on the desk contains over a dozen very rare antique fountain pens. Years ago I mentioned that you have an interest in them. She'd searched for the rarest, most valuable at auctions and in antique shops throughout the world. Each is tagged with the date of one of your birthdays. Maybe she hoped one day to be able to give them to you. It might have been her way of telling you she cared. Even if it's a gift from her grave, she wanted you to have her message."

My mother handed me the package.

"Mother, I still don't understand. Why didn't she just tell

the truth?"

"I'm speculating she didn't feel as though she could. It meant she must risk losing me. And certainly losing my father's esteem. She required his admiration. It was her very breath."

"*Tu as sans doute raison,*" I told my mother she was probably correct.

"You're speaking French," she noted with a smile. Her arm went around my shoulder. "For years I've encouraged you to speak French. I'd hoped you hadn't forgotten it. How about a walk in the gardens? Barefoot, naturally."

"The sky looks as though it might rain."

"*Is ne va pas pleuvoir,*" she denied it would rain.

"*Moi, j'ai vraiment l'impression qu'il va pleuvoir.*

"Well," she relented, "if you truly believe it will rain, we shall take an umbrella." Suddenly she embraced me. "I'll never again allow the rain to harm you."

"I'm no longer your *jeune fille,*" I answered with tears. "I no longer need to be sheltered."

She walked to the window. "But if given the opportunity, I can offer an umbrella from time to time, when you need it."

"Yes. Yes, that would be nice."

She turned. "Randa, allow yourself to love. Not only when love doesn't stand up to the intensity of the rain. Trust your love. Love is the sweetest part of life."

She knew all along. "Do you think I'll ever learn to give my heart away? Do you think I'll remember how to trust?"

"I did once. And if you can forgive, you can surely take the chance on love. Trust someone worthy of your love. I loved your father. And we've all forgiven your grandmother for making us distrustful."

"You had more to forgive your mother for than I did. And in the end, you forgave." I approached the doorway. "Mother, let's save the walk for another time. It's been a long day. I'd like to be alone. There's nothing like a drive in my Z to clear a cottony head."

"I'll call you in the morning. I love you, Randa. If it were only yesterday once again."

"I love you, too, Mother."

Perhaps, I considered, there was yesterday in each of our todays.

* * *

Garbo was directed toward Denver's nucleus. I'd turned off the stereo's smooth jazz so I could listen to the raindrops that pounded against the T-top panels. There was the automatic thought of the mountain storm the day Jona died. That violent pelting rant had been produced by roiling, churning clouds. Now the summer rains fell gently. With a heavy layer of clouds overhead, I knew the night skies would be sans stars. I also knew I wouldn't be searching the heavens for newborn stars. Not tonight.

The lyrics of rain seemed to be about flowers, courage, wilderness, and an ability to trust my own soul chatter. Knowing that much meant love would certainly locate me. I turned the music back on, and listened intently.

I thought about Nevada's smile. I was overwhelmed with her warmth for a moment. Then I knew – there are always conversations that couples shouldn't have. Learning them is just part of love being visible. Honor and truth are incorruptible. Yet vantage points are different.

Giving love a chance was up to me. Human frailties, differing opinions, and foibles that would never match - they should never be what makes love evaporate. Understanding each sequence of life's charm seemed the secret. Knowing that those who love do the best they can possibly do – well, that may be the key. My smile had reappeared.

I would wait for Nevada to go off duty.

Then I would phone her. She had promised that she'd be waiting. I trusted she would be. Enforcement and news media would always be adversarial. But it shouldn't be a reason to crush love. Our feelings were something special.

Perhaps we could twirl a small globe together. We both needed a vacation from doubt. I wanted to know Nevada better, trust her better, and love her better. Better than I'd ever known, trusted, or loved anyone before.

The End - Por Fin & La Fin

Kieran York

Author Kieran York

Kieran York

ABOUT THE AUTHOR

Kieran York has authored both Sapphic fiction and poetry. Her lesbian mystery series, *Timber City Masks,* and *Crystal Mountain Veils,* featuring Royce Madison, were originally written and published in the mid-1990s. A second edition of them was recently released by Scarlet Clover Publishers. *Shinney Forest Cloaks* was published in 2015 and is the third mystery of the series. All three Royce Madison mysteries have been on the Amazon 100 Best-Seller's List – LGBT Mysteries. And *Shinney Forest Cloaks* was Amazon's Hot New Release.

York's fiction also includes *Appointment with a Smile,* published in 2012. It was a 2013 Lambda Literary Society Award Finalist in the Romance category. *Careful Flowers* was released in 2013, followed by 2014 releases – *Earthen Trinkets* and *Night Without Time.* In 2015, *Touring Kelly's Poem, Loitering on the Frontier, Primrose,* and mystery *Trevar's Team:1* were released.

In 2014, her volume of poetry, *Blushing Aspen,* was published as Sappho's Corner Solo Poets book of poetry. It won The Rainbow Award Honorable Mention for poetry, and was a Finalist in the poetry category of Golden Crown Literary Awards. In 2015 the poetry book titled *Realm of Belonging,* was published by Scarlet Clover Publishers.

York has had two collections of lesbian short fiction. The first was entitled *Sugar With Spice,* and was published in 1989. The second was released in 2015, and was called *Within Our Celebration.*

Previously, during the seventies and eighties, Kieran worked as a reporter and reviewer for both newspapers and magazines, and was a magazine publisher for three years. She also wrote and performed songs with a regional woman's band. She has been guest lecturer and panel member at various events, including Rocky Mountain Book Exhibition and Colorado

Musician's Series. She is a member of Lambda Literary Society and Sisters in Crime.

She has written for *Journal of Mystery Readers International.* In addition, she has given numerous campus and coffeehouse poetry readings, as well as taught poetry and creative writing workshops. She graduated from Fort Hays Kansas State University, and attended Mexico's University of the Americas her junior year.

Kieran lives in the Rocky Mountain Foothills of Colorado with her schnauzer, Clover. She enjoys music, literature, and art. She considers her valuables to include Clover, and her other family and friends, her library, her antique typewriter collection, and her guitars.

Additional information is available on her websites: http://kieranyork.com and www.scarletcloverpublisher.com – in addition, you can find her Amazon Author's Page at: www.amazon.com/author/kieranyork/ .

SCARLET CLOVER PUBLISHERS
COMING ATTRACTIONS - 2016

BALLAD OF RAINDROPS

Troubadour Magnolia 'Nolie' Cassidy's existence had always been unorganized. Although Nolie's life had periodically settled down, it was now once again disrupted. Events had suddenly shouded Nolie's life. Her precious old Irish setter had died. Her inkwell had dried up, and her guitar was in hibernation.

She was in love with Libby. But Libby had let her down when Nolie was at her most vulnerable. She was once again a vagabond. But now she was without a song, without a lyric, and without love.

Nolie previously wrote poems and songs that came from some magical Muse. She believed that it was her Muse that had gone missing. That was until Nolie herself became lost in the middle of the Rocky Mountains. Then she realized she was the one that had gone missing. And she was assuredly lost.

To be found, it took a storm, the friendship of a dog she despised, and the love of a woman who never gave up on Nolie.

SCARLET CLOVER PUBLISHERS
COMING ATTRACTIONS - 2016

RASP MEADOW CROSSING: Royce Madison 4

Sheriff Royce Madison has always wanted to solve a cold-case mystery. It had been a mystery that had perplexed her father decades ago. It had always remained in the back of Royce's mind. The summer was getting too complicated for her to find time to look backward.

She had been dispatched to assist in fighting one of the rampaging wildfires in Colorado's back county. The unrelated murder of a gun merchant interrupted her tour – and she returned back to Timber City. Crime in Timber County hadn't taken a vacation while she was away.

Could any of the crimes be connected? If so, how?

Add to that, her personal life was unraveling. This time, she was almost too busy to notice.

www.ingramcontent.com/pod-product-compliance
Lightning Source LLC
Chambersburg PA
CBHW060535260626
47161CB00003B/907